The Name I Chose

ALSO BY NAIMA HAVILAND

Bloodroom
The Bad Death
Night at the Demontorium
Aunt Téa's Addiction
People Like Us
The Tiger Tamer and the Ranch Hand
Independence Day
The Surface
The Escape

To those still hiding, who don't know
how wonderful they are

CHAPTER 1

MORDECAI

Mordecai detected no native talent in the girl playing the piano at his side. He hadn't expected it, though in all his years of teaching the daughters of the rich and the sons of the poor, he never took a new pupil without hoping for the best. Because Mordecai was generous, he looked for and was pleased by the slightest talent, indeed. Promise was enough. Interest was enough. A narrow gateway by which he might introduce a person to the joy found in music.

But Mordecai needed a salary and took anyone. The joy-deaf. The clumsy-handed, the resentful, the bored. He seldom found these among the poor, those boys whose parents saved and sacrificed to buy a piano. They always stood over their son and made sure he did not stare at Mordecai but straight down at the keys. They made sure he listened instead of screaming or crying. They dragged him back if he ran. And if the boy shook uncontrollably; well, coal was expensive and wood scarce. Did they not all shake from cold?

And if the boy laughed – God help him if he laughed – for learning to play the piano gave no cause for hilarity no matter how Mordecai looked. It was serious business. A boy who grew into a skilled pianist could support his parents by teaching. And if he proved a wunderkind! A wunderkind could pull a family from the ghetto; fly as if on a comet's tail across continents in a blaze of fame and fortune. Such were the aspirations of the poor.

Mordecai never found laziness in their meager parlors, never stood over a son and saw his fingers stumble through lack of practice, never heard a sour note. And he never encountered daughters of the poor, except fleetingly as they peeked in to steal a glimpse at Mordecai, before they gasped and fled.

No, it was the daughters of the bourgeoisie Mordecai saw often. The sons apprenticed in their father's offices. The daughters must learn to play prettily to win a husband. He'd no doubt this very ambition burned in the bosom of the girl who played with such placid determination beside him at this very moment. They were of a type, these girls. They must sing prettily, make pretty conversation, and look pretty. None of this prettiness came cheap, but the investment paid off. A rich husband secured the family fortune. A socially prominent husband pulled a family up to his level. It was rare but not unheard of that a pretty daughter landed a titled husband. Such were the aspirations of the wealthy.

Mordecai never found laziness in their over-furnished, overheated parlors. He never stood over a girl and saw her fingers fly over the keys in a composition of her own making, never heard an improvisation. What he saw and heard was rote perfection, for nothing less than perfection would do. There was never a bump in the nose, for a nose could be scalped, ground down, and reshaped. Never too thick a waist, for denial of food and the correct number of purgings brought a waist into proper circumference. Never was hair too thin, too coarse, too straight, or too curly. A foot pressed to a piano pedal was never too flat or too large, for contraptions strapped onto a girl child's feet enabled the development of a pleasing shape.

No one stared at Mordecai, for a direct look was unfeminine. No one screamed or ran, for a sharp-eyed grandmother was always present to remind a girl that a husband could be uglier than Mordecai, inconceivable as that seemed. She must never run from, scream at, or look upon too boldly any man, be he handsome or hideous. And if she laughed – God help her if she laughed.

Mordecai found his new pupil no more talented than the rest and no less pretty. Her previous training had been adequate. Her playing was dutiful, docile, and dull.

Bored, Mordecai looked out the window to the beautiful landscape of this country estate. He'd taken the solitary commission to escape the city, where a cholera epidemic was at present killing off his poorer students. Inventive use of new technology – aeroplanes trailing banners that advocated protective face covering, hovercraft spraying perfumed or antiseptic mists – proved as useless at slowing cholera as modern medicine was at curing it. Even piano tutors of his caliber did not command a salary sufficient to fund refugee operations, but Mordecai could not quell a bitter sadness over leaving his slum protégées behind to die.

His new employer's coach had come for him at dawn only two days past and found him packed and ready, his attire spotless, boots polished, collar starched and ascot tied, top hat pulled low over his misshapen brow, the myriad imperfections of his face hidden beneath thick makeup. Nothing to be done for his profile but mitigate its protrusions with a bushy false mustache, a monocle camouflaging the misalignment of his eyes. Mordecai's innards did not allow him to sleep the night through and the coach's long journey, made slower by the burden of his excessive baggage, afforded him a cat nap whenever he could get his posture angled just so. He'd wakened to fresh air and winter sunshine.

Mordecai was watching fluffy white sheep graze on a distant hill when his pupil struck a note that brought his head around to look at her.

Miss Paulson kept her eyes on the sheet music, playing, playing. A pretty piece with deft little climbs and swan dives and curlicues that sounded harder to play than they were.

It hadn't been an off note. It hadn't been a true note. It had been an original note.

If any feature of his body functioned properly it was Mordecai's ears. He had perfect hearing. He had heard a note not written by the composer but slipped in by the player. Not an extra note, either; that would've ruined it. A replacement note, an unconventional note that for one second turned the conventional piece into something special.

"Stop," Mordecai said. She did. "Turn back." She turned the sheet music back a page. "Begin."

She played the piece over and this time it was perfect, a dull piece for dull people easily charmed and quick to applaud. He'd imagined the original note. How could one credit inspiration to a girl of such uninspiring prettiness? He looked at the childish curve of her cheek, the pert nose, the smooth curls that lay along the swan's curve of her neck. His eyes slid down her slender arms to her fingers playing nimbly over the keys, and then to her fingernails.

They were bitten to the quick.

CHAPTER 2

The days fell into a predictable but not unpleasant pattern. Miss Paulson took her lessons with Mordecai every morning. That left his days free to do as he liked. He roamed the grounds, made use of Mr. Paulson's extensive, if underused library, and played the piano for hours. It took all day for a morning edition of The Herald to arrive by post, but once Mr. Paulson had done with the newspaper, Mordecai read it.

All these activities he did in solitude, for no one looked at or spoke to Mordecai if they could help it. The Paulsons kept a polite distance, and the servants knew their place. Stuck between the upstairs and downstairs classes, he and the governess might have been compatriots but she avoided him. One didn't dine with an employer's family, so she dined alone.

This projected invisibility gave Mordecai the vantage point of an observer, and he couldn't help learning more than he cared to. Miss Paulson's parents had never sent her to boarding school. People reckoned they never would now she'd reached the age for marrying. She went to balls but they forbade her to dance anything lively, which kept her dance card empty. They discouraged social calls lasting longer than a few hours. With so few opportunities to forge bonds among those of her own class, she had as her closest companion an old duenna who rarely left her side.

The crone had served the mother and then the girl, from birth. Still, in Mordecai's observation, the nurse showed little affection for her charge, but treated her as a feral creature that must not be let too far afield. Mrs. Paulson, a woman of cold, well-preserved beauty, kept her daughter at a distance from which she'd have the best perspective to assess her appearance and demeanor. Mr. Paulson kept to his study, attended to matters of business, rode, or went shooting.

The family came together at dinner, a formal affair even when they didn't have guests. More often than not they did, as there was serious matchmaking underway. Young men from neighboring estates who passed muster at dinner received invitations to tea. Mordecai had seen a few of these high teas in passing, for they took place in a sort of atrium below a mezzanine that led to the library. Windows soared to cathedral heights, sunlight beaming in to pick up the honey highlights in Miss Paulson's hair and warm her skin until her cheeks flushed a delicious pink. The lace at her bosom and wrists glowed the pure white of a dove's wings. She made pretty conversation with her suitor under the watchful eye of her grandmother. She poured tea without spilling a drop and passed the China cup and saucer in graceful hands clad in decorative gloves that hid her bitten nails.

The great house had nothing so open as the atrium. To attain any room, Mordecai traversed labyrinthine halls while trying to ignore information not intended for his ears. Gossip, flirting, strategizing, complaining, orders, and excuses drifted through open transoms or doors left ajar, through hallways, up dumbwaiters and back staircases in a crosscurrent of sluggish drafts that made it impossible to guess from which direction the overheard words originated. When he first heard the piano, Mordecai stopped walking.

It wasn't the Paulsons' habit to engage musically at this hour. Stranger than the timing, something in the music, itself, gave him pause.

Mordecai cocked his head to catch its tempo. He closed his eyes to concentrate. He started moving, blind, letting his hearing guide him. Seduced, he obeyed the tantalizing notes. They grew gradually louder, and he knew himself on the right track. Following the music, Mordecai tried to identify the tune. He could not, and this drove him forward.

Before long, he gave up applying education and experience to the mystery. The name of the music eluded him, even as the instrument and the maestro who played it remained out of reach. Who in the surrounding area played with such virtuosity? Mordecai decided he must meet him.

The melody was melancholic but transcendent, the notes lifting, skipping, deepening. It brought to mind a beautiful bird taken to glorious flight, only to hover just beneath the apex of a lofty cage. But oh, the defiant tenderness of such a creature! Who, in this stale environment, had wit to conceive it, put pen to page and fingers to keys and give the bird wings? It must be a visitor, Mordecai thought, one of the endless stream of Miss Paulson's suitors. He must meet the man, no matter what shock his appearance may cause.

By now, he'd drawn close enough to hear every note as crystal ornaments comprising a brilliant whole. Mordecai knew every composition published. This beautiful piece was original, unknown. The secret longing expressed in each chord struck a responsive beat in his heart. He could barely breathe by the time he reached the door. It was only slightly ajar, limned in sunlight.

The music began again without stopping. The player was improvising on the improvisation now. Mordecai savored it, tried to anticipate the next note. Maestro though he was, he could not guess it. The surprise bested his expectation.

The composer must be alone, waiting for Miss Paulson and her hawk of a grandmother, for no one played in so unrestrained a manner before an audience. Mordecai placed a hand to the door, deciding to steal in quietly and wait for the right moment to make his presence known. He slipped inside.

He found not a piano but a spinet. Not a parlor but a bedroom. No suitor of Miss Paulson's but Miss Paulson, herself.

Alone and in a state of undress, she stood with her back to the door. She bent forward slightly, her camisole open to the small of her back. As her fingers tickled over the spinet's keys, he saw every struck note in the subtle play of muscle and shoulder blades.

With her free hand, Miss Paulson balanced across her shoulders a long bar from which hung an assortment of false legs. The bar curved but Mordecai thought this had more to do with the flexibility of its wood than with the weight of the legs. Something about them made them look hollow.

He felt he was dreaming, for it made no sense at all. *Why should Miss Paulson carry empty legs?*

Miss Paulson held the bar steady while she continued to play a second tune of her own devising as exemplary as the first.

Her spine looked a straight string of pearls beneath pale skin. From her tiny waist, petticoats flounced. Sunlight made the white muslin transparent, silhouetting the one leg upon which she stood and her other leg that ended just above the knee.

One leg ending above the knee. Shock made him witless. He thought, *well that doesn't happen.*

She stood straight on her single leg, no leaning for balance. Her exquisite posture was natural. She looked born to it.

Born to it. This realization broke his paralysis. Mordecai gasped or moved. Miss Paulson's fingers lifted and she turned her head. And saw him.

And looked around wildly, flailing to grab something –

a blanket, a shawl – while fluffing her petticoats to hide her missing leg. Her actions caused the bar to fall from her shoulders with a hollow clatter of false legs colliding. Mordecai kept the bar from falling to the floor with one hand and caught Miss Paulson with the other, in order to prevent her falling, as well. His palm absorbed the satin warmth of her bare shoulder. His rescue brought her so close he could see sweat beading her forehead. Her camisole gaped to her waist. She gathered it closed as she twisted in an effort to minimize his view of her half leg.

Mordecai's mouth went dry. His heart thundered. "I beg you do not distress yourself—"

"Go!" Her eyes met his wildly, the pupils dilated. "Go!" she hissed, pushing him toward the vast windows.

Mordecai hid behind the heavy drapes as the old maid came in holding a corset. Peeking between velvet panels, he saw the crone halt with a snort of disgust. "Ye've not put your leg on!"

"I wanted to play the spinet," Miss Paulson murmured.

"Ye've excited yourself," the duenna scolded, mopping the girl's brow. "Which leg?"

"That one." She pointed without looking.

Watching the old lady prepare the false leg, Mordecai tried to get over the shock.

He'd never seen a disfigured woman among the bourgeoisie. None existed. Rumors of a tragic accident befalling this house or that sometimes arose. The impenetrable surface of a family's self-protective silence deflected these arrows. It remained a private shame and financial burden to have a daughter maimed irreparably. He'd never heard of a bourgeois child *born* disfigured.

Birth defects only happened among the lower classes, unfortunate evidence of their inferiority. Yet here it was. The familiar grace with which Miss Paulson stood on her only leg suggested that she'd never had to unlearn the ease of standing on two. An upper class girl born disfigured exposed her family lineage as a sham. She cast suspicion on her family's genetic code.

Which of her parents carried the propensity for birth defects? Their generation had married in blind faith, genetic testing having not yet advanced sufficient to merit common use. It had since become a social requisite to announcing a betrothal. In fact, genetic testing before marriage had become so common, it was fast becoming something only *common* people desired. Aristocrats made a show of waiving it. Perhaps the Paulsons counted on that. They were aggressively matchmaking, while keeping their daughter's flaw secret.

What alternative did they have? What man would marry such a girl and risk siring legless sons? And who, among a class of perfect people, would trouble themselves to know the Paulsons once their genetic imperfection came to light?

These were Mordecai's ruminations as he evaluated lifelong assumptions. *The Paulsons cannot have been the only members of society carrying genetic affliction.* Yet, exposure as such could only mean sudden and irreversible social ruin, followed by a related financial descent. If upper class women birthed imperfect infants who could not be known to exist, what happened to those babies? Mordecai supposed they were left at the doorsteps of foundling homes. Why Miss Paulson had not met this fate in infancy was a mystery.

Mrs. Paulson may have been told she couldn't have another child. They may have feared trying for another, feared another birth more defective than the last.

How Miss Paulson's earliest memory must have been shaped by this secret! Every social interaction couched to protect it. In Mordecai's mind, the disparate pieces of information overheard during the past days now fell into a pattern; her never going to boarding school, never overnighting with a friend, forbidden to dance anything more demanding than a waltz. People thought these restrictions the whims of overprotective parents. He was sure they'd no idea what the parents were really protecting. Only the duenna knew that.

The secret would come out on her wedding night but what would her husband's family do? Expose itself to society's ridicule? Her secret would become their secret.

The secret was the price Miss Paulson paid for her life, and she paid it well. She was dressed now, the leg strapped securely to her thigh. A full petticoat flowed over the half petticoat and a dress flowed over that. She was ready for the hairdresser as the final preparation before meeting her dinner guests, another family with excellent connections and an unmarried son. She looked like any other girl.

But Mordecai knew better.

When Miss Paulson, her duenna, the hairdresser, and the maid had gone, Mordecai stepped from the drapery and looked around. Without the bustle and chatter of women the place seemed loud with quiet. He'd never been in a lady's bedroom before but had a notion décor differed depending on her personality and experience. This was a virgin's bedroom. A simple canopy hung over a four poster bed. Blossom sprigs patterned the wallpaper. Children's books filled the shelves. The powdery floral scent of Miss Paulson's perfume, which he'd never noticed before, lingered faintly. The spinet took pride of place in the center of the room, the instrument of expression for the girl's longing. Nothing in her musical compositions matched her perfume or this room. The room caged an imaginary creature concealing the real one, as the rosewood cabinet concealed her inventory of legs. He'd seen the duenna lock them inside it before the hairdresser and maid arrived. A silver comb and brush lay on a marble-top table, morning sun turning a strand of Miss Paulson's honey brown hair to a burning filament of gold. As Mordecai reached to touch it, his reflection in the glass above the table startled him.

The moment he'd seen Miss Paulson's secret, he'd

forgotten his ugliness for the first time in his life. He paused to confront his reflection.

He'd learned he was ugly sometime between the ages of two and three. Before then he'd thought he was just a bad boy, that something inwardly horrid made his mother hide her face and his father kick him, made girls shriek and other boys throw rocks. He'd had to learn what the words meant to really understand.

Hunchback. Crooked Eyes. Beak Nose. Pinch-head. Spots.

One-Leg. That's what they would call her behind her back, in sniggers.

If they knew.

CHAPTER 3

Miss Paulson struck a discordant note. Her grandmother looked up from her needlepoint with a frown.

Her fingers trembled over the keys.

She's afraid. I have seen her and know her secret. He said, in a tone of stern indifference, "Again."

Her round shoulders stiffened with resolve. She began again. This time she didn't botch it. But it was bland beyond endurance, of nursery rhyme simplicity that mocked the complexity of her own compositions. Mordecai sighed.

She looked sharply at him. The note ended, but the resonance held.

Was this all that was to become of her, then? Perhaps she'd compose music in her own home, overheard by a husband who resented her tricking him into marrying her. Mordecai's lips thinned beneath his false moustache.

"You try the maestro's patience, Philomena," the grandmother said.

"'Tis of no consequence," Mordecai assured her. To Miss Paulson, he commanded, "Again."

She did not begin again. She trembled more violently than before. Diamond tears glittered in her lashes. Mordecai's heart moved heavily, weighted down by pity. He put fingers to the keys and began to play. Miss

Paulson's gasp went unheard beneath the mellifluous flow of music. How it filled the room, the notes curling like vines in summer and clinging to the senses, rooting the listener into the deep and fertile earth of imagination.

"A singular composition," the grandmother remarked. "Is it your own?"

"'Tis another's, ma'am," Mordecai spoke as he played, while Miss Paulson clasped her hands tightly in her lap. "I heard it but once, yet it claims the remote region of my heart where reside all things known that I shall never speak of."

"Indeed." In a single word, the grandmother expressed society's general opinion that music teachers had no business speaking of the heart or asserting that they even had a heart – with remote regions, no less! He could feel the old lady's eyes on him, but his eyes remained on Miss Paulson's hands.

They sprang from her lap and took up the reins of her composition, fingers flying over the keyboard in ecstasy. Watching her play her own music, music from the heart and mind of genius, Mordecai kept from smiling by an extreme act of will. A delicate pink bloomed in her cheeks. Her round shoulders rounded still more as she leaned in. Her arms jumped. Ringlets danced about her ears.

The grandmother half rose from her chair, setting needlepoint aside. "This is most irregular."

"An exercise only, my good lady." Mordecai gave her his blandest expression, "to limber up the fingers." He began to play and Miss Paulson sat back, listening to his variation on her theme. He sensed tension leaving her body as her expression grew thoughtful.

A thrilled undertone gave texture to her shy assertion, "Maestro, if I may ...?"

She played a variation on his variation that sent a dart of joy through his heart. He strove to sound detached when he said, "yes ...yes ..." For several moments, he and she played back and forth, each playfully daring each other to the next improvisation. The music grew more intricate and light at each new level, rising to the lofty ceiling like bubbles in champagne until it became giddy, almost silly. Mordecai felt he and his pupil should burst into laughter at any moment. This would never do, for the grandmother eyed them warily.

"I think your hands warmed enough by the exercise," he stated gravely, "that you may attempt the lesson now with more success."

Her shoulders drooped.

"The second coda, if you please," Mordecai said in his teacherly voice, monocled gaze straying to the large window through which he could see sheep rooting for grass on a distant, snowy hill top. "Begin."

She played faithfully, each placid note of the parlor music distinct in mediocrity. It mollified the grandmother, who sat down again and picked up her needlepoint.

A suitable young man and his parents dined with the Paulsons that evening. Mordecai heard their dull conversation as he left the library with the book he'd chosen as his solitary dinner companion. Something bright in Miss Paulson's voice made him pause. The young man replied animatedly, no doubt responding to her brightness and confident in the belief that he'd inspired it. Mordecai knew better. She'd been in this unusually bright mood all day, her sunny voice finding his ears no matter where he went. He realized now that her voice had rare beauty, as if discovering one secret flaw had made known to him all her obvious advantages. With proper training, she could have been a singer of great renown, just as easily as she could have been a world famous concert pianist. She would be neither. She would be the wife of this young jackass or one just like him.

Dinner had finished by the time Mordecai returned to the library in hopes of finding a more uplifting topic.

They'd adjourned to a drawing room, where stood a grand piano. Miss Paulson began to play a popular tune of such bland charm it drove Mordecai away.

Later, he came out of the water closet and found her standing in the hallway. Mordecai looked back at the WC in a second's wish to find escape there. She'd been waiting for him. That much was obvious. Her brown eyes shone.

"Mr. Michaelson."

"Miss Paulson."

"I wish to express my gratitude – no, don't look like that!"

At the start of her declaration, he'd glanced around anxiously.

"In all our years living here, I've made a study of the house. This bend in the hall is one of few places that holds sound."

He slowly came around to look at her. In the gloomy hallway, her deep honey hair looked almost black. His candle and her candle formed a pool of light between them.

"So ..." she spoke his words from yesterday, "I beg you do not distress yourself." She stepped into the light and he got the impression such a move took courage, for her chin looked stubborn and her eyes uncertain. "Nothing we say can be overheard."

With some annoyance in her naiveté, Mordecai glanced at the shadows beyond her, where anyone could be lurking. "There's nothing you can say to me alone you cannot say in company."

"Oh, but there is!" She took another step forward. "You must allow me," she said in a rush, "to tell you how earnestly indebted I am for your silence on a certain matter."

"Think nothing of it," he said flatly. "In point of fact, I'd already forgotten it." Her beauty stung him and he turned away. "Good night, Miss Paulson."

"It's not for my sake alone that I value your discretion."

She sounded nearer! As if she followed him! Mordecai stopped, incredulous to hear, close enough to feel her breath on his neck, her quavering murmur, "If they find out you know, I daren't think how they might check you."

The fear in her voice reminded him that every aspect of the Paulsons' life depended on keeping their daughter's secret. They'd destroy him to keep the secret. He turned back, "Would that trouble you?"

"Exceedingly." Her downcast eyes lifted, gleaming with unshed tears, pupils large in the dim light.

By launching a teaching career from his concert success, he'd escaped the insult of public astonishment that anyone so ugly could produce music so beautiful. Since then, Mordecai had worked diligently to achieve a comfortable existence. He aimed to enjoy it in solitude to the end of his days. "Then, Miss, I repeat – do not distress yourself."

She made no reply but her soft mouth trembled.

"All is forgotten. Quite." He did leave then, before he lost his temper.

They'd spared no expense in time or money to make her as pretty as a bowl of sugared fruit. He imagined the young man pawing her on their wedding night, undressing her to find her less than perfect. Had they prepared her for *that*?

CHAPTER 4

Sleep never came easily or lasted long. This night it apparently had no intention of arriving at all, for hours passed while thoughts of Miss Paulson tormented him. He'd no right to concern himself with her happiness or mourn the waste of her talent, for the gulf in society that separated them rendered such considerations pointless.

Mordecai reached for his water glass in the moonlit darkness. As cool liquid sluiced his throat, reason doused his defiance of fate. From birth, life had singled him out for a travelling carnival as one of its penny-a-view freaks, or as a beggar in the streets. Still, fate had surprised him with a golden apple. His virtuosity had afforded him respectability and a comfortable living. Perhaps, fate held a consolation prize in reserve for Miss Paulson. *It will be children, healthy boys and girls as beautiful as she.* Here, imagination failed him, for to fully visualize children as yet unconceived, one must know the features of the father as well as the mother. The father of Miss Paulson's children remained as yet a blank, though Mordecai had no doubt when he appeared, fortune would give his looks every advantage.

Sudden restlessness compelled his legs over the side of his bed to shove his feet into slippers. Mordecai donned a robe as thick and long as a cloak. Unable to keep still, he left his room without benefit of a candle and took to the labyrinthine halls of this mansion like a restless spirit.

From his daily wanderings, he knew the passages so well he didn't stumble in the dark. Moonlight slanting through windows turned the interior into a geometrosphere of gray, black, and indigo shapes. Night made the house more beautiful, obscuring with shadows the glaring excess of furnishing that was the uniform error among the nouveau riche. His slippers on the carpet runners silenced his footsteps on the stairs. Mordecai descended, traversed the mezzanine, descended again, and walked on. His footsteps slowed when he saw golden light flickering around the music room door.

Unable to stem his curiosity, Mordecai walked toward it. And once so near the door, he could not resist turning the knob. It swung open without a sound on its oiled hinges.

Miss Paulson sat at the piano with her back to the door, as ignorant of his presence as she had been in her bedroom. By candlelight, she pantomimed playing the piano. Though her fingers stayed an inch above the keys, never touching down upon them, Mordecai knew the chord of each key and could see, and thus hear, a concert of Miss Paulson's composition. Whenever a hand moved beyond his view, that portion of the concert went silent for him. He guessed at the missing notes, but it could not satisfy, and Mordecai moved to widen his view of her hands.

Her fingers stilled.

Mordecai retreated a second too late – she startled upon sight of him, her satin robe sliding from her shoulder to catch in the crook of her arm.

Mesmerized, he beheld the girl in her state of undress, the lace-trimmed white linen nightshift no more substantial than sea foam, and her hair woven into a single braid without sufficient care to draw it back from her face.

The rising color in her cheeks reminded Mordecai of his own appearance. How must he look to her, with no makeup hiding his spots, no monocle balancing the misalignment of his eyes, no fake mustache mitigating his hawk nose, and no corset to force the stoop out of his back? He saw his unadulterated monstrosity in the shock transforming Miss Paulson's face. In the agitated workings of her throat, he could see all chance of his escape disappear. In the next moment, it would release a cry to tear the blanketing silence that held this house in stillness, raise the alarm and bring its inhabitants running. Everything about this tableau was irredeemable if someone discovered them. What perspective would they take of his standing over her? Miss Paulson's eyes widened, and her open mouth grew wider still. Mordecai braced for the scream that would end his career.

A smothered gasp broke free, "Mr. Michaelson—you're my age!"

Every muscle in his body jolted inward then shuddered loose individually, unraveling as comprehension of her words dawned. He gathered his wits, grabbing for dignity behind a stone demeanor. "I am three and twenty."

"I shall be twenty in July!" Her brown eyes danced merrily, brimming, he imagined, with laughter at him.

His brows snapped together. "Turning twenty in July, you ought know better than to be so jolly when a man surprises you in your undergarments."

"Oh, Lord!"

"Ssh ...!"

Miss Paulson pulled her robe up her arm, yanking the lapels to her chin and scrambling for the ties while hot color suffused her face to her hairline.

Her mortification sent Mordecai's umbrage dwindling to uncertainty. She hadn't realized the state of her clothing until he'd jabbed her about it. She unsettled him, and he knew he'd dealt a low blow, unsettling her in return. He made quiet amends while she knotted the sash with a violence that shook her lapels open. "There is no error on your part." She caught the lapels in one hand and fought with the other to pull the slippery satin closed over her knees. "Be at ease, I shall leave you."

Miss Paulson looked up. "Don't go," she mouthed.

The despair in her eyes put the burden of reason on him. "Neither of us ought to be here," he told her under his breath with his hand on the music room door. Turning to leave, he heard her whisper, "I've written something new."

His head turned a fraction of an inch.

"Should you like to hear it?"

He whispered back, "You cannot play the piano tonight."

"I did not play tonight," she persisted in a hush, "but you heard all the same."

Mordecai leaned toward the door, thinking to propel himself from the room by good intention but it didn't work. "Play it tomorrow," he said, "at your lesson."

"Grandmother won't want to hear it." With his back to her, he sensed she leaned forward. "No one cares to listen but you."

"But why are you here, Miss Paulson, with a spinet in your room?" He turned back in time to see her drop her eyes.

"You play here."

Mordecai turned to her fully, eyes narrowing.

Miss Paulson turned to the keys, her fingers rising above them.

Mordecai watched her fingers begin a slow dance through the air.

Her music's first moves wove intrigue and he could not anticipate where next it would take him. "That is a chancy beginning, Miss Paulson."

"Some beginnings are." She darted looks at him beneath her lashes.

The notes brought to life in the space above the keyboard entranced and delighted him. When her fingers stilled, bringing the silent music to an abrupt halt, Mordecai realized he now stood right behind her. "That cannot be the end of it."

"It is not."

He smothered a frustrated laugh. "You must finish it."

"I cannot – well," she allowed, "I haven't composed the ending. Perhaps ..." Her head tilted shyly downward but her gaze slanted up to him, "you might help me with it?"

Mordecai sat down beside her. "It is a grave mistake," he said—*to be here with you*—flashed through his mind and winked out in the dark, "to leave a masterpiece hanging." His fingers spread above the keys. He thought a moment. Then he began to play above the keys, the music taking shape in his mind and flowing to his fingertips. "This might ..."

"Oh, yes, I think so ..." she whispered, hands lifting. She struck the air above a key, followed it with several more.

Mordecai hummed in deep satisfaction. His fingers moved over the keys in a counterpoint improvisation.

Her body leaned with his when he reached for the farthest keys.

They played together in a silent duet, seeing and therefore hearing the nocturne as it formed itself, note by note, from the meeting of their minds. Four hands moved from the far ends toward the center of the keyboard; musicians so lost in the music, they did not notice the progress of their fingers until suddenly her left hand touched his right.

Both hands fell to the bench, an expanse of needlepointed cushion between them.

Mordecai's heart thundered. It was cold in the room but his body burned. He tried to breathe soundlessly, though it seemed when he tried, he could get no air. He took a mental count to regain command of himself. He had heard that in experiments with electricity, if a man touched a *live* wire the force rooted him in place. Though in danger of his life, he could not let go of the wire. Behind closed eyelids, Mordecai saw girlish fingers moving with nimble confidence across black and ivory keys. And his heartbeat accelerated still more. Words rumbled in his throat, "Miss Paulson, let go of my hand."

"But you are holding mine!" Her urgent whisper drew his attention to the space of bench between them.

With his senses in riot, he'd not apprehended the transgression at its moment of commission. He saw now that his hand crushed hers, but like the man with the live wire, Mordecai could not let go of it. In fact, he was bending down, or bringing her hand to his face; he could not tell which. Then he was kissing her bitten nails, the raw quicks and scabbed cuticles, as if by the touch of his lips he could heal them.

Her fingers straightened in his grasp and brushed across his face. The fingers of her other hand slid up his temple and buried deep in his thick, dark hair.

She's pushing me away. The realization plunged him into frozen waters, cold clarity rushing in. Mordecai's very presence in this room, alone with her at this hour, violated every boundary of class and propriety. To *kiss* this girl's bitten fingertips revealed a self-destructive strain of lunacy in his character that astonished and horrified him. Mordecai shrank from her, but his retreat must have unbalanced her for it seemed she swayed forward. He felt the stir of her breath as she whispered, "I love you."

Mordecai leapt to his feet, banging his hip on the keyboard and stumbling backward, made a grab for the piano's frame and pushed away from his pupil.

She'd kept from falling in the wake of his sudden retreat by grabbing the bench in both hands. Her braid had come undone, and her hair tumbled past her shoulders in long, loose curls. Her smooth skin shone with lingering heat. Mordecai stared with smarting eyes at this excess of beauty. He blinked several times.

"Now, see here." His voice died when she met his gaze. Her brown eyes glowed hazel with desire. A sense of unreality came over him at the same time his body stirred with renewing ardor. *This is all wrong. I'm ugly and she is not blind.* Did her inexperience trouble her? Was Miss Paulson experimenting, like the man with the live wire? Again, Mordecai felt unable to move, trapped by temptation. Now he knew himself a dog, because his incoherent imaginings placed her beneath him on the bench, and devil take the consequences.

"Mr. Michaelson," her soft, sweet voice trembled, "did you hear me?"

He admired her. He desired her. He could not also ruin her. He began helplessly, "Philomena ..."

Her eyes flashed. "You *do* feel some affection for me!"

Good Lord, had he really uttered her Christian name?

She urged, "Please give me the words."

Had he lost his mind?

"It might help me later ..." she trailed off with a sigh.

Mordecai backtracked with a cool apology, "I showed undue familiarity." *An understatement, to be sure.* "I beg your pardon."

She looked mutinous. "I should like that you beg anything of me but my *pardon*."

"That is all I have a right to request," Mordecai asserted. "You can have no illusion as to my place in society – indeed, I have none."

"Oh, but you do have a place!" she murmured, touching a hand to her chest.

"Do not touch your heart," he clipped, "as if society had any care for the feelings residing there."

"But do you care?"

Yes, Mordecai's heart said. *Yes. Yes. Yes!* His lips said, "No."

Philomena's eyes widened, brimming with sudden tears.

Mordecai cleared his throat carefully, painfully, around unnamed emotions that seemed to have crystallized there. "You presume a choice in the matter," he grated.

"But I do not choose what my—"

"Your world, to its innermost orbit, cares only for choices that advance its own fortune."

"Yes, I know but ..." Color deepened in her cheeks. "Cannot you and I—"

"What?"

She looked about the room, struggling for words.

"They decided your future in advance of your birth. I cannot change it, nor can you."

Philomena bent her head.

The forward tumble of her shining hair begged his caress. Mordecai clasped his hands behind his back. He looked away.

"What shall I do?"

Her despairing little question wrenched him with such force that he wondered he could find his voice at all. But in rejecting her hopes, he'd removed the beam upon which she'd been leaning, so he knew he must answer. Mordecai searched his mind for the markers that had turned his path so far from the only destination the uncaring world had assigned him. "Persevere, Miss Paulson." It meant nothing, but in his entire life, it amounted to everything. It was all he could give her.

CHAPTER 5

Next morning's lesson was a disaster. Whatever tune he set her playing, she segued into one of her own compositions. "Stop!" Mordecai barked.
Her grandmother looked up.
Philomena's hands stilled. They were gloved, one cotton fingertip spotted with fresh blood.
Her soft cheek flushed. A stray curl twined down her neck. The flowers in her hair emanated an exotic yet innocent scent. He longed to soothe with soft kisses the puffy, faintly purple smudges beneath her eyes. Her dress had tiered skirts of some gossamer fabric that he itched to rub between his fingers. Her nearness filled him with restless heat.
"Play only the music I set before you, Miss Paulson," he said flatly.
She began dutifully, with none of her characteristic skill. The notes plodded one after the other like a dimwitted child learning to walk.
Mordecai stared out the window. The sheep didn't bother grazing today. Sunlight glittered on the frozen hills.
When he'd walked into the music room this morning, Philomena looked as if she didn't recognize him. He realized she'd anticipated the real Mordecai, sans makeup and false moustache. She must have pictured him thus all night while sleep eluded her.

Mordecai had managed to sleep – finally. He'd dreamed such visions of mutual delight between himself and his pupil that he'd wakened to find his bedclothes sticky and warm.

While staring into the distance and repressing his fevered dreams, he became aware the piano piece had ended. He glanced past the grandmother to Philomena's averted face.

Her lashes trembled. Her gloved hands fidgeted.

"It's fine," he pronounced. The non-committal judgment conveyed displeasure.

"I have a ...slight headache," she murmured.

"I should not think it relevant," her grandmother scolded.

"'Tis well enough, madame, I assure you," Mordecai said tiredly.

The old lady's eyes glittered at his contradiction, but she considered her granddaughter for a moment before saying, "Very well, you may go."

Philomena fled.

"I ask your pardon, my good lady." Mordecai addressed her deferentially, mindful that he'd made a gaffe, "I find overtaxing a student hinders further learning. Miss Paulson is at such a point in her training, but I did make the point with undue bluntness."

"Oh, it's no matter now," the dowager said with breezy indifference. "She played poorly, I'll grant you, but she was distracted, as any girl would be in her situation."

"I'm afraid I don't follow ..." Mordecai trailed off, feeling dread gather in his stomach.

"The young St. Claire begged a moment alone with Philomena last night."

Did he, by God?

"Such a request can have but one objective," the old lady breezed on, "an objective confirmed in private conversation with Philomena's father directly afterward.

Yes, confirmed and soundly agreed to."

Agreed to hours before a midnight walk to the music room.

"A proposal by any gentleman might distract a girl from lessons, but an offer from this particular gentleman is her dearest wish and the culmination of her family's every hope. I shouldn't wonder she's given herself a headache from excitement. I doubt she slept at all!"

Mordecai stood when she stood and bowed as she passed. When she swept out of the room, he didn't straighten. The news bent him double as if by a physical blow. He couldn't breathe and for a moment, sight deserted him. He heard only the thick pounding of his heart. He ground his teeth, struggling to put down a violent surge of tangled emotions. He wanted to steal Philomena, hide her from all eyes save his own. He could not abide the alternative, the very real and *confirmed* alternative of her belonging to another.

Vision cleared with his sudden resumption of breath. He caught sight of something beneath the piano bench. Bending further to retrieve it caused the bench to obscure his view of the object and thus, for a moment more, keep its identity a mystery. Mordecai felt it as a silky sliver caught between his fingers. Rising caused a thousand twinges in his malformed back. At last, he stood completely and held to the light the strip of scarlet silk that had slid from her braid last night.

Caught in its knot was a bright filament, a long strand of her golden-brown hair.

CHAPTER 6

Mordecai had always supposed Hell to be a fiery place threatening only those on the brink of traveling there. But Philomena's betrothal kindled the edges of his life, embers eating inward and consuming him by inches. The sight of his rival leaving the Paulson residence with triumph in his every step shot through Mordecai's heart like a flare. Worse, to see them leaving together on social visits.

Charlie St. Claire, like any adventurous young man of means in this miraculous age, motored himself about when in the country. He took as much proprietary interest in Philomena's preparations to ride in his extraordinary contraption of brass and leather as he did in the vehicle, itself. He fastened her motoring coat with a care Mordecai envied, fitted goggles to her face and tied the scarf beneath her chin while bending his head to speak to her as the social equal Mordecai could never be. It stung his eyes to watch the other man place a hand on Philomena's waist to aid her ascent into the motor car before he jumped in and roared off in a fusillade of tire-thrown gravel and clouds of steam.

Mordecai hated this man for reasons beyond his control. However, he could control the manner in which he pined for a girl beyond his reach. He resolved to sicken himself no longer with spying. Mordecai avoided visual provocation, but there was no avoiding Philomena's music.

Now she'd given her family the outcome they craved, they gave her free rein to play anything she wrote. He thought they must have turned a deaf ear to the music, for how else to explain their indifference to the obvious genius of its creator? Only Mordecai knew these were new compositions, each more haunting and sorrowful than the last. The hallways channeled it everywhere. The high domed ceilings held and amplified it. Mordecai knew Philomena's music was her way of speaking to him. He sat alone and listened, with her ribbon curled in the palm of his hand, the single strand of her hair shining bright.

Mordecai hid this secret love token inside his waistcoat when he packed his belongings. He made preparations to leave in concert with others, as part of a coordinated and large-scale operation. The successful event of a society wedding had become the household's overriding ambition. It necessitated a change of scene, as well.

Lest a country wedding cast them as country people, subject to condescension from the smart set for decades to come, the Paulsons set their sights on London. Mordecai knew they had the added burden of ensuring they never gave society cause to believe they hid Philomena, else people should cast about in whispers for the reason they might have hidden her. In swift order, they lit out for the city.

Their caravan of coaches diminished in elegance according to the rank of passenger, with the family's lavish coach in the lead and the lowest servants still deemed essential at the tail end. Mordecai rode somewhere in the middle, in company with the governess. Now that Philomena's education had achieved its most ambitious aim, they had both to seek employment elsewhere. Perhaps this predicament obsessed the governess as she stared out her window. Mordecai kept eyes steady on the rolling fields outside his own window, as he recalled his last encounter with Philomena's father.

Mr. Paulson had wanted a celebratory drink with another man and having no one of his own class to choose from at the late hour, he'd invited the piano instructor into his study. Mr. Paulson had handed the tumbler of whiskey with care not to touch Mordecai, then lifted his own in a toast without looking directly at him.

Long accustomed to ignoring slights of this nature, Mordecai gave his congratulations on the upcoming nuptials without the slightest sign he found them repugnant. He smiled placidly while Mr. Paulson extolled the virtues of the match. Philomena's future father-in-law was a captain of industry, and in securing his son, she linked her family with a fortune immeasurable.

Mordecai had wondered how they'd resolve the matter of genetic testing prior to betrothal announcement. By custom, a girl's family offered to have her tested at a laboratory chosen by the boy's family. It had become fashionable for the boy's family to make a show of declining the offer, as a gesture of faith in the girl's pedigree. Still, the St. Claires had been in their right. But it seemed their son was too smitten to entertain doubts regarding Philomena's genetic code.

"He likes her playing," Mr. Paulson told Mordecai, "says she looks very pretty at the piano." Flushed and perhaps more drunk with his daughter's conquest than with his fine whiskey, the man felt inclined to be generous. "She won't take lessons anymore now she's got the wedding to plan, but your contract's not up. You may stay on til' you've found a situation."

Mordecai ground his teeth in memory of this offer, as if he could bear to stay and witness Philomena fitted with a dress and trousseau for her marriage to another man. Could he touch a piano without the side of his body craving the companion warmth of hers? The promise of a musical life mocked him. All music but Philomena's sounded insipid to him now. Mordecai's future stretched out before him as a lonely passage of time in a blur of days and years.

The Paulson's four-story stone mansion stood close to the street in a row of mansions similar in character. Beneath each of its forty front windows, wrought iron baskets spilled evergreen vines down its brownstone facade. The caravan, running brilliant to shabby like a molting snake, curled around the city block into a narrow alley to fill a cobblestone courtyard at the rear of the Paulson residence.

Footmen opened the door of the first coach and helped the Paulson women out. Mr. Paulson jumped down, danced like a pugilist in his spit-polished boots and rolled his shoulders to loosen the kinks in his back. He passed a satisfied glance over his mansion, cooling in its shadow where it blocked the setting sun, then strode indoors. Mordecai stepped out just in time to see Philomena disappear into the house. She looked back over her shoulder and met his gaze.

Her wide-eyed glance of longing and despair struck him motionless and set his heart hammering. *It's no dream. She cares for me, but they will give her to another.* A dark fury worked through him with such force he thought himself a changeling, a malevolent stranger as internally misshapen as the outer shell of his twisted body.

Mordecai walked into the house, strode through the immense, marble-tiled foyer past the spiral staircase, out the front doors, and into a street that blinded with the reflective brilliance of countless windows set in a continuous run of stonefront mansions.

He kept walking, as streets narrowed and buildings shortened and the air grew dank. He walked until he found a neighborhood that matched his mood. He entered a public house.

He ordered one pint after another until he felt heavy in his chair, but his mind remained cursedly clear. In the few moments it had taken him to walk through the Paulsons' city mansion, his mind had recorded every detail of its infrastructure. The activities of the household revolved around the spiral stair at the house's core. Each floor was a mezzanine onto which all the doors of its outer rooms opened. The foyer rose fifty feet to a multi-paned skylight.

He knew exactly how such a house was run, how little secrecy it afforded. Still, the floor plan's very openness allowed concealment, with no one save the mother and grandmother entering Philomena's rooms without the duenna's permission. It ensured close observation of every inmate who might otherwise discover the girl's secret.

He knew that he could not stay there. Mordecai feared the strength of the changeling newly resident within him and the direction in which it might pull him. Instead, he took a flat, and sent for his things.

In no time, he found new pupils – all in the bourgeois class, for cholera was so rife in the slums that he taught there at risk to his life. His salary from the Paulsons continued. This, added to fees paid by the parents of new students rendered Mordecai every material comfort, but he suffered agonies in spirit. Each pretty, perfect bourgeois pupil was so like Philomena in demeanor and dress that it beguiled his senses to fantasy. Sometimes he turned his head and did see Philomena; ogled her soft cheek, her graceful neck, the sunlit gold strands in her brown curls. Gradually, the very real, very different girl who sat in Philomena's seat replaced the vision and Mordecai despaired of his sanity.

Once, while sleeping in his narrow bed, he felt her turn over and throw an arm over him. She pressed her body against him. He felt her warmth and shape. He heard her whisper, "I'm yours." Mordecai woke to the cold darkness of an empty room. He stared into his loneliness and felt it devour him.

Mordecai began to doubt his memory. Had Philomena's backward glance truly expressed longing for him? Sleep deprived, hollow eyed, and frayed in daylight hours, Mordecai faltered in trusting the very reality of her. Perhaps, Philomena as he'd known her – shy, sweet, sensitive – had been nothing more than a fair guise concealing an imp who'd chosen him to tease and torment. She rode his shoulder, whispered in his ear, beat the very blood through his veins at her whim, and strode the dark corridors of his mind as he'd once strolled the dark corridors of her country house. He could not rid himself of wanting her. He hadn't strength to try. He became dimly aware of his descent but hadn't energy or will to slow his fall.

But one day while listening to her play another of those dull, conventional piano pieces instead of one or her originals, he'd snapped, "Have you really nothing for me, then?"

A startled silence answered him, then a hesitant, "Mr. Michaelson?"

Mordecai's gaze slid sideways and took her in. She was someone's daughter but not Mr. Paulson's.

He felt the grandmother's eyes on him. She wasn't Philomena's grandmother. He'd have welcomed that gorgon if it gave him back Philomena for an instant.

His gaze dropped. *It will never do.* He told himself to worry. There was something to worry about, after all. If word got out he'd gone barmy, who'd hire him? What should he live on? He tried to care, but his head swam. He rose unsteadily from the bench. "Forgive me." And stumbled away. "I'm unwell."

He arrived home to find something in the post addressed to him, the envelope a thick stock of such quality its texture looked like cream. He drew out the paper and read the short, imperative note from Theodore Paulson, a summons to play piano at his daughter's betrothal party. The note made clear in Paulson's economical style that he expected Mordecai to fulfill his contract in this way if not the other. Not that it mattered to Mordecai.

He crumpled the note.

There had never been any question but that he would go to her.

CHAPTER 7

Mordecai plunged into musical fanfare. On cue, Philomena stepped into view on the mezzanine to ecstatic applause from the guests below. Though he'd thought himself hidden behind the crowd, her eyes found him first. His notion that she was only an imp sent to torment him vanished. Her spontaneous smile was for him. It lit her entire being. It shone in her eyes. Mordecai cut his eyes to the crowd, and his visual warning made her look at them.

Liking her acknowledgement, they cheered all the more. It was not the first round of champagne to fill the flutes they now held high in tribute. Mr. Paulson had opened his wine cellar far in advance of his daughter's entrance, and Mrs. Paulson had arranged Mordecai's sheet music with meticulous attention toward steering emotion along a trajectory. Their combined efforts met success to a degree that rendered Philomena's beauty immaterial to the outcome.

An adoring atmosphere held her aloft in a golden bubble. Mordecai mellowed his tune from triumphal to sentimental, following the script from Philomena's dramatic entrance to her pause for admiration. Diamonds glittered in her curls and sparkled at her ears and neck. Her pale blue dress shimmered like a thousand daylit stars.

He doubted her mother's judgment. Ought they

manipulate the collective gaze on Philomena, just at the moment she must descend a spiral wrought iron staircase? The long train on that glittering dress could prove disastrous. Mrs. Paulson perhaps banked all on the fiancé at Philomena's side, on the strength and guidance of that crooked elbow into which Philomena had tucked her small, gloved hand.

He'd avoided it, but now Mordecai made himself take his first look at the man, up close.

No one could fault his height or build, and his clothing stood a credit to his tailor. Convention held him to be handsome, for it valued smooth skin, regular features and blond hair brushed to gleaming. He seemed an easy-mannered gentleman, to be sure, willing to stand in full view of an admiring crowd for as long as it required him to receive its congratulations, while a pretty girl clung to his arm. Did his easy manner derive from arrogance, rather than affability? Did his smile span within a hair's breadth of a smirk? Mordecai did not like to think so for the elemental reason that Philomena's lifelong happiness depended upon the young man's character. Philomena's fiancé inclined his head to her, and his blue eyes roved her lovely face.

His expression gave Mordecai a chill.

Could possessiveness and boredom coexist in a lover's gaze?

Mordecai hoped the impression owed more to his jealousy than to intuition.

With a slight movement of his arm, the young man turned Philomena's attention from her guests to the stairs. She murmured assent, and they moved as one to the precipice.

Or so it seemed a precipice to Mordecai. The long train to her dress flowed heavily and silkily, as if with a serpentine will of its own.

Philomena took the stairs with practiced grace.

Mordecai perceived no undue pressure on the arm beneath her hand. Her fiancé guided her down the iron spiral with the exquisite care of one bearing an ornament of spun glass.
He knows!
It struck him like a plug of brandy. It hit his stomach and flushed his skin and made him dizzy.
Fearing to hope, Mordecai dared to wonder.
Could he know she walks with the aid of a false leg?
Mordecai did not know anyone who believed deformity existed above a certain caste. The society present held it as taboo. A mark of inferior breeding caused immediate expulsion from their ranks. *Yet he must know. Why else handle her so tenderly during the everyday act of descending a stair?* He'd found out, somehow. Philomena may have confessed it.
He knows, but loves her anyway. Perhaps, all the more so.
Mordecai pounded the keys in jubilant exclamation at the moment the couple stepped off the last stair – just as Mrs. Paulson had directed him to do.
The champagne-fueled well wishers engulfed them.
Philomena's mother and grandmother exchanged a look that read, *We have done it!*
This fleeting glance of mutual congratulation undermined Mordecai's certainty. It had been a furtive connection between conspirators. Conspiracies exist in secrecy. They have no reason to exist, otherwise.
The muscles grown taut with exhilaration collapsed as Mordecai drooped inwardly. He tried to rally. Perhaps Philomena's fiancé kept the secret at her request.
Mordecai looked around at the men puffed up with their own importance, at their sons already melting into plumpness induced by overindulgence of food and drink. Their daughters conversed without listening, while their attention roved the room. These maidens held nothing in beauty compared to their mothers and grandmothers.

Cosmetics and creams, knives and hairline stitches ensured timeless allure. Barbed strips caught muscle beneath the skin and pulled a face back up to its original position. Light applications of acid burned away wrinkles. Surgeons inserted pliable cushions into the breasts of these aging Aphrodites and vacuumed fat from their flaccid arms. Perhaps Mordecai could have stood up straight, slept through the night, and seen the world through the unified vision of matching eyes, but these remedies didn't exist. The science of vanity outpaced the science of compassion, and all sciences catered to an income far above his own.

Could anyone in this crowd love Philomena as she was? As Mordecai loved her?

Her betrothed would have to be an extraordinary young man to overcome the prejudice of his upbringing.

The signal was given for dinner, and the young man offered his arm to Philomena's mother, who accepted the courtly gesture with a triumphant glance at her smiling mother-in-law.

Mordecai watched them go, willing him to be all that Philomena deserved in a husband.

With nothing left to do, but contracted to stay the evening, he kept his seat at the piano near the front door. The open door behind him showed the shadowy interior of a parlor, from the depths of which came the sonorous toll of a grandfather clock. Dinner stretched on for the guests, but Mordecai didn't envy them, for he had no appetite. He began to play Philomena's music as a means of having her near. The clock had struck two more times before he heard the distant noise of a midsize orchestra tuning up in the ballroom, but he cared as little for that as he had for dinner. Losing himself in the music of his most beloved composer, Mordecai lost track of time. He forgot his environment completely until someone sat down beside him with a swish of silk and chiffon and a subtle cloud of powdery, floral perfume.

"You should be with your guests."

"I thought you were calling me."

He had been, though until now he'd played her compositions with no awareness of his ulterior motive. Unable to resist their favorite preoccupation, her fingers ran alongside his over the keyboard. Playing companionably together was sweeter than anything Mordecai could imagine.

She said beneath the music, "He'll tire of me."

"I never should."

"But he's not like you," she said through a smile of pleasure, blushing. "No one's like you." She played counterpoint to his point. "He'll tire of me, and after I've had children—" Her fingers faltered on the keys. "If he wants to have children after he sees—"

Mordecai's hands stopped. He drew a heavy breath. "He doesn't know."

Her head turned swiftly in his direction. He felt her astonished stare. *No, of course, she wouldn't tell him.* She would have been brave, indeed, to overcome the prejudice of her upbringing.

"Who wouldn't want children with you?"

Philomena gestured toward her legs, her words running over each other in terror – "If he'll even still want me—"

"He'll want you," Mordecai grated. "What man could help himself? If you only knew how I—"

Her sudden grip on his hands cut him short.

"Oh Mordecai, don't you see?"

He looked up from their joined hands to see her face flushed as if by fever.

"He'll tire of me!"

Had any woman said such a thing before and sounded so happy?

"He'll leave me to my own devices, my own interests, my own friends!" Her breath caught on a tiny laugh as if she found his incomprehension amusing. "What care he

40

then if his wife hires a music teacher?"

She put his hands to her heart. Beneath her warm skin, its fierce rhythm drummed into his palms. Mordecai's breathing grew shallow, and he had a moment's difficulty hearing Philomena.

"Naturally, my children shall have a music teacher." Her voice deepened to a husky whisper, "I'll have my dear maestro with me once more."

Mordecai bent toward her hands where they held his to her heart. His lips moved reverently over her fingers. He felt her cheek nestle in his hair. Mordecai's hands slipped beneath hers and slid down.

Her corset-bound, warm and definite shape brought clarity to his fogged brain. With a harsh intake of breath, he broke away from her, eyes darting about the massive open space. Anyone could have seen them. Yet, the mezzanines were empty, the doorways empty. They'd been lucky. That was all.

Philomena's cheeks burned with hectic color. Her brown eyes gleamed, a thin ring of color blazing around the high-gloss black of her dilated pupils. Her visible arousal struck him such a blow that he almost reached for her again. Instead, he warned raggedly, "Have a care."

Her eyes widened in belated realization of the risk.

Mordecai shifted away from her on the bench. "Leave me."

"I don't think I have the strength."

"Then play something."

She joined him in the composition he'd renewed.

The caress of her face against the top of his head had disarranged a few curls from her artful coiffure. Mordecai chuckled and tucked the errant strands behind her ear.

"Philomena?"

The male voice brought their heads up.

CHAPTER 8

Her fiancé stood at the entry of the hall that led to the ballroom. He'd not been there a moment before. Mordecai was sure of it.
Philomena blurted, "Charles!"
"He touched your hair."
"It was disordered from dancing."
"Indeed not." Charlie's eyes glittered coldly. "I danced with you last, and should know." He walked into the foyer.
Philomena began playing a charming little parlor piece, a ludicrous thing that would have made Mordecai wince under different circumstances. "Mr. Michaelson has been my piano teacher for years."
Mordecai hadn't thought her capable of dissembling. It surprised him. But she'd read her fiancé's narrowed eyes. Training for the rest of her married life, she reinforced her lie, "Why, he's almost like a second father."
"He touched you as a lover."
"Naturally he'd straighten my hair," she prattled on, "he still thinks me a child."
"Can you really enjoy that freak's touch?"
The piano blared as her fingers plunged. Her eyes spat fire. "How dare you speak of him in that manner!"
"You'll not embarrass me." The young man's face constricted to a mask. "Stand up and come back with me now."

Mordecai saw now how the marriage would be. Philomena saw it, too. "I cannot marry you."

"I'll say what you can and cannot do." His clipped tone turned lazy. "I'd just as soon marry you now, as ever. A girl who fools around with the help can have no undue expectations of *my* behavior."

The piano bench scraped the floor as Mordecai shot to his feet. "I warn you, sir."

Charlie didn't spare him a glance. "Philomena, if you do not rise, I shall drag you."

"I cannot rise." She was turning and twisting on the bench, trying to free her voluminous skirts from its legs. The long silky train had twisted around the piano's pedals.

What Mordecai saw from his position, Charlie could not see from his. Two bright spots bloomed in the man's smooth-shaven cheeks. Knuckles turned white in his tightening fists as he lunged at the piano.

Mordecai stepped into his path. "You frighten Miss Paulson."

"I mean to," Charlie retorted, scowling at her. "What do you mean, tossing your skirts in that idiotic way?"

"Philomena, where are you?"

The imperious tone froze them in place.

"Here, Grandmother!"

The lady appeared as if materialized by the tension around the piano. Her shrewd gaze comprehended Mordecai and Philomena instantly. Then it landed on Charlie with the full force of her charm. "Mr. St. Claire, I see you've arrived just in time to rescue my granddaughter."

"I have, madam," Charlie said with a flash of teeth.

"Her old maestro is fond of her playing, to be sure," Mrs. Paulson waved at the piano as if it were a trifle. "She's no interest since making your acquaintance, but she hates to disappoint him."

Mesmerized by her grandmother's machinations,

Philomena struggled blindly to free her skirts. Mordecai gently moved her shaking hands aside before making the attempt himself.

The old lady shot to his side. "I shall assist her."

But he'd met with some success and would not be diverted. Mordecai held Philomena's foot to pull her skirts' twisted silk free of it.

"Mr. Michaelson, release my granddaughter this instant."

He felt hard, smooth wood beneath her slipper's thin kid leather.

"You heard Mrs. Paulson." Charlie barreled into Mordecai, knocking him backwards, upsetting the bench and sending Philomena back with a cry and a tearing of fabric.

"Charles, no!" Philomena cried.

But he grabbed her foot to jerk the dress from the pedals.

Forgetting the dress, he gaped at her foot.

Then he shoved his hand up her leg, even as she tried to squirm away from him.

Shock ripped through his face. "She's got a fake le—"

His head jerked sideways in a spray of blood. He crashed to the marble floor.

Philomena screamed.

Her grandmother stood over the fallen man, clutching a heavy candlestick that dripped gore.

Orchestral music rushed through opening ballroom doors, pulling Mrs. Paulson's head around.

Philomena stared in horror at the blood spreading from beneath her fiancé's head. "Is he dead?" she quavered as Mordecai felt for a pulse.

Voices and footsteps overtook the escaping waltz.

Mordecai confirmed the worst with a grim nod.

Mrs. Paulson threw the candelabra in his direction and let out a shattering scream.

"Grandmother, what are you doing?"

A running crowd rounded the corner. Mrs. Paulson flung an arm. Rigid from shoulder to manicured fingertip, she pointed to Mordecai. "Murderer!"

CHAPTER 9

Philomena threw herself at him. "Go!"

"I am innocent!" he protested.

"You cannot be, for if you are it ruins everything for them." She pushed him through the nearest doorway; not the front entrance, for the piano obstructed the path, but into the parlor at Mordecai's back. Her young face drawn into a mask of desperation, she pleaded with him, "No court will take your word against hers." Panic gave her strength as she lurched forward, beating at him and pushing. Running footsteps grew in number down the hall. Philomena's voice thinned with panic, "Go!"

He collided with a closed window. Philomena pushed up the sash. Cold air buffeted his back as sounds of a mob filled the foyer.

The grandmother's voice rose over all, "He's fled through that room!"

Shock and outrage made him witless and weak. Philomena was able to shove him backwards out the window before he knew her intent. Gravity pulled him, and resisting Philomena's thrusting hands stole the last of his balance. He fell as if thrown, in a pinwheeling flail of arms and legs, landing on mossy ground and rolling down an incline. He got his feet under him and wobbled to stand. Something hit him in the leg like a bowl into pins. His knees buckled but he braced himself and caught Philomena in the bargain, yanking her upright with a growl of incoherent temper. Concern replaced irritation. "Are you alright?"

She didn't hear him. She was gazing up to the window. The wooden sash had fallen, trapping the fake leg between window frame and sill.

Caught at the ankle, it extended far outside, dangling leather straps and buckles. It was a doll's leg that Mr. Paulson raced to conceal with a flare of his dinner jacket's tails. His back blocked view out the window from the interior. Mordecai heard him shout, "He has gone!"

Philomena's shoulders went slack, and Mordecai reckoned by his proclamation the man had just dealt the fatal blow to what remained of his child's respect. It's generally assumed even indifferent fathers make some attempt at catching a daughter who falls or leaps from a window. But assumptions of this nature do not account for the precedence of lineage over offspring, the irreversible death of reputation once perception of a family's genetic infallibility has withered.

"His bluff can't hold them back forever." Philomena's head whipped around to apprehend their predicament in a sweeping glance.

Party guests flowed into the street, eager to spot a fleeing murderer.

They mustn't catch her up without two legs beneath her. With her fiancé's shocked revulsion upon discovery of her wooden leg fresh in his mind, Mordecai refused to lose her to the collective scorn of a crowd. Philomena must never learn shame as he knew it.

A high wrought iron fence bisected the long and narrow grassy corridor between the Paulson mansion and its neighbor. Midnight cloaked the fugitives, and ornamental trees gone skeletal in winter screened them. Next door, closed shutters parted. Light sliced outward. Mordecai drew Philomena back.

Anxiety quavered in her voice, "Oh, Mordecai, where to go?"

He bent and swept her up into his arms.

Down the length of the landscaped strip, gaslit orbs topped iron lampposts in a series of flickering moons. Passing each one marked off in increments the distance from his would-be captors. Moving within shadows against the wall, he dared hope he yet escaped view, but voices grew louder behind them as some deserted the street for the side garden in search of him here. The slight weight of Philomena's trembling body and the trusting clasp of her arms around his shoulders leant him strength and speed. He passed the last barren tree and iron lamppost, turned a corner and stepped onto cobblestone.

Here they were confronted with the next obstacle to their freedom: coaches filled the courtyard, horse nose to back bumper. Firelight cast them in silhouette, for coachmen and footmen had a good blaze going in a barrel. They waited for their masters to leave the party, a shift that may come soon or not til' dawn. At their own disposal in the meantime, they amused themselves with drink. Mordecai couldn't see them, nor they him. Far away they were, near the courtyard's gated entrance. He could tell by the pitch of their voices and the range of their laughter that merrymaking had reached its zenith. This in no way meant they were too drunk to chase him should they discover Mordecai carrying Philomena. She was of the gentry. His twisted form gave evidence that he was not. The appearance was that of a kidnapping and there would be a fine monetary incentive for them in thwarting that; all the more so, if guests coming up the side garden alerted them of a murderer on foot.

In the diminishing time afforded him, Mordecai snuck around coaches, careful not to startle the horses who dozed into their feedbags. A sudden lean of a powerful body could knock him to the ground. A diving hoof could crush his foot. Mordecai held Philomena tighter, lest such an accident bring her injury. To his surprise, she reached out and laid a tender hand on the nearest flank. As Mordecai hastened by, Philomena caressed each horse, gently soothing them to acceptance of the interlopers.

In this way they quietly reached the means of their next escape, the coach parked nearest the courtyard's open gates. A family crest gleamed with glossy paint across the coach's door, shining reflective of the barrel fire when Mordecai opened it.

Despite the danger and urgency of their errand, Mordecai was loathe to relinquish his lovely burden. He settled her quietly, carefully into the vehicle's opulent interior, already missing the warmth and shape of her. Mordecai set his mind against sensuality and self indulgence and trained it on his mission. Closing the coach door, he thanked a thousand gods for oiled hinges, dozing horses, and men distracted by the bottle. Climbing up to take the reins, he refused to contemplate his complete ignorance of handling a coach and horses. These horses, two bays resting in their latent power, were as yet ignorant they should soon be called to duty, for his stealth gave them no warning. Theirs would be a rude awakening, but wake they must and at a gallop.

Recalling past observation of coachmen at duty, Mordecai flicked reins across their backs. They jumped to violent wakefulness, causing Mordecai to make an involuntary snap of the reins that sliced the horses' withers.

In reaction, the bays exploded out of the open gate, throwing Mordecai on his backside. Alarmed, his reflex was to rein them in, but he snapped the reins again and again, pushing them to racecourse velocity. Too soon, there erupted behind him, cries of "Thief!" Whipcracks and the maddened neighing of horses, shod hooves ringing out on cobblestones – all tumult beating Mordecai's pulses to hammering force at his temples. The bays ran with only the slightest tug on the reins as Mordecai's senses ran riot along with them. Every jostle of the vehicle beneath him, every sharp turn and startled pedestrian, every shout from his pursuers heightened his fear. The horses, intuitive beasts, took fright from his terror. And poor Philomena, who depended on him as her rescuer, was almost certainly afraid. It was insupportable.

Mordecai calmed himself by picturing in his mind the street patterns of the neighborhood. His vision mapped outward. He mentally traced the confusing snarls of byways and highways, selecting and rejecting from their number until a route arranged itself. As he strategized, it seemed the noise behind him dimmed. The horses calmed and grew more responsive to his demands. Their slower gait did not bring him within reach of his pursuers, as he'd feared. Listening for them and seeking them out as he turned corners revealed his success in giving them the slip.

The coachmen had given up, but he was not fool enough to think the Paulsons and their guests had done so. The map his mind perused contained thoroughfares filling with police wagons, detectives and lookouts. These he must avoid as long as his path to a certain address allowed it. He kept to back streets and alleys. Sleepy neighborhoods and shuttered mercantile districts may trouble him little. Peril presented itself in the bright avenues to which those seeking diversions, respectable or otherwise, gave custom. Mordecai had never taken notice of coachmen on duty. Now he set his mind on it, for though he wore no livery, the night might well disguise him if he played the part. Affecting the ruse, Mordecai traversed the small city's dense, complex and varied environment, his mind ever steady on a place he felt sure should admit him.

CHAPTER 10

At Mordecai's insistent knocking, the door finally opened.
"We're closed—" The man stopped abruptly when he saw he saw Philomena. Jaw dropping, he goggled at her. Meeting the eye of the man who carried her, his consternation deepened.

"Mr. Michaelson, what can you mean calling at this hour, by alleyway?" He glanced quickly up and down the alley. "And with a ..." His quick assessment of her proved the first impression as he beckoned them in. Gazing after Mordecai as he closed the service door, he finished speaking in a tone of wonder, " ...with a lady ..."

Philomena clung to Mordecai as she looked around the tailor's shop. Bolts of wool and silk covered every wall. Paper patterns and other accoutrements of the trade piled atop every table and chair.

"I was just tidying up." Their host lunged at one such overloaded surface and swept all aside.

Mordecai seated Philomena.

The daughter of privilege and the stocky workman gazed at one another in open curiosity.

"A lady!" the tailor marveled. "Here!" His ginger brows snapped together. Mordecai bearing her through an alley at night suddenly connected in the worst way possible. "You've run away with her."

"Not for reasons you suppose, Mr. Bloom."

"I could scarcely credit my suspicions – for reasons that flatter you and others that insult you." He cut himself off with a half shake of the head, an impatient glance at Mordecai. "But what complexion can I place on such a matter?"

Mordecai leaned a hip on a table, folded his arms across his chest. "We've known each other a long time, have we not?"

"Years."

"You've come to know me as a man of character?"

"Sterling, sir."

"There's been a blunder. I mean to mend it."

Philomena's head came up with the cry, "Blunder?" while Bloom scowled and demanded, "Who made the blunder?"

"I took her from danger. Its specific nature you'll hear of soon enough, but not from me."

"Much obliged if you tell me nothing to which others may hold me accountable."

"He didn't do it!" Philomena blurted.

Bloom cut a glance her way.

"She's a witness," Mordecai said.

"Unimpeachable?"

"Vulnerable."

The tailor took a deep breath. "Only say, Mr. Michaelson, has the danger passed?"

"For the lady, it can pass," he answered, "with your help."

Mr. Bloom laughed in self-derision. "Indeed, sir? I, a tailor to gentleman of misproportions, help a lady? She is – if I may say so, Miss – quite beautifully dressed already."

"I know you to be an artisan of a different sort, the finest in the city."

"You flatter me."

"In the entire country, I shouldn't wonder."

"But how can—"

"Miss Paulson," Mordecai spoke with calm authority, "if you please, lift your skirts."

Mr. Bloom gasped at the request. Philomena blushed furiously. She bit her lip and looked to Mordecai in appeal.

His gaze glinted. "Show Mr. Bloom—"

"I cannot!" she squeaked. "No one must see." Her features thinned in anguish. "It's a secret!"

His voice deepened in texture, "Do you trust me?"

"Yes..." she sighed brokenly.

The tailor looked from one to the other intently.

Drawing strength from Mordecai's steady gaze, Philomena lifted the shimmering blue tide of her evening dress inch by inch. Mr. Bloom saw first the pointed toe, then the entire of one exquisitely embroidered kid slipper. Light seemed to trace her delicate ankle in the silk sheen of her stocking. The fine silk gleamed along her sleek calf. There was fascination in the tailor's gaze, for if he'd never seen a lady up close, he'd never expected to see one expose her leg to him, but kindness and patience also lingered in his eyes. Watching him, Mordecai saw the exact moment the man registered the absence of the other leg.

Philomena held her hems far above the knee, her cheeks flaming. Silk garters held the mauve silk stockings. One contained her beautiful leg from mid-thigh to toe. The other was full at mid-thigh but its shredded end fell flat as a deflated balloon where her lower thigh would have met her knee.

Bloom's face contorted as he tried to reconcile reality with the impossible.

Misinterpreting his expression, Philomena let out an anguished cry and pushed her skirts down. The beaded silk slid heavily beneath a cloud of chiffon to hide her lifelong secret.

"Nay, Philomena—" Mordecai rushed to enlighten her, as the tailor with the lift of a placating hand, murmured, "Easy, lass ..."

Then Bloom declared, full-throated with shock, "There's never been a lady missing a limb!" He backed up, staring at the floor. "I'm not what you'd call on intimate terms with the gentry, but certain things are known—" His head came up. "It doesn't happen to them!"

"It happened to me," Philomena murmured.

"A tragic accident, perhaps," Bloom suggested. "I'll own that even people of quality can be unlucky. That's what happened to you, Miss, eh? A tragic accident?"

"The tragedy was my birth." Philomena kept her eyes on her lap. "I've never had two legs. If I had—" her voice broke to a whisper, "I'm sure I'd remember."

"But you're—" He looked to Mordecai, who said nothing to interrupt the man's emerging revelation. It did not surface without struggle. "But they're better than us! It cannot happen to them if they're better than us!"

"Turn the sentence inside out," Mordecai said, "and you may have the real secret, after all."

"A secret kept for centuries without a murmur of suspicion?"

"A whisper now and then, if one is close enough to overhear," Mordecai allowed, "but never proof."

Both men looked to Philomena.

She embodied living proof.

The tailor shook his head at the implications. "What methods they employ to protect a secret of this nature I shouldn't like know!"

Rigidity of face and figure betrayed her tension. Mordecai cursed himself for allowing their conversation to reach her ears. *We've frightened her. Let my next words reassure her.*

"It is your method I mean to employ, Mr. Bloom." Mordecai held his gaze. "I trust your discretion and am bold to insist you make haste, whatever the price."

Diamonds glittering at Philomena's ears and throat caught Bloom's eye. He gave an infinitesimal shake of his head.

Mordecai read the man's thoughts. "You'd draw less attention pawning a coronation crown," he agreed with a grim chuckle. "I shall pay."

"I might have guessed it," Bloom replied with a lift of his brows. Then he said with tired censure. "I've warned you about the danger of carrying large sums on your person."

"It's a good thing now that I do."

Philomena's curious gaze moved from one man to the other.

Bloom gave her a fatherly smile. "You need concern yourself no longer, Miss." He slid panel doors in opposite directions to reveal another room entirely, its walls hung floor to ceiling with wooden limbs in various stages of construction.

Philomena's lips parted on a cry. "I thought—" Her eyes filled with tears. "I did sometimes wonder – " They spilled over and ran down her cheeks. "– if there may be others, somewhere, deficient as I. But I had never met any, nor seen a false leg that was not my own. I felt …"

"Alone?" Mr. Bloom asked gently.

"Yes!"

"Not a bit of it, my dear. Why, there are many – and none of them deficient, no more than you! They are …" He searched for a word, then brightened when he found one. "Augmented!"

Mordecai picked her up and carried her to a bench in the anteroom, where he sat beside her and drew an arm around her shoulders. Mr. Bloom watched this transpire with a look of sadness that Mordecai apprehended as pity.

Though missing a limb, Philomena Paulson was a lady. Mordecai was not only a working man, but one with – how had Mr. Bloom so kindly put it? With misproportions. The tailor held him in high regard, but Mordecai knew the man had no illusions as to society's regard.

While yet in the privacy of this workshop, Mordecai was free to let his feelings for the young woman show openly. In this moment, she needed his care, and Mordecai gave it gladly from the depths of his heart.

Mr. Bloom picked up a short bench and placing it before Philomena, seated himself upon it. "If Miss Paulson would be so good as to raise her skirts to the place where the new limb is to be fitted?"

Keeping her intact leg modestly covered, she lifted her skirts again on one side until she revealed her truncated thigh.

With the delicacy of a surgeon peeling back the skin from a wound, Bloom's fingers peeled away the gossamer web of her torn stocking. He clucked sympathetically at the signs of chaffing on her tender flesh. "I daresay you've never had a custom fitting before."

With downcast eyes, Philomena shook her head.

He caught Mordecai's eye in brief acknowledgement of her isolated upbringing.

"If you look up, Miss, you'll see I've several legs in stock not far in size to yours. Altering one for your use can be done in a jif, and I'll wager you'll find it more suitable than any you've worn before."

"So many!" Philomena's gaze wandered the walls festooned with false legs, her lips parting in wonder. "How is it possible there are so many?"

"My clients are, in the main, young men injured while fighting far away in defense of the empire." He'd risen as he talked and was moving about his shop. "They get younger every year …" The artisan gathered his tools and as he set to work, he began to spin tales of adventure and peril as they had been related to him by his soldier clientele.

Philomena's eyes rounded as he described acts of heroism and daring. Forgetting herself in her fascination with his stories, she allowed him to fit the prosthetic to her bare thigh again and again as he measured and turned back to his work table to make minute adjustments. Finally, he and the lady declared satisfaction with the limb's fit.

Taking his proffered hand, she stood.

Holding her skirts to her thighs, she bent at her knees.

Mordecai watched the ball joints at the juncture of false calf and false thigh roll smoothly in imitation of a real knee.

Philomena stood on her toes.

Mordecai saw each false toe bend on hidden springs.

She rolled her ankle, turning the foot left and right. Cautiously, she walked in ever-widening circles until she traversed the entire room with confidence. She beamed. "Mr. Bloom, you are an artist of the highest order!"

The face, gone plump with the good living his dual profession afforded him, now grew ruddy with bashful pleasure at her compliment. "You're too kind, Miss. And brave." He removed his spectacles and polished them with a chamois cloth. "Yes, quite as brave as the soldiers, in your quiet way." He cleared his throat, replaced the spectacles on his nose, and drew the wires behind his ears.

"Capital work." Mordecai approached him, drawing a fat wallet from inside his waistcoat.

"I don't know what's afoot or where you're going," Bloom spoke close to Mordecai's ear, "but you'll not escape notice in your present attire."

Mordecai knew his evening clothes would make him conspicuous on the run but it couldn't be helped. "I've money only for—"

"Never mind that. The suit you commissioned is close enough to finished, and I know you're good for the bill upon your return."

Mordecai almost confessed ignorance of the date of his return or if fortune should favor his return at all, but Philomena's dancing with an imaginary partner in further testing of her new limb had diverted Mr. Bloom's attention. He wore a charmed expression but had worried eyes. "Were I a seamstress as well as a tailor, I might replace that finery with something more suitable for ..." Bloom trailed off in avoidance of any further inquiry into their plans.

A loud and sudden pounding against Mr. Bloom's door brought them all to swift attention.

Philomena attempted levity, "Is it always this lively?"

"That's my residence door they're abusing."

Philomena's eyes met Mordecai's, knowledge passing silently between them.

A coach parked outside a residence may not draw much attention, but this one bore that glossy crest identifying the family that owned it. And on this night, the crest identified the coach as stolen and its thief perhaps not far away. In point of fact, the thief stood in Mr. Bloom's workroom.

Again, the sound of a fist pounding with authoritative force against wood reverberated through the hallways and rooms of Mr. Bloom's premises.

Bloom passed Mordecai a parcel on his way forward.

Mordecai bunched it closed without looking and took Philomena's arm with a casual, "Let us away, dear."

"Yes, I think we may do," she agreed with equal aplomb, though her eyes had rounded.

CHAPTER 11

He was more aware than he had been of the alleyway's grime now that Philomena walked beside him. He grimaced to know there was no more barrier between the filthy cobblestones and her foot than a delicate satin slipper. She held her skirts clear of the ground, looking down in an effort to make out the uneven terrain in the surrounding darkness. Arm and arm with her, Mordecai matched Philomena's pace but kept his sight fixed forward on the kaleidoscopic colors moving with frenetic energy at the alley's end.

While they were in the tailor's shop, the evening had indeed advanced sufficient to see the district's nightlife rise to fever pitch, but Mordecai imagined beneath the clashing noise from all its sources, he could still hear the small taps of Philomena's bare wooden foot on the stones. Her earbob swung with her every step, diamonds flashing in the alley's gloom. He bade her stop a moment, gently unclipped her earbobs and dropped them into Mr. Bloom's parcel. Though exceedingly pretty, the girl might just escape notice if they hid the bright evidence of her status.

"Oh, la!" she exclaimed in a cross between a whisper and a horrified laugh, "I might just as well shout my name to the skies!" Philomena unclasped her necklace and watched the shimmering strands disappear into the parcel's depths. "Is it as easy as that to become someone else?"

"It's a start." Mordecai led her out into the full crush of working class thrill seekers intent on trading modest wages for a portion of the myriad diversions attainable at this hour.

If Mordecai thought she'd escape notice, he'd reckoned without the competitive scrutiny second nature to women. Shop girls, maids, and factory workers parted with hard-earned coin to acquire ready-made imitations of the latest fashion plates. By this exchange, they believed they elevated their place in society. Transformed thus, each girl assessed other girls for confirmation of their inferiority to herself. They catalogued every detail of Philomena's appearance, but all her attention fixed on concealing her wooden foot behind her hemline. It was left to Mordecai, alone, to dread the moment their collective scrutiny became recognition of her identity as a lady of quality.

There dawned in every pretty young face, an identical expression combining pity, scorn, and abrupt dismissal.

Relief so acute it felt like agony flooded through Mordecai. His life's experiences had taught him well the prejudices of every caste. He read their assumption about Philomena as just this: she was a maid favored by her mistress with the gift of a magnificent gown, but she lacked the money to purchase any jewelry – nor even a cloak or hat with which to complete the outfit. What's more, she'd emerged from a dark alley with this twisted sort of fellow who'd taken liberty with her person, as evidenced by her hair having tumbled from its pins. They averted their eyes as if her apparent fall from grace pained and bored them in equal measure. The young men who led these girls out for an evening's entertainment commanded their attention as before, and the lot of them were much diverted by a great commotion at the intersection ahead – sharp whistles, men shouting and women crying out, horses' hooves clattering on stone and all in confusion. A break in the congestion gave Mordecai a quick glimpse of constables and police on horseback.

"What goes there?" enquired the girls excitedly, nudging their beaux forward. And if ready-made fashion had made them ladies, haberdashers had woven a similar spell to give stableboys, barkeeps, and mill workers the arrogance of lords. They elbowed and shoved one another to pull ahead of the pack, demanding to know the meaning of all the disruption ahead.

"Murder" was the answer that came down the block.

Murder! Who's been murdered?

The news bounced back, over the shoulder, over head and overheard. Stretched out in proportion and distorted in detail from one trip through the ranks to the next.

A gentleman, they say. Murdered near Hyde Park. *Hyde Park?* And the bobbies think the murderer's here? A stolen coach outside a tailor shop?

What?

A gentleman's stolen a coach.

No, it's the gentleman's coach – the one's been murdered.

A gentleman's murdered a tailor! Beneath the noise and gossip beat a pulsating drone growing ever louder, like an audible rising tide. But as yet, one sound made itself heard above all others in two distinct beats, the word, "murder."

It made the pretty girls shudder violently. One might cover her open mouth behind her gloved hand. Another might hide her face against the arm of her gentleman friend. However differently they signaled distress, they all had the same bright eyes. *Murder!*

It made the beaux laugh in brash indulgence, with reflexive protectiveness in their puffed up chests. A lad might tighten his arm around his girl. He might brush a kiss near her ear, assuring her with such like, "I'll protect you, lass! You've naught to fear while I'm here, 'ave you?"

They found police agitation engaging indeed, quite as good as concert hall high jinks or the wax works' latest horror tableaux, and they made haste to reach it.

A rising drone came suddenly to its apex in a pulsating roar that deafened, as gale winds bent people double and bright light blinded those who squinted up at it beneath upraised hands. Rotating blades sliced the night sky, a metallic body at its center like a giant insect ringed with fire. Torchlight blazed behind its multiple glass eyes.

Mordecai moved backwards, drawing Philomena with him as he sought the darkness beyond the steel bug's roving spotlights. But the men behind the torches had trained not only to fly the insect but to spot the anomaly in any crowd. Mordecai knew this but ran opposite the crowd's direction, anyway.

He made for a hansom cab standing idle at the curb. The horse driven to madness by the fire and thunder of the insect, reared and tossed its head from side to side as the hansom driver tried to blindfold it.

Mordecai laid a hand on the man's wrist. "One moment," he shouted over the din to the cabbie, "I've fare!"

He darted to the cab's door, and in repetition of their journey's beginning, helped Philomena inside it. Philomena hugged Mr. Bloom's parcel to her midsection as she fell into a seat inside the unsteady vehicle. Mordecai met her frightened eyes with a reassuring wink before closing the hansom door.

He paid the driver the going rate for a private ride, cupping a hand to shout instructions into the man's ear.

The hansom jumped forward as the horse lunged beneath the driver's whip.

Philomena whirled in her seat to look out the small rear window.

Mordecai stood at the curb. He saw her turn for the cab door.

"No," he ordered her in a groan subsumed by the noise of the steel insect's wings. His unheard demand that she not jump from the moving hansom to run back to him was favored by the speed of the cab, which knocked her back in the seat. She turned yet again, staring out at him with accusing eyes.

His return stare begged her to understand. By Mr. Bloom's expertise, he'd seen to Philomena's restoration. The hansom would deliver her home with her impairment still a secret, as far as her family could know. The Paulsons would take her back, hush up all talk that she'd ever been from home, and marry her off to another fiancé. It was not an outcome she'd welcome but it was better than life on the run with an accused murderer. She must see that, and forgive him someday.

Mordecai's vision strained for a last glimpse of Philomena but great white flakes flew between them. He swatted them impatiently out of his field of vision, by touch understanding without caring that the obstructions were paper. In his peripheral vision, he saw they were handbills, whole or sliced by the steel insect's blades. Mordecai batted them aside, hungry for sight of her face, which grew smaller in the distance.

CHAPTER 12

PHILOMENA

Why had Mordecai not attempted the door? Philomena stared out the cab's back window at strangers crossing the street.

In her mind's eye she still saw him, standing in the center of the cobblestone street as straight as his physical singularities allowed, while the crowd's turbulence blew the ends of his white evening scarf about his rigid shoulders and knocked his beaver hat to a slant over his monocle. Sheets of paper falling from the sky obscured him from view.

Philomena spun forward, staring at the empty seat facing hers as she struggled for breath. She could not feel a beat in her chest. She struggled inside a body gone dead with shock.

It had never been his intention to elope with her, and as he'd told her nothing of her destination, she knew exactly where the hansom was taking her.

She imagined entering the Paulsons' home, pictured her parents standing at the foot of the wrought iron stair. She'd try not to cringe beneath their appraisal as she walked on a marble floor washed clean of her fiancé's blood, the tapping of her bare wooden foot echoing in the enormous foyer. They'd demand every detail, plot how to silence Mr. Bloom. Silencing Philomena would be easy, as always. She could feel her grandmother's arms already closing around her.

Breath returned in a long, rusty inward rush of air. Philomena fumbled for the eyehooks holding her bodice closed at her back. Shaking fingers struggled with the tiny metal things to no avail. She stopped to peel her long kid gloves down her arms and tossed them aside before attacking her gown with renewed vigor. Her body pitched and fell with every jolt of the vehicle. With a smothered scream of frustration, she tore at the gathered satin and felt it succumb to her assault. She swiped at the curtains and sent them sliding over the windows. In privacy, she pushed her bodice down to her waist. She was able to untie her corset's knot at the small of her back, but her duenna had laced it so tight, the string seemed fused to the metal holes through which it laced. Resigned to the corset, Philomena pushed her dress and petticoats down her hips. She tugged at bows and ribbons and thus freed, kicked the hated skirts way from her legs.

Layer by discarded layer, tulle and silk rose from the floor in a growing cloud. She dove beneath it, searching blindly for the paper sack she'd carried from Mr. Bloom's shop. Her lips compressed on a moan when fingers closed upon her prize.

Carefully, lest she unwittingly free the jewels she'd hidden within, Philomena drew out the clothes tailored for Mordecai. Finery rose and flowed and covered her as her movements on the hansom floor displaced the cloud of finery. She'd fallen under in a flurry of silk ribbons and lace with her long hair streaming over her bare limbs.

She rose as something hybrid, an unclassifiable being that balanced with surprising ease in the roll and pitch of the coach. Philomena ran a hand down her tight-laced curves concealed by the loose linen shirt and a three-piece suit of wool tweed.

Clutching to her chest the paper bag now made smaller by its reduced contents, she registered the slow pace of the hansom stalled in evening traffic. She listened to the tumult all around it. The pitch of collective excitement outside matched Philomena's insides. She reached in the dark for the door's handle.

Philomena stepped out into chaos.

CHAPTER 13

MORDECAI

When the hansom turned left and disappeared around the corner, Mordecai lifted a handbill he'd unwittingly caught. It read:

WANTED

That heading took up the top fourth of the page above a daguerreotype of Mordecai's face. Beneath his sinister countenance ran the words:

FOR MURDER

A ball of fiery rage clogged his windpipe.

It could have read differently, such as WANTED for questioning in a murder case. But, no. The Paulsons had gotten right to it and left no room for doubt. Beneath FOR MURDER ran Mordecai's full name and a description of every unfortunate distinguishing feature he possessed.

Phrenology had its detractors, but the scientific theory that an abnormal shape of the head indicated depraved morality still held sway over general opinion. Mordecai might declare himself innocent of killing Charlie St. Claire – and the dowager Mrs. Paulson guilty – but a direct comparison between Mordecai's misshapen contours and her symmetrical features would render a guilty verdict in the minds of many. Only the rich could afford cosmetic surgery to correct abnormalities, and thus attain for themselves the regularity of features attesting to an upright character. This point of fact made scant impression on popular assumption that criminality was a character flaw from the middle class down.

Text announcing the reward for his capture filled the handbill's lower third. It was not a large sum to the St. Claires and the Paulsons but it presented a fortune of life-changing significance to most of the city's inhabitants.

Mordecai felt tempted to go to the police, account for himself and declare his innocence despite the heavy odds against him. It galled beyond measure to be accused of such a horrible thing as murder. To run was cowardly and dishonorable. It was the kind of thing a murderer would do.

On the other hand, accusing the Paulsons would embroil Philomena in scandal of a different sort. He felt caught in this conflict as an insect preserved in amber.

The great metal insect above bladed its way south, its drone dulling with distance. Then a shrill cry rang out from somewhere up the block, wrenching Mordecai from his ruminations, "It's him!"

Mordecai stepped outside the range of a gaslit lamppost, but it was too late to evade interest.

Heads turned in Mordecai's direction. Someone shouted, "Where?"

"There!" shouted the first man, who'd advanced several paces towards him with the handbill aloft. Mordecai backed into the shadows. People studied their handbills while others followed the man's pointing finger in great eagerness to compare the likeness to the wanted man, himself. Handbills littered the street. People swept them up as they hastened forward.

Farther north, the intersection of Mr. Bloom's shop still

moved with mounted police and constables. Mordecai's opportunity for a calm surrender, during which time he could employ a solicitor to slow injustice and temper the indignities of a biased process, had passed. Here, a new crowd formed, led by the first man with the handbill, the one who'd just broken into a run.

A police whistle shrilled in the distance, small beneath the battle cries of, "It's him!" and "After him!" Momentum surged – urgent, disorganized, and growing more powerful by the second.

His monocle and top hat fell to ground as Mordecai ran. Pursued by a danger too immediate to allow fear, he knew only the bare instinct of any hunted animal to dive underground. If the crowd caught him it would tear him to pieces. They weren't even thinking of a reward; they'd remember it when he lay dead at their feet.

The nature of a riot is chaos and in this Mordecai held the advantage. He knew the subterranean was only a block away. While these clods crashed into each other and chased mistakenly after any man who appeared to be an outsider, he'd disappear down the steps leading to the omnibus that ran underground. The handbill's identifying phrase *in evening dress* deteriorated in oral retellings to "a dress" or "dressed in". With his back to them, Mordecai was just a hunched figure in a black suit. This part of town had its share of dandies and swells. He could be any one of them – or so he thought until the original shouter, fancying himself a ringleader, broke to the front ranks and pointed at Mordecai, shouting, "It's him in evening dress! Michaelson! Murderer!"

Michaelson! Murderer! became the chant of the crowd.

CHAPTER 14

PHILOMENA

A drone in the distance grew ever louder and took on definition as cries of "What's he done?" collided with "Murder!"

What care I? Philomena raged inwardly. *He abandoned me!* Then a cold realization sluiced through her hot emotion. *He never invited you.* She had jumped out the window, after him.

Philomena turned in circles, searching for Mordecai, but she only saw excited strangers. People shouted, "He is near!" and "Which way?" Conflicting news of the fugitive's whereabouts set people running in different directions. Mounted police blocked the intersection, their horses bucking beneath them in uncharacteristic reaction to the mayhem.

The pandemonium set Philomena's teeth on edge. *It's my fault,* she thought, *all of it. Oh, that he'd never met me. He should not be hunted now!*

The hansom bearing her wardrobe homewards traveled in stop-and-start fashion through obstructive traffic. Philomena had no regret for quitting it but where to go now? What to do? She wished for sanctuary in Mr. Bloom's shop, but police swarmed the tailor's establishment. Philomena set out in the opposite direction.

Her nature had so long ago relented to the constraints of etiquette that shouldering her way through a crowd felt subversive in the extreme. Such behavior from a street boy surprised no one, but this *boy's* long honey-colored curls trailed down *his* neck from the ruined coiffure still anchored to the top of *his* head. Philomena felt acutely aware of this flaw in her disguise.

A break in the crowd occurred just long enough for Philomena to spy a man's bowler hat fallen to the cobblestones. She dove for it.

"Oi!"

The man seized her with such force she feared he would pull her off her feet as he spun her around.

Philomena saw a visage black with anger for the briefest moment. Then he got a look at her face and his expression went blank. She cursed the features so prized on the marriage market, her long lashes and curvy lips and hated most of all the silken honey-blonde hair tumbling from beneath the hat, for none of it matched her disguise. Stolen hat. Stolen clothes. A paper bag full of diamonds.

The man's brows snapped together over narrowing eyes.

Sudden caprice prompted Philomena's cheeky smile.

Color flushed his cheeks as a confused wonderment clouded his eyes. "Alright, little gentleman," he mumbled, dropping her arm. "Keep it if it pleases you." He bumped into people behind him but could pay them no mind with his attention fixed on her. "S'only a hat, after all..."

As she fled, Philomena heard a distant feminine enquiry, "Did you not find your hat?" She didn't wait for the man's reply. Soon afterward, the loud *thwack thwack* of revolving metal wings deafened her.

The street flickered bright and dark as the aerocraft's blades intermittently obscured the torchlight shining from its fat round metal body. Their turbulence beat down, blowing dirt up from the cobblestones, rippling through clothes, and snapping awnings over shop windows. The whirlwind whipped the falling handbills into a white cyclone that people snatched at. Holding the hat on her head, Philomena crouched into the rotating wind.

She swerved through the crowd of people who looked up to the metal spy machine instead of watching where they were going. One said so close that it amounted to a scream directly into Philomena's ear, "It's searching for the murderer!"

Under momentary darkness in the shadow of a blade, Philomena caught a handbill from the sky.

The blade passed. Torchlight sliced across the page.

Philomena read: WANTED above a daguerreotype of Mordecai's face.

She felt kicked in the stomach.

Darkness moved over her. Philomena steadied herself against people jostling her.

Light bladed free. She could see to read:

FOR MURDER

Heat flushed her cheeks.

The Paulsons hadn't wasted any time.

I am Paulson in name only! she protested to Mordecai in absentia. *Oh, why could you not trust me to run with you?*

Reason asserted itself. She could not run without aid of a prosthetic, and Mordecai had limitations of his own. She must be grateful she did not slow him down. Under passing light, Philomena scanned the handbill for mention of herself and saw none. That was something, at any rate. He was not accused of kidnapping. He surely would be, if discovered with Philomena in tow.

She crumpled the paper and stared up into the torchlit sky with hot, angry eyes. Could he not have risked it, to keep her by his side? The blades darkened her rebellious face. Reason overturned revolt. *Selfish girl! Place him before yourself if you love him as you claim.*

The great metal insect above bladed its way south, its drone dulling with distance. Then a shrill cry rang out from somewhere down the block, "It's him!"

Someone shouted, "Where?" but everyone was shouting and to Philomena the din lost all meaning.

Her eyes strained to read the catalog of Mordecai's unflattering distinguishing features. The words said nothing of his talent. Indeed, why mention his stern sense of honor? It credited the Paulsons nothing to make his redeeming features known.

Someone bumped her hard in passing, knocking her sideways into someone else who dashed her aside with the violence of his own locomotion. Her absorption with the handbill had robbed her of awareness that the people all around had ratcheted tenfold in their frenzy. Occupied thus, she couldn't reach out for balance. The surging crowd spun and bumped her to such a degree she became dizzy. Impossible to brace herself in such turbulence, for she must hold tight her hat and precious paper parcel.

Philomena cried out in pain when someone stomped her flesh-and-blood foot. She tried to pull her wooden foot closer in, for she feared they'd trample and break the toes free of their delicate springs. But the self-protective posture undermined her balance.

Philomena reeled between jostling strangers and tried again and again to recover, hunching her shoulders in an instinctive urge to self protect. She recalled her parents forbidding her to dance and suddenly understood their strategy. The crowd spun and crushed and battered her with no more mind or effort than if her slight body were made of paper fashioned into human form by twisted wire. She feared falling, knew a peremptory terror of being trampled to death beneath the stampeding herd intent on capturing Mordecai. She closed her eyes in dread. She felt her hat knocked off her head and, reaching to catch it, felt her parcel tear free of her fist.

The paper rent and diamonds spilled. People ran over them without noticing. Philomena watched in horror as the delicate metalwork broke and brilliant gems scattered on the cobblestones.

Suddenly, the crowd passed. The horde directly in front of her rapidly left her behind in its mindless pursuit. Philomena dropped to her knees and flattened on the ground, arms sweeping out to recover the broken bits of her priceless jewelry. She didn't register the rhythmic clatter growing nearer until it grew to thunder. She looked up to see mounted police bearing down on her.

Level with her eyes, hooves dashed cobblestone. Horses' knees pistoned in a rapid battery as behind their flying manes, faceless metal masks rendered their riders inhuman. Elbows rose and fell robotically, smartly snapping crops to horseflesh.

Unable to gain mastery over her legs, Philomena darted across the cobblestones in a crablike scramble. She scrunched her eyes shut and braced her body for impact. The cavalry's thunderous advance overran her.

Dirty wind blew through her hair. She choked on dust. Wool tweed scratched her skin as she shouted noiselessly into her knees.

Stillness enveloped her.

Noise receded.

Philomena lifted her head.

Knotted tightly into herself on the ground, she watched the horses gallop down the street after the running populace.

The crowd had not only run after Mordecai but from the police who perhaps chased them as a means of crowd control or in hopes their alert on the fugitive might prove legitimate.

Philomena ground her teeth in frustration at the physical disability and frailty that prevented her following them.

The diminishing rhythm of hoof beats thrummed in her heart a repeated refrain: *if only, if only.*

If only she could find some way to help Mordecai! His singularity of structure made conventional escape difficult. Her brow furrowed. She chewed a cuticle.

Please, please, she begged providence, *protect him.*

Though Philomena could not aid him, at least she did not hinder him. Clutching the hat containing diamonds to her heaving chest, she rose painfully on one flesh-and-blood leg that trembled so badly she feared it would buckle beneath her.

She evaluated her mismatched feet. Bruises darkened her flesh-and-blood foot. The torn silk stocking sheathing it and the grime-smeared blue satin slipper with its tattered ribbons endangered her, for like her long hair, it betrayed her true gender. The man distracted from his rage by her smile could not account for everyone. Philomena had never heard of a girl dressing like a man, but she felt with dread certainty that respectable citizens should find it an outrage sufficient to justify savage expression.

As for her other foot, by some miracle, her wooden toes remained attached by unbroken springs. Mr. Bloom's kindly reassurances to the contrary, experience had taught her a faux leg signaled inferiority in her genetic code. Should others know of it, they'd see no shame in hounding her to death. If tempted to doubt the bloodthirsty inclinations in human nature, she could take as living proof the mob running Mordecai to ground this very moment.

Philomena transferred bits of jewelry to various pockets. Then she tucked her hair beneath the hat. She turned her back to the mounted police and the mob heading south. They'd left in their wake an empty cobblestone street littered with WANTED handbills and flanked by dark storefronts. Philomena walked north, stepping around and over Mordecai's image with an almost superstitious dread of looking down.

CHAPTER 15

MORDECAI

Heart pounding, lungs burning, Mordecai lurched to the subterranean's entrance. He overshot the first step. His stumble became a tumble. The world spun in jagged revolution, jarring his skeleton as he hit tile steps after tile step. He reached time and again for the stair rail, but missed and his fingers brushed the tile walls. His head cracked on the steps and his vision exploded in stars.

He managed by force of will to remain conscious. The mob's shouts rang off the tile, its footsteps pounded down steps above him, and the whole narrow tube of the stairwell became an echo chamber for the many who, united by excitement and trumped up rage, became as one beast.

Mordecai threw himself forward, launched to his feet, turned a corner, and ran.

... Into people standing in queues to buy their tickets. Standing stock still, in fact, because the mob's amplified noise in the stairwell had startled them. Their bemusement turned to offense when Mordecai barreled into them. A woman screamed and a beefy workman grabbed his arm, growling, "What gives?"

"There's a fellow with an ax!" Mordecai panted, pointing in the direction of the unseen stairwell. "He's felled several people already. For pity's sake, save yourselves!"

A screaming stampede for the pay gates ensued while a cross current of thrill seekers made for the stairwell, determined to get a look at the mad ax murderer. Overwhelmed, the ticket takers shouted for police. A constable came running from an opposite stairwell some fifty yards away. If the noise in the stairwell was loud, the noise in the tile-walled terminal was thunderous. Mordecai rode the momentum of the crowd climbing over turnstiles and rushing down the stairs. The wave carried him past women clutching the handrail and pulling their skirts from beneath trampling feet. As if caught in gale winds, the women lost their grip on the handrails, falling forward with parcels, children, and skirts clutched to their bodies. Mordecai flew forward when a knee jabbed into his back.

His head bounced on his neck, and he saw at a glance the man behind him was falling, ass over ankles beneath the panicked surge of those above him. It was his knee that had dealt Mordecai a blow to the kidneys. Mordecai thrust an arm under the man's armpit and hauled him along until he found his feet again.

A voice boomed from above, "Idiots!"

Mordecai looked up to see the terminal ticket gates were now far distant, a constable standing at the rails bellowing down at them from a megaphone, "The fugitive is among you! Stop!"

But people in confusion and fear don't register insults or process new information quickly.

Mordecai's feet hit the stone floor. The crowd at his back plunged into the new void toward the platform and the train that would steal them away to safety.

But the omnibus was pulling away.

A screamed protest tore his eardrum, "Unhand me!"

Mordecai realized the stabilization he'd blindly clutched for was the skirt of the female screamer. He dropped it immediately, running for the others after the omnibus as he shouted over his shoulder, "Pardon me!"

But the lady pointed at him, yelling, "That man assaulted me!"

A whistle blasted his other eardrum. Wincing, he whirled to see a constable reaching for him.

"Come with me, sir," the lawman demanded, adding a bored sneer, "– if you please!"

"It's him!" The accursed instigator of the riot shouted from the stairs, pointing. "Michaelson, the murderer!"

The original crowd, out for blood, flowed down the stairs.

Mordecai fled the constable, but the young policeman was athletic and gained fast.

Mordecai came within reach of the closing door. The train's churning wheels roared as it picked up speed. Its whistle blew and its chimneys belched black smoke. Mordecai lunged for the omnibus doors. Hope soared, for he thought he might reach it.

But the constable cut him off, swung his club with a satisfied, "No, you don't!"

Desperate, Mordecai leapt. He landed half inside the omnibus doors as the passengers shrank from him with a collective gasp. The landing knocked the wind from his lungs. He rolled onto his back, gasping for air, as the doors closed on his body.

The train pulled from the platform, with his legs outside in the firm grasp of the determined lawman. Mordecai kicked and flailed. Hard hands grasped beneath his arms and pulled him inward as the doors knifed and retreated, knifed and retreated. His legs throbbed from the bruising impact and outside the train's turbulence blew at him. He felt his shoes leaving his heels. Night swallowed the train as it plowed into a tunnel. The constable lost the tug of war, but the doors still automatically insisted on closing. A gruff voice rumbled in Mordecai's ear, "Take hold of the doors, man!"

Mordecai caught each, grimacing and gritting his teeth in his effort to force them farther open. He managed to pull his legs in just as his fingers slipped and the doors crashed closed.

For a moment, he could only lean against the omnibus wall, his eyes closed and his face stinging from a hot sweat, as he caught his breath. He opened his eyes to meet a cold, blue stare.

"You'll not thank me when you learn why I've aided you."

Mordecai waited in bone-tired confusion and bodily pain for the man to enlighten him.

"I don't know what you've done," a hard smile briefly exposed a neat row of tea-stained teeth, "but to cause an outcry like that, you'll fetch a fat reward for me, I am sure."

CHAPTER 16

PHILOMENA

The intersection ahead glowed with light and sparkled audibly with the renewed interest of a people past the novelty of chasing down a wanted murderer. Philomena knew she couldn't risk their fleeting attention alighting on her, with the one foot wooden and the other trailing ribbons. She stepped into an alley just shy of the intersection. Hidden thus, she gazed wistfully across the street to Mr. Bloom's shop. How she longed for the old tailor's protection, but again she resisted the urge to seek shelter there. They had put him under scrutiny of the law, and she must not repay his kindness with more trouble.

Resolute, Philomena stepped carefully over the loose stones and weeds of her chosen path. This back alley frightened her so much more than the other one had for the simple fact that in this one, she walked alone. At least, she had achieved the aim of hiding her feet, and she told herself to keep her eyes open and her wits about her so as not to miss the next opportunity to improve her situation.

In short order that opportunity appeared as an opening door through which stepped a woman wearing a frilly blue dress that glittered in the interior light. She was followed by a burly man dressed in the bottom half of a donkey costume. Before the door swung shut, the man extended one of his furry donkey legs and kicked a brick into the gap.

Heart hammering and with a steadying hand on the brick exterior of the buildings Philomena passed, she drew closer within cover of darkness.

The show people leaned against their wall, passing something glowing between them that sent pungent tendrils of smoke on the wind. "Empty house tonight," the frilly woman remarked in a tone that suggested she was holding her breath as she did so.

The donkey-man coughed a great gust of pent-in smoke. "Word is there's a murderer loose."

The frilly woman's head swung around, painted eyes going wide. "A murderer – *here?*"

He passed her the glow with a shrug. "'He's not likely to take in a show, now, is he?"

"He might do!" said she, in her airless manner of speaking before releasing her smoke in a nervous shudder "Or hide in an alley!"

The donkey-man gave another of his shrugs before dropping the glow and grinding it beneath a hoof. He opened the door and, with a great final exhalation of smoke, followed his frilly costar inside.

Don't, don't, don't ...

Philomena's mantra must have worked. Despite a passing concern about roving murderers, the smokers forgot to kick the brick out of the way. Philomena stole through the narrow entry.

Her first impression was of raw wood and ropes and a space intermittently partitioned by heavy, dark drapes. She heard a full, if marginally talented, orchestra playing somewhere distant. Its tempo; urged to frenzy by horns, bass, and kazoo; reached a crescendo, followed by sporadic applause. Then she heard performers running offstage into the wings.

Moving in direction opposite to those on the other side of the drapes, Philomena found herself within view of a room that seemed empty. She pivoted around the door jamb and flattened against the interior wall. A mirrored wall opposite the door betrayed her presence to anyone passing. She might have closed the door had an upright piano at the room's farther end not stolen her attention.

She wondered how a piano would sound in this big, empty environment of wood and mirrors. *Very different, I should think, than back home where furniture and plants fill every portion of the place.* She stared at the piano, lost in thought while the back of her mind caught sounds outside the room drawing near—

"No one in the seats, make it hardly worth the effort ..."

"... evident *you* think so, at any rate."

"Treasure, aren't you? Perhaps *I'll* murder you."

"D'you suppose they caught 'im yet?"

Philomena knew she ought hide, but their breathless voices and swishing skirts became musical in her ears, like violins and wire brushes on drums. The sounds wove themselves into a piano score creating itself in the forefront of her mind. *Perhaps they'll walk past the room?* She simply couldn't resist leaning over the bench to try her new composition as it formed. *Oh, just one moment ... then I'll go —*

"WHO THE BLOODY HELL ARE YOU?"

Philomena whirled.

Two penny divas stared at her from just inside the door.

Philomena stared back, partly because she knew herself caught dead to rights, partly in shock at the clash of orange and red comprising their costumes.

One diva stepped forward, narrowed her eyes and raised a brow. "I asked you a question, boy."

And the other said, "He's wearin' a girl's shoe ..."

Philomena sat and swept her legs under the piano bench, her fingers returning to the familiar comfort of the keys.

Touch became the tune that had sprung to life in her mind before the interruption. Unable to resist, Philomena turned fully to continue her new composition. The less aggressive of the two divas tapped her foot in time with the beat.

The other said, "Filling in are you? Percy is so unreliable. Where's 'e gone now?"

"P'raps," suggested her friend, adding a little shoulder shimmy to her improvised two-step, "He's in pursuit of that murderer."

"He ought reconsider 'is priorities," the other sighed, turning away. "That boy's not half bad ..."

Philomena played until they'd gone, finished with a flourish and reluctantly left the piano.

Careful to avoid people, she made her way through a maze of backstage curtains. She found a room so crammed with costumes of every conceivable type that anyone entering it became impossible to find. Philomena flung skirts and coats and animal suits out of her way as she felt along the floor until she'd found shoes of a masculine shape small enough to fit her feet.

Philomena parted the hanging garments to examine the brown boots she'd donned.

Her victory felt anticlimactic. She had shoes. Did that mean she could run? Could she catch up with Mordecai?

How far had he gotten by now? Had he evaded his captors? Philomena shredded a cuticle in her teeth, worrying for Mordecai.

She heard people coming and shrank back behind hanging costumes.

She heard chair legs scrape the worn floor, items sliding about on a surface, and conversation. *Another show's coming up.* Philomena started in on another cuticle.

Through nonstop banter, actresses provoked each other to annoyance or laughter. Some sang together, while others begged a loan of face paint and stockings or ribbons or the curling tongs. When hands thrust into her hiding place to grab costumes from their racks, Philomena quickly retreated deeper into the collection. Hidden, she tamped down her impatience, gnawing at her fingertips and waiting, waiting. Her fingers blazed fire but she couldn't help it.

After eternity, the room beyond the costumes emptied. Blood dripping from her fingertips left a spotted crimson trail behind her as she emerged.

Tables topped with all manner of theatrical clutter lined mirrored walls. With nothing like a piano to distract her as before, Philomena had cause to notice her reflection and was startled.

She saw a white-faced boy with flushed cheeks, big eyes, and bloody lips wearing a good suit too big for his skinny body and a bowler pulled down low over his ears. The boy reached out with bloody fingertips and fished scissors from a pile of ribbons.

Abandoning her male doppelganger in the mirror, Philomena bent double. The bowler fell off her head and her hair fell free in a glorious riot of honey-brown curls. The small diamonds that had once pinned her coiffure into place must have fallen in the street during the mayhem.

Philomena cut close to the scalp as quickly as she could, surprised by her spirit's inner rebellion against the assault. It felt like killing herself, losing that hair. It was the last of her identity. Waves of it shone on the floor. *I should keep it.*

Why, for God's sake? Memory provided the answer. Her mother and grandmother wore hair pieces and sometimes her father complained of the cost.

I could sell it.

But she carried a fortune's worth of diamonds in her pockets.

A scream interrupted her inner debate. Philomena sprang upright and whirled about.

She took the woman in costume for a singer, as there

seemed no end to her lung capacity. Each scream rose from its predecessor without pause for air, as her painted mouth swallowed the lower third of her face and her eyes rolled beneath false eyelashes. Women rushed into the doorway and froze in shock. Costumed in a variety of fantastical characters, they played supporting ensemble to the singer whose scream found the words, "It's the murderer!"

"I killed no one."

Philomena's small voice broke the spell of background silence.

Fauns, fairies, goddesses, and princesses grabbed each other in a screaming chorus of varied messages on the same theme: "There's blood everywhere!"

Philomena saw *spots* of blood everywhere, to be sure.

"Oh God, we're next! Stay back!" They cringed behind raised arms and splayed hands while at their center, the singer pointed to Philomena in dramatic fashion.

Though she was the cause of the commotion, Philomena had the odd sense of being secondary to the purpose.

The singer's gloved fingers shook. Her whole arm shook. Paste jewelry jangled all up her arm. Her body vibrated with terror. Her feather headdress shook.

Behind her, the chorus cried, "Won't someone save us? Simon! Percy!"

A big man shouldered his way into the room. "What's all this?"

The singer's answer rose and fell on swells of hysteria, "*HE'S* got the *INSTRUMENT* of his *MALICIOUOS* trade *IN HAND!*"

"Scissors?" the man scoffed.

They'd no appreciation for his tone. "Protect us, Simon!"

"From a little boy?"

"He's got blood on his hands!" a fairy snarled.

"Be a man!" they chorused. "Do your job! You're stage manager!"

The singer shrieked, "He's killed a woman!" She pointed to the hair on the floor at Philomena's feet. "Scalped her like a savage! I shudder to think who among us is next!"

Simon said, "Look, you're all wearing wigs," but it was too late, for the damage was done and the pitch had increased.

"OhmiGAWD!" and "Who's missing?" and "Whose hair is that color?" and "Who's next?" and "Simon, take him in hand!" and "Someone call the police!"

Philomena ought be scared, and she was, but she'd never seen performers up close, in heavy paint, at full volume. They fascinated in their agitation. No one ran away, but everyone screamed and kept on screaming, except for Simon who looked flummoxed and put out, and a woman who bellowed from the hall, "What're you sluts on about?" as she fought her way in.

Philomena recognized the penny diva who'd confronted her by the piano.

"It's the murderer!" they shrilled in answer. "The one escaped! The one they been lookin' for!"

"Percy's understudy?" She laughed.

"He's covered in blood!" the singer yelled at the diva. "Look you there, Sandra – he's got scissors! He'll kill you next!"

"You daft cow," Sandra scoffed. "Mordecai's Michaelson's the murderer."

Philomena protested, "He didn't kill anyone!" at the same time the singer cried, "*What? The Maestro?*"

"Simon, tell them," Sandra demanded.

"It's on them handbills flung all over the streets," Simon said, "why there's no one here watching the show."

Unified disbelief met this news. "Couldna done!"

"Who's this then, I ask you? Who's this?"

"Mr. Michaelson, with the funny little twisted up body?"

Philomena yelled, "Don't you dare describe him thus!"

"The freak?" they asked each other.

"He's no freak!" Philomena yelled.

"He hasn't the coordination!" They hooted and crowed at the very notion of it, tears of mirth tracking through their face paint as they amused each other by imitating Mordecai's stiff, awkward gait while Philomena's face flushed. "Him?" they cried, pretending to wield a murder weapon in palsied fashion while every fiber of Philomena's body tightened in a fury. "The murderer, that little abortion?"

Philomena charged with a lioness roar.

They screamed and fell back.

Simon hooked Philomena beneath the armpits, tore the scissors from her hand and hauled her off her feet, calling for aid. "Percy!"

While Simon dragged her off, Philomena kicked and struck out at the women who'd maligned her beloved.

"Show's over, brat." Simon thrust Philomena at a big, tall man in the hallway.

Percy launched her over one shoulder without losing hold of the giant donkey head cradled in his other arm. She hung, limp and shaking in the aftermath of her violence while blood rushed to her head and the floor flew past her vision. Fake donkey fur brushed her face. Empty donkey legs swung in her peripheral vision. Impervious to his twin burdens, Percy reached the door still held ajar with a brick and kicked it open. Cold air hit Philomena with a suddenness that made her gasp.

He leaned her against the brick exterior and watched her buckle and grab her knees.

Philomena grappled with thoughts too weighted by grief and anger to speak aloud.

Oh, this world was the worst. People were the worst. Her family was the worst, and what did that make her? Was it any wonder people came out twisted up and missing parts in a world like this? She could have stabbed those women without a care in the world. It only took an instant to reveal the worst.

Her nose wrinkled as a pungent trail of smoke curled into her nostrils. Philomena straightened against the wall and noticed Percy beside her, still wearing his donkey bottoms. The upper donkey half sat on the ground. He held something out to her tipped with glowing embers.

She frowned at the twisted stub of smoldering paper, put the unlit end in her mouth and drew in a draught of exotic taste.

"Hold it," Percy said.

She snorted involuntarily, but managed. Squinting, she passed the glow to Percy.

He took a quick hit and said through held breath. "He couldn'a done it."

"Why not?" Smoke expelled on Philomena's bitter reply, "because he's a freak?"

Percy's head swung her way. He caught her gaze and held it. "Because he's kind ...and patient." He held out the glow.

Philomena shook her head, confused.

Percy took a contemplative toke. "He taught me everything I know."

Philomena turned suddenly in his direction.

Smoke escaped on his rueful laugh as he pinched out the glow and stuffed the bud in his shirt. "As much as I *could* learn, anyway."

"You're the piano player!"

Percy brought the top half down and shoved his arms through the forelegs.

"But you're dressed like a donkey!"

The big donkey head muffled his words, "Not everyone's a prodigy, kid."

CHAPTER 17

MORDECAI

Horrified that his savior had aspirations to be captor, Mordecai staggered to his feet and backed away from him. "I'm innocent." He looked around to find every passenger in the train car staring at him. "I am innocent!"

The short little man stepped in front of him to address them. "I shall account for this man. You saw me catch him, fair and square." He turned to Mordecai, looking up. His bottle brush moustache twitched as he pronounced with newfound authority. "Take a seat there, and we shall have no quarrel between us. I only want what's mine, fair and square."

"Fair?" Mordecai responded indignantly. "I am unjustly accused!"

"You may tell them so at the next stop," the man said, "for they're no doubt rushing that way to apprehend you."

Mordecai looked at the window seat pointed out to him. The unctuous twit meant to hold him by taking the aisle seat. Mordecai stepped back.

The man's brows snapped together. "Where are you going?"

Mordecai moved swiftly down the aisle.

"Give up," the man called after him. "You're trapped."

Passengers shrank from Mordecai, wide-eyed, thinking him a madman. But Mordecai, who once cared about his reputation, found conviction by public opinion of murder had liberated him. Indifferent to public reaction, he reached the end of the car. The man, guessing his next action, ran forward with a yell.

Mordecai's fingers curled around the lever of the car's rear door. He yanked, then pushed. The door gave. He leapt into wild speed and black oblivion.

Mordecai crash-landed in the cage-like platform between the last car and the next, pain exploding through him on impact. Mordecai choked and coughed on the thick, scorching air, his stinging eyes flowing tears. The omnibus churned through the dark tunnel at relentless speed, powered by coal furnaces that burned at a furious rate. He felt his ankle manacled between iron bars, his foot blown back by the turbulence. Frantic to save his foot from injury, Mordecai pulled his leg with both hands. This unbalanced him as the omnibus rounded a corner. He clutched a bar in desperation to avoid gravity sucking him into the void.

He continued working with his ankle. Sharp and dull pains brought his teeth together in a prolonged grimace, but intense relief at his success quickly followed. Mordecai sagged against the bars, limbs flung out on the barred floor. The little intra-platform served as an open enclosure in which he might rest a moment and catch his breath. If only every breath did not burn from the hot smoke chugging from the omnibus stacks. His air passages felt raw. Tears welled in his squinting eyes. Mordecai opened them to blurry darkness.

Sparking embers in thick black smoke glittered like demonic fairy dust above him. The cars' interior lights shone through their glass windows, but the dark ate it. Mordecai should have welcomed a glow from windows set in the rear doors, but the doors were not equipped with such, so the dark swallowed him also.

Golden light sliced down the rear of the car from which Mordecai had escaped. The light expanded and the silhouetted form of his captor leaned out, moving his head in search of his quarry. The man's greedy persistence provoked a sudden rage in Mordecai. He stood without thinking. The train's turn around a bend threw him sideways with enough force to nearly send him over the platform's short wall. He caught the top of wall's top bar. At this angle, light through the open door reached him. Mordecai glared at his enemy's silhouette.

Whether fear of falling into the speeding void or of the wild picture Mordecai presented – quite possibly of both – the man's aggression sounded like a bluff. "Where d'you think you'll go?"

Bent double, Mordecai pulled himself along the barred walls until he could stand before the door of the next car.

The man strained to be heard over the noise of the train, "I'll grab you at the next station!"

"Step outside—" Mordecai dared, "and grab me now!"

The man hesitated.

Mordecai laughed. He opened the door behind him.

Light flooded out to illuminate the disbelief in his captor's face.

Mordecai climbed up, backwards and with no small difficulty, into the next car.

The man looked down at the metal platform between the cars, observing how its open frame shook in the train's turbulence before looking up at Mordecai.

Mordecai met his eye, grinned, and shut the door.

He turned to face a car load of shocked passengers. Something tickled annoyingly at the corner of his lip. He swiped at it, discovered his false moustache, now hanging by a remnant of theatrical fixative, and threw it aside.

As if he'd thrown a mouse, a woman shrieked and jumped away from it, falling into the lap of the man beside her.

The man tried to free his newspaper from beneath the woman's rolling bottom. "Madam, I implore you!"

Mordecai walked down the aisle in a purposeful stride. Passengers shrank as he passed. He felt their eyes on his back. It was unlikely they'd seen a handbill or witnessed the riot in the subterranean's terminal. To them, he was just a smoke-smudged stranger, but they feared him on principle. No one passed between cars when the omnibus ran. It was too dangerous. Anyone attempting it was clearly deranged and not to be provoked to further acts of madness. These suppositions suited Mordecai just fine.

Upon reaching the opposite end of the car, he pushed the door open and stepped into noise, into hot wind smelling of rock and smoke and soot. He landed at a crouch on the metal platform, which swung from impact of his landing, and held his place with a grip on the widely spaced metal bars beneath him. Light snuffed out as the car door swung on oiled springs to crash shut behind him. Mordecai made his way carefully through darkness. He felt across the back surface of the next car. Finding a lever, he pulled open the door and stepped up.

New car. New shocked faces.

Mordecai repeated the process, and each time he emerged from the hot, black void into another lighted car, he felt more estranged from its inhabitants and less regretful for the estrangement.

At last he opened a car's exit and felt no presence beyond it. He stepped down onto the metal floor of an open deck. The door behind him swung shut on light and humanity. Mordecai felt for the deck's handrail, grabbing it for balance in the increased turbulence at the train's end. Wind tore through his hair. His chest expanded with an intake of dirty air that burned his lungs.

It felt good.

When the omnibus reached the next stop, its end would

extend far beyond, deep in the tunnel. Still, while the train rested to allow boarding passengers, police would enter and search until they reached him.

As if in answer to his thoughts, the omnibus slowed with a scraping of metal and the hum of wheels on tracks. The tunnel grew gradually lighter, darkened in patches by the train's farting blasts of smoke. Mordecai leaned over the handrail to look ahead down the row of cars. His hair blew back from his face. Soot particles stung his eyes. His teary squint perceived the lighted platform far ahead. As expected, among the waiting passengers stood ramrod rows of police.

The train still moved, but ever more slowly. Mordecai climbed over the handrail and held it, feet braced on the deck's steel floor. He rode outside the deck, his trousers rippling and coat tails dancing desultorily in the slowing turbulence. Mordecai picked his moment arbitrarily and jumped without a clear view of where he'd land in the murky shadows.

It was a short drop but made while moving, and he landed badly. Rocks cut into him. Wincing, he scrambled away from the train. He rose as carefully as he could to keep from tearing his clothing. He stumbled over a train track. A metallic scree split the blackness, and to his horror, he found the omnibus reversing. He leapt away just in time to prevent being run over. The train stopped with another high screech and chug of smoke.

Mordecai retreated until he felt a tiled wall at his back. He turned and made his way deeper into the tunnel, into darkness.

CHAPTER 18

PHILOMENA

Philomena left the theater's alley with a lighter heart. Mordecai couldn't have murdered anyone, Percy had said, "because he's a good man." That made two people who knew Mordecai was innocent. Philomena was no longer alone.

She had a second reason for walking on air. Percy's skill at the piano signified so little he must double as a costumed stage buffoon. Yet he felt Mordecai had valued him no less for his lack of talent. Indeed, Philomena suspected he may have given Percy more time and attention than Percy had given the piano. The teacher esteemed the student above the instrument. This new insight into Mordecai's character was a gift more precious than the diamonds hidden in her various pockets. *I could be all thumbs, and he'd still be kind.*

Such a man is worth saving, despite impossible odds.

She surveyed a street littered with possibly hundreds of handbills falsely accusing Mordecai of murder.

Well, no one's reckoned on me.

She passed a hand over her shorn head, feeling odd, as if lightning flashed through her veins. As she bent to tuck Mordecai's over-long trouser legs into her stolen boots, a breeze blew a handbill over her toe. She picked it up, gazing at Mordecai's image and asking, as if he could answer, "Where have you gone?"

A clue presented itself neither by lover's telepathy nor a sudden stroke of genius, but by her view of the middle distance where police and pedestrians gathered. Philomena hoped this congregation indicated the fugitive remained at large.

Her approach went unnoticed, as all remained preoccupied with the manhunt that had left them behind. People loitered with visible eagerness to overhear conversations between constables and mounted police. When they got too close, the lawmen waved them away with a riding crop or a bully stick. Adults drew back with a studied air of nonchalance. Boys ran away laughing, only to edge ever closer again to provoke another rebuff in a game that never failed to amuse them.

Hungry for stray information, Philomena joined the loiterers. She overheard, "He disappeared down the subterranean." Having never heard the word before, Philomena guessed its literal translation was *below ground*. Had the earth simply swallowed Mordecai? She moved around the perimeter of the crowd, searching with dread for a sink hole or some similar mishap of nature.

Instead she found a doorless entry in a stone building. Here, stone steps descended into the earth. *Like a cellar. Like a storehouse.* The Paulson homes all had cellars into which servants descended to retrieve preserved food or cleaning instruments. Was the subterranean a sort of common cellar?

As she stood pondering this, a young couple brushed past her. She heard the young man tell his lady friend, "Let us see for ourselves if he entered the subterranean."

The lady gasped in excited horror at the suggestion. "Suppose he *is* underground menacing the general populace?" Shuddering, she cried, "Oh no, I should not like it!" Nevertheless, she took her companion's arm and hurried down the steps beside him.

Philomena followed. Why should the general populace gather in a public cellar? And why should Mordecai seek out such an obvious trap?

The steps led to an indoor dwelling of stone and tile where people moved in aimless circles, unable to move forward. Separate conversations echoed to collective resonance that made difficult the perception of singular words. Hoping for clarity, Philomena hastened to the bottom step. Nearing the couple she'd followed, she heard the male demand of the crowd, "What is happening?"

"Is he caught?" the woman asked eagerly. Someone must have answered in the negative, because her companion pounced with, "Where has he gone?"

Philomena thought she heard, "He's boarded the omnibus," and searched her memory for any reference to a vehicle of that name. Perhaps it was a kind of motor car, but she thought as yet those were just an expensive hobby. Perhaps an omnibus was a type of aerocraft? Philomena knew of two kinds of aeroplanes, single-wing and biplane. They were small, their flights but limited in distance. She could not picture them taking to the air from a place below the ground.

The Paulsons traveled overland in a private coach. On rare occasion, they'd traversed the continent by train. Could a train be an omnibus? No, it could not be; for *omni* meant *all*. The Paulsons reserved a train car for themselves only – there was no *all* about it – and no train in which they traveled ever ran underground.

Still, all who were not on level with the Paulsons traveled by different means. Their country servants purchased a seat alongside others on a common coach in order to travel home to visit family. Philomena reasoned that in the city a common coach might run underground. Apparently, unbeknownst to her, they had done so all the time. The gulf in life experience between herself and Mordecai struck her with sudden force. She'd never even heard of an omnibus, and he had made his escape on one!

"Boarded!" exclaimed the woman. "How can it be so?"

"'S'only what I heard ..."

"He cannot have done," the man scoffed. "What? Past all them constables – Oi!" he yelled at a trio of boys. They were knocking into people as they ran through the crowd, without a care for the impertinence of such an act or for the lateness of the hour. Where were the parents of these boys? Philomena wondered, envious of their freedom. Then a thought struck her. They weren't much shorter than she, and hadn't the theater people mistaken her for a boy?

Philomena left the couple to follow the boys. Hoping to blend in with them, she bumped into people at a heightened speed. Her rudeness incited angry protests, but she affected the careless disregard for censure displayed by her new role models. Joy bubbled in her chest. She laughed. To be jostled by others had terrified her, but to slam into them – how jolly!

Her progress took her past the stalemate to the very reason for the stalemate, itself. Would-be travelers were detained and organized into separate queues. A constable stood at the head of each queue interviewing possible witnesses one at a time. Philomena skirted around the queues, hoping to escape notice while straining her ears for any information about Mordecai.

A constable asked, eyes on his notes, "You were at the turnstiles when the murderer jumped them?"

"That's right," a man confirmed. "A fair mess there was then, to be sure. Hysterical, the lot of them." He sniffed disdainfully.

A woman in another line reported, "He manhandled a lady," while the constable scribbled in his pad. "Touched her bum!"

The constable's pen lifted.

"Aren't you going to write that down?" Her shoulders rolled back as her bosom swelled. "I should have given that criminal a stout taste of my carpet bag had he the accosted me in such a manner!" The woman's bright gaze collided with Philomena's glare. "Never you mind the story, little guttersnipe!"

"Get along, sonny." The constable swatted Philomena aside with his notepad. "After his ...interference with the lady," the constable asked, "did you see where next he ran?"

"He disappeared under the crowd, for the whole lot of them stumbled and tumbled –"

"He took the Holborn line," a man behind her interrupted.

The woman's double take caused the man to look down his nose at her. The policeman's pen poised over his pad. He looked at the man. Philomena stood as stone, all ears.

"Aye." The man nodded. "For I watched at the rail, having intended for Holborn myself but not wishing to be swept into the melée. They very nearly tore him in two."

"Who did?" demanded the woman.

"If you recall nothing else, madam." The constable nodded her aside but she remained.

For the constable's benefit, the man answered the woman's question. "The police on the platform and a passenger in the car," he reported. "Quite a tug of war, I'd say, but the passenger won. The car sped away with the fugitive – and without me, which is a good thing as I'm now here to aid in the investigation."

The constable asked, "You're sure it was the Holborn?"

"I understand there's a reward ..." replied the man.

Philomena trembled with excitement to hear Mordecai had boarded an omnibus on the Holborn line. Here was the first useful clue of the evening, for she knew the place, if only by hearsay.

She'd learned of Holborn when Charles and his parents

had dined with them not so long ago. As is typical after many courses and many glasses of wine, gossip grew salacious. Conversation had turned to a certain member of society who'd recently deserted his wife and children. Everyone understood he should never return for his heart now belonged to a beauty of almost supernatural charisma. Sure enough, by the time the man and his beauty were spotted in a Moroccan gambling den drinking absinth from a common glass, his solicitor had set terms of divorce that cut matters to the bone.

"I do wonder," Philomena's grandmother said idly, "how on earth the wife shall get on."

"Visit Holborn, I expect," Philomena's future father-in-law remarked to the general amusement of all.

"Quick!" Mr. Paulson chortled, "Restore emeralds to fashion, else she'll not get a quid for them!"

"Draw it mild, dear," his wife admonished with a smile.

As her fiancé bid her goodnight, Philomena had asked, "Will Mrs. Rasmussen bargain well for her emeralds, do you think?"

"You booby!" Charles had laughed. "T'was a joke. Ladies do not visit Holborn."

"Oh …" Philomena considered this, feeling very sorry for Mrs. Rasmussen.

"She'll contract an agent," Charles said with a kiss on her cheek, "one known for discretion in such matters if she's any hope to preserve her dignity."

Holborn jewelers traded with agents of unfortunate ladies in high standing. Philomena was such an unfortunate. Mordecai had boarded an omnibus on the Holborn line, which meant he headed in that direction even if he did not disembark there. She had two reasons to wish herself in Holborn.

Beyond the constables and people, she saw a tiled little booth inside of which sat a bored woman behind a glass window. On the walls around the window hung timetables and destinations. Philomena had overheard servants mentioning these destinations when discussing the comings and goings of their personal lives.

In that moment, Philomena's world view revolved until it stood upside down. She'd always thought herself more fortunate than the servants. After all, they had to perform service for their livelihood while she was the one they served. But she'd never been to these farflung destinations to which the servants referred so casually. Girls of Philomena's class always traveled with a chaperone, only to destinations approved beforehand and in the vehicles provided them. How limited her fortune compared to the servants who, for the price of a token, traveled anywhere they wished!

The prices posted on the tiled walls of the ticket booth might well have been a king's ransom, for she hadn't coin to buy a token.

"Oi!" The ticket lady shot out of her seat, shouting, "Police! Mind them boys!"

The boys ran down the steps to a lower floor, but constables, taken up entirely with the task of interviewing potential witnesses, could do nothing about it.

Aggravation contorted the ticket seller's countenance. She sat down in a huff.

Philomena meandered.

The ticket lady's narrowed eyes followed her.

By seeming happenstance, Philomena found herself near the turnstile at the head of the steps.

The ticket seller stood.

Philomena crouched.

The lady shouted, "Grab that boy!"

The nearest constable did try, but Philomena scrambled beneath the turnstile too quickly to be caught.

She overshot the mark and fell down the hard stone steps, crying out in pain as she attempted to grab hold of the stair rail. She finally did, stopping her descent with a suddenness that wrenched her arm in its socket. She looked up to see the ticket lady coming after her.

"You little blighter!" The lady held her skirts high, skipping down the stairs rapidly with a steadying hand on the rail.

Philomena had no hope of outrunning her, so she hiked her body upward to sit on the rail and shoved off. She sailed down the long trajectory with a speed that brought the bottom platform racing into view. Her hands burned with the effort to slow her descent. Caught between a scream and a laugh, she clung to the newel post as her body slid off the end of the rail.

From a distance above, the ticket seller shouted to the constables below, "Catch that boy!"

Her demand went unheeded. As above, so below. Constables interviewed witnesses. Street boys ran through throngs of people, slapping them on the rump and laughing.

Philomena's eyes traveled over walls of shiny white tile. Here and there, long blue tiles with white lettering spelled out the name of the neighborhood: PICCADILLY. Some eight feet above the floor and every two feet along the walls, gas lights flickered inside black metal cages. Down the length of the platform, benches and metal waste bins stood bolted to the stone floor. The platform's width ran from the wall to an abrupt end, like a cliff. Across the tracks, another platform rose identical to the one on which Philomena stood. Between the platforms, tracks ran from one tunnel to the next. Each tunnel formed a void that gaslight could not penetrate.

One tunnel suddenly brightened. The rumbling roar of the approaching omnibus reverberated through her chest, building anticipation for the beast's emergence from its black cave.

Its appearance disappointed Philomena. She'd expected something akin to the fantastic, but here was nothing more than a train, iron black and lined with small windows. She saw its passengers rise to their feet. With an earsplitting screech, it came to a halt in the platform. Large doors slid open – that, at least was something more than above-ground trains possessed – and passengers stepped out onto the platform.

Constables tried to keep people from boarding the train, but everyday concerns and goals of these would-be interviewees took precedence over civic duty, the drama of a fugitive paling by comparison to personal matters. They were not under arrest and so could not be detained. New passengers rushed to the train.

Philomena joined them.

CHAPTER 19

MORDECAI

The lightless journey robbed him of time and place. He walked without awareness of direction.
Underground remained silent until those times when a sudden roar filled his senses, an omnibus exploded into his tunnel and wind blasted his face and body as he clung to a rocky wall. Then noise retreated, replaced once again with nothingness.

CHAPTER 20

PHILOMENA

Green leather seats with brass fittings, two on either side of a center aisle, ran in rows to the back of the omnibus car. Philomena took in the sight of them until someone nudged her forward. She slipped into a paired seating and slid over to the window.

Soon the omnibus lurched forward and, with an uptempo of its chug-chug rhythm, picked up speed. The tunnel swallowed them. The tiny gas lights running along the tops of the car's walls kept the interior at a varying golden glow. Soon it seemed to Philomena that the omnibus flew, it went so fast, and she couldn't help smiling. Her smile faded when she looked out the window, for the tunnel's darkness turned the window to an obsidian mirror reflecting her wan visage.

Her eyes looked like hollowed shadows. Her hair stuck out in short spikes no longer than a bristle brush, but here and there sprang random tufts that curled. She looked a lunatic, and surprised herself by laughing. Curious eyes turn her way. *Am I acting lunatic, as well?*

Philomena winked at her obsidian reflection. It was a lunatic path set before her and only a lunatic could traverse it.

At every stop of the omnibus, Philomena looked for a blue tile with its white letters that would tell her the neighborhood it had reached. With every stop that was not Holborn, she grew more impatient. By the time she'd counted ten stops, she'd begun to gnaw her cuticles again.

"Pardon me!" she called to a matronly woman passing by with a tired expression. The woman frowned at Philomena's eccentric haircut, but her visage softened when she apprehended the anxiety in the boy's big, dark eyes.

"When does the train reach Holborn?"

"This is not the Holborn line," said she. The group of people making their way to the opened doors moved the woman along as part of their number.

"But ..." Philomena stood and leaned in the direction of the disembarking woman. "What is a Holborn line?"

"Consult the signage, boy," said a man in line behind the woman.

Philomena followed his gesturing hand to a diagram within a frame hung on the omnibus wall. Multicolored lines ran at angles, intersecting and diverging from each other. The diagram swelled in her perception and made her dizzy. The omnibus lurched forward and Philomena fell sideways into her seat, staring at the inscrutable diagram.

She could make no sense of it. All she did know was that she could not reach Holborn on this omnibus. Mordecai had boarded the Holborn line at the selfsame platform from which she'd boarded, but somehow this omnibus was not the Holborn line. What was a *line*, anyway? And how to find the right one? How did one learn? Which of these strangers could she trust to ask for help? None looked receptive enough to ease her misgivings.

Philomena sat back in her seat, bringing her head to rest on the top edge of it. The train entered another black tunnel. The terrain's rough-track vibrations ran through her body in tandem with her shivering nerves. *Philomena, contain yourself*, she thought, lifting her head. *No one is born with an understanding of rail lines. They learn, and so shall you. Somehow.*

Calmed, she still felt dizzy. Her stomach hurt awfully. A man two seats ahead of her ate a baguette, while bread crumbs fell like snow into his lap. Philomena could not take her eyes of that baguette. Her stomach growled and her mouth watered. She had a strong urge to seize the baguette for herself. How long ago had she sat to supper in her own home? Hours. Even then, she hadn't eaten much.

The omnibus stopped and the man rose, tossing the baguette aside. As soon as he'd vacated his seat, Philomena seated herself there. She'd too much pride to make a move toward the baguette until the man had stepped out of the train. Then she snatched it from its place on the floor beneath the seat. Grimacing, she brushed a stray hair off the baguette. She pinched away the floor-blackened surface of its chewed end and brushed dust off the whole of it. Turning away from the car's new passengers and hunching her shoulders, she hesitated but a moment before hunger overtook revulsion. She devoured the bread stick. It was too little to assuage her hunger and only served to make her thirsty in the bargain, but she told herself it would sustain her far better than nothing. She scanned with eagle eyes for other passengers enjoying a snack. When the car stopped at the next platform, Philomena searched the abandoned seats and was rewarded with more leftovers. She closed her mind's eye to visions of mouths and tongues and teeth masticating the meal that was now hers. She must take her luck as she found it.

With hunger soothed, Philomena thought she may have regained her wits sufficient to deciphering the mystery of subterranean lines. Philomena moved to the seat next to the diagram of colored lines delineating omnibus routes. If she stared long enough, perhaps a useful pattern would emerge.

If only her eyelids didn't feel so heavy. Her view of the diagram grew hazy.

CHAPTER 21

MORDECAI

In this boundless void, Mordecai went a little mad.
He did not find it unpleasant.
As if looking into a mirror of polished obsidian he saw reflections of his beloved everywhere. He watched the play of emotion over expressive features, followed the expert dance of her bitten fingertips over piano keys. He walked blindly in the dark and saw her walking ahead of him as gracefully as would any girl with both legs.

Following her at his leisure, Mordecai found solace in his own disappearance.

By overcoming life's considerable challenges he'd never expected to find happiness, but he had striven to become respectable. Now respectability was lost to him. He'd never get it back, for the only witness to his innocence was Philomena. Mordecai hoped she kept quiet. If she opened her mouth, he feared that murderous grandmother would close it permanently. But if he eluded capture, Mordecai could avoid provoking that outcome.

Without a courtroom drama followed by the sideshow allure of Mordecai's public hanging, perspective on the murder might soften to romantic legend. If society believed one of their own had died defending Philomena from a maniac, eligible men would compete to win the tragic heroine's hand in marriage. Mordecai believed she'd adapt well to it. Philomena hated pretense, but there existed in her nature a subversive streak that inspired her to turn insupportable events to her favor. She'd learn to enjoy material wealth and find joy in loving her children.

CHAPTER 22

PHILOMENA

She woke with a start.
How long had she slept? During that time, the subterranean's clientele had changed considerably in character. Where once there had been working class people on their way home from late-running jobs, the car was now completely empty save for a few adolescent boys with particularly nasty auras. They had hard, hollow-cheeked faces, pock-marked skin, and sallow complexions. They were none too clean about their persons, though their attire had a certain style. They wore caps pulled low on their foreheads and neckerchiefs knotted at jaunty angles.

Something whizzed past her nose and – *thock!* – struck the framed diagram of omnibus routes. Philomena looked sideways and saw a dart quivering, its point caught fast in a circle beside which read: Piccadilly.

"Piccadilly – just as you said, mate!" Two boys each clapped his hand to the other's. "And here I thought dead sure you'd pierce the little boyo's nose!"

"If I'd meant to do, I should'a done," said the boy whom Philomena assumed had thrown the dart. Beside and just a little above the Piccadilly dart, another pierced the diagram.

It had been the sound of that first dart striking home that had awakened her.

"Let's 'ave another go," a third boy said, taking aim with his dart. "Bet five bob I hits Avon square."

"Five bob!" hooted his compatriots to one another. "He's not seen five bob together since Friday, last."

Dart poised, the marksman scolded, "Yer scarin' the boyo."

They rushed to the seat before Philomena's. Five boys crowded together, staring into her stunned face with feral glee.

"We scarin' you, boyo?"

'S'matter – don't like darts?"

Philomena had never seen street boys in her life. Up close, they looked dangerous as stray dogs. She prayed fervently they truly believed her a *boyo*. If they guessed she was a girl, she suspected the encounter should become unimaginable.

"You lousy?" one demanded.

Philomena couldn't stop a little frown gathering between her brows. She'd no idea what it meant to be *lousy*.

The boy ran a hand over his head, alluding to her amateur haircut. "They scalp you, on account o' lice?"

Philomena thought it wise to nod.

"Cat gotcher tongue?"

Another phrase she'd never heard of.

They eyed her eagerly, considering ways to make sport of her.

The omnibus slowed to a stop. Philomena pulled herself along the seat and stood with difficulty, every inch of her body sore from sleeping such a long time in one position.

The boys rose as one and followed her. She could feel their eyes on her, noting every detail of her awkward gait as she regained her footing.

"You lame?" one asked, from right behind her.

Oh, no! They mustn't guess it!

She traversed the empty platform without a clue as to what neighborhood stood above ground. She heard the collective footsteps of the boys trailing her.

"I said 'was you lame!'" the boy shouted in sudden temper at her silent treatment.

Philomena's eyes closed briefly. If only the platform were not deserted at this hour. She might have found a rescuer, or the boys might have given up the prospect of any deed that did not bear observing. But they had her to themselves and could do as they liked.

"If he outruns you, he ain't lame."

The pack broke into a run.

Philomena's heart slammed against her ribs as she ran to the best of her ability.

"Lame!" she heard one proclaim.

She hadn't a chance of eluding them, but she tried anyway. She beat them to a large sign standing upright in a wooden frame and took refuge on its opposite side.

"Step out from behind that sign and take yer defeat like a man!" another taunted.

"Wonder if he's got any dosh on 'im."

Dosh? Money. They had to mean money, and she thought of the diamonds.

They'd stopped running. She heard their boot heels striking the stone floor at a leisurely pace. She was trapped between the sign and the tiled wall directly in front of her. They had her and could take their time while they figured out what to do with her.

"Got any fags, d'you think?"

A derisive laugh answered this question. "With skin like that? Boyo don't smoke."

Philomena's stomach had sunk to her shoes. She wouldn't survive manhandling by this pack of hyenas, not after they discovered her tight-laced curves.

"Hey boyo!" they called.

"Got any bad habits?"

"Does being yellow count?" a boy sneered. "Hiding behind an advert …why, I oughta clout him a good one for it. I hate a coward."

Philomena's fevered gaze alighted on a small step set into the platform at the edge of the tiled wall. In the shadows, the step should escape notice to distracted passers-by, but her fear sharpened her focus. This small step leading down to the track, right at the mouth of the tunnel, presented her only possible escape.

Philomena went for it.

With a shout, the boys gave chase.

They'd catch her, of that she was certain, but she could no more stand placidly in wait for a beating than she could fly. Philomena tumbled down steps made invisible in the darkness and landed in rocks and dirt.

The boys gave a sharp yell at her abrupt disappearance.

She felt her way blindly along the tiled tunnel wall. Her fingers encountered a corner. She ducked into a depression, feeling pipes and cables at her back. Philomena stood as a statue in her unlikely shelter, barely able to breathe from fear.

She heard their feet scrunching in the rocks at the track.

"Aw, fer chrissakes …" one complained as others muttered mutinously.

"Turn back?" another scoffed. "Fine fellows! You can no more commit to a …" The rest of his words disappeared in the upsurge of the omnibus's engine as the vehicle charged forward.

A moment later, coal-dust blew across Philomena as the omnibus roared past. It seemed an age before the noise receded enough for her to lower the shield of her hands and arms. She remained in place, listening for any sign the boys had given up pursuit of her.

Who could say they were not hiding out of sight on the platform, perhaps upon the first few stairs leading up to the next level of the subterranean? How long should it take for those jackals to grow tired of waiting for her to emerge?

Philomena stepped forward, toeing her way in the pitch black of the tunnel until she encountered the iron rail of the track. She paused to consider her options.

If she climbed back up onto the platform, she risked encountering those street boys.

Might she not walk along the track to the next platform, instead?

Setting her mind to it, she soon fell victim to lack of sensory input. The dark void played tricks on her. She thought she heard someone else out there. Philomena stopped, listened.

CHAPTER 23

MORDECAI

At times it seemed he heard the footsteps of another traveler through the tunnels.
    Mordecai stopped walking. He stood still as stone, listening with his entire being for some blind sense of the place.

After several moments of complete silence, Mordecai gave up the fantasy of an unseen companion on a parallel journey. He must have imagined this in his loneliness. He continued on his way.

CHAPTER 24

PHILOMENA

She hadn't imagined it!
From a distance, she heard the hesitant but regular crunch of footsteps on rocky soil. The gait gave audible witness to an imbalance. Though pronounced, the instability had predictable rhythm; else Philomena should think the hiker inebriated. Drunk or sober, did the distinction make any difference in the danger posed to Philomena? Certainly not.

After all, what respectable purpose had one to walk through subterranean tunnels? None!

Philomena sought the tunnel wall again, found a depression, and hid.

She sat in the depression she knew not how long before her mind made a canvas of the darkness, presenting to her a panorama of horrors.

They were not imaginary, but sprang from memory.

Philomena remembered a slice of light growing vertically in the darkness before widening to illuminate a glimpse of her grandmother.

Philomena, sitting on the floor, begged, "May I have my leg?"

"What use have you for a leg, Philomena, when

confined to a closet?"

"Am I to stay here much longer?"

"Long enough to contemplate the error of your willful ways. Savages must be tamed."

"But I'm not a savage!"

"Indeed? Who but a savage should take off her stockings for all to see?"

"But Cook's children took off their stockings to wade in the pond."

"You are not like Cook's children, Philomena. You are not like anyone. You cannot wade in a pond. You cannot take off a stocking. You must never let them know."

"May I have my leg?"

The slice of light thinned.

Wild panic clawed up Philomena's throat. "Please! I cannot walk without it!"

"Perhaps you ought never walk again, Philomena," Grandmother closed the door and turned the lock, "if you cannot be trusted."

After all the day's shock and danger, it was the subterranean tunnels that threatened Philomena's spirit. She had the feeling now, as she had whenever they'd locked her in the closet, that she should never see daylight or people again. Philomena sat against the tunnel wall in the darkness and stifled a sob against her knees.

But then her mind's eye conjured the image of Mordecai from the encompassing darkness. She considered the challenges arising from physical malformations. How mean the array of opportunities presented him, yet he'd built a career that earned him a comfortable income. How cruelly people may have treated him, yet in his chosen profession Mordecai helped people flourish.

Philomena dried her tears with the back of her hand. She stood, felt about in the dark for the track, and began once again to follow it.

Mordecai persevered, and if she intended joining her life

to his, she must match him. *He thought you too delicate. Prove him wrong.*

Though she had much to make her anxious, Philomena gave preference to reliving the pleasure Mordecai's infrequent smiles had afforded her. When they composed together at the piano, her soul frolicked with its sympathetic twin. Despite his physical asymmetry, his form fit perfectly with hers when he embraced her. Though absent at the moment, his presence sustained her.

CHAPTER 25

MORDECAI

It came to him that his environment wasn't black but gray, a place of shadows. At first, he thought his eyes had acclimated to the darkness and had given him the discernment of night vision.

But the gray continued to lighten. Gun metal became the gray of an overcast sky. He gradually made out the shapes of rocks in the tunnel walls, a curving jagged embrace around dirty air that smelled of smoke and dust. A roar filled the tunnel. Mordecai winced as a bright shaft of light pierced his pupils.

He jumped back. Wind blew his hair and turbulence vibrated through his body. The rocks dug into his back as an omnibus thundered past.

Smoke filled his lungs. He fell, choking. His eyes streamed tears. His chest heaved. He bent double, coughing. He dashed a hand across his eyes. He peered at the blurred string of lit windows in the speeding train. Mordecai pulled his ascot free of his collar and held it to his nose, breathing through it.

The omnibus seemed endless in length; segmented into cars, it resembled a mechanical centipede. It disappeared around a bend at an astounding rate. Ten years past, such vehicles existed only in theory. Now they moved inhabitants of this tiny island nation from one shore to the other as easily as the nation's armies overcame continents and its navy dominated the seas. Soon motor cars, hoverbugs, and aeroplanes might traverse the globe; for the Crown put its purse to this aim as a means to expand its supremacy.

Was there a corner of the world beyond Her Majesty's influence or the reach of her laws? His disappearance ensured Philomena's happiness. Few places facilitated one's vanishing more effectively than the omnibus tunnels, but he couldn't stay, unless he fancied dying of hunger and thirst.

The speed-blurred outline of the cars' windows took on definition as the omnibus slowed. When he finally saw the last car, he broke into a low crouching run.

CHAPTER 26

PHILOMENA

Philomena walked in darkness for an immeasurable amount of time and at length, a pattern emerged in her progress.

At the first faint rumble of an omnibus approaching, she'd move as quick as she could to the tunnel wall. Unable to gauge its speed by its noise, she feared being overrun. She'd flatten herself against the wall to avoid this outcome, turning her face away from its ever-brightening light. Its engines' raging energy roared through her flesh, making her skin vibrate and her scalp sting. Black dust filled her nose and throat as the engine's roar filled her head so completely as to make its own queer silence.

When two trains approached through cross tunnels, Philomena's fear doubled. She felt no more than a shivering animal in the face of violent death.

In the wake of such onslaughts, awareness of her body crept in slowly. She released the breath trapped in her lungs. The painful pounding in her chest eased in strange symmetry with the diminishing thunder of the passing trains. When strength returned, Philomena pushed away from the wall to find the track again and continue on her way.

During one of these blind treks, a sudden thought stopped her.

Philomena's fingertips went to her teeth.

The trains that came out of side tracks – from whence did they run?

She had followed the track run by the trains that came up behind her, assuming the straight path to be true and the others but tangents that were she to follow, should misdirect her.

Suppose she'd been wrong?

The straight path had yet to deliver her to a train platform.

Did the side tracks come from the platforms? Had she wandered one line interminably, while the end to her journey could have been reached several times already?

Philomena could have thrown herself on the ground in despair at the very idea that her solitary, endless walk led nowhere.

Now, stop that. She gave herself a good talking to. It was never too late to have a good idea. *You may have struck on the very thought that will change your course for the better.*

The next time an omnibus by its noise and light announced its entry from a curving side track, Philomena's physical reaction stemmed from excitement rather than fear. When the omnibus disappeared, she searched out until she found that side curve. Eager to test her new theory, she let it guide her in the dark.

CHAPTER 27

MORDECAI

His body ached at every joint and his muscles screamed in agony, for he'd been walking a journey of hours. Now he made the unreasonable demand of his mortal flesh that it move with the speed and grace of an athlete. By some strange twist of fate, it obeyed him.

Near the platform, Mordecai slowed to a stop. How far had he wandered? He watched beleaguered, shabby people step from the omnibus onto the platform, wondering if he dared walk among them.

Mordecai hopped over train tracks, leapt up stone stairs set into the tunnel and stepped onto the stone platform.

CHAPTER 28

PHILOMENA

In time, she saw with soaring heart, a gradual lightening in the atmosphere ahead of her. In short order a large square of light appeared in the distance on the tunnel wall opposite her. She rather thought that square of light marked the shape of a platform. Philomena felt her way against the wall toward that light. Soon she discerned a patterned surface on that highlighted wall, and as she crept closer, white tiles distinguished themselves from a background of blue tiles. Closer still, and she could see the white tiles formed letters that read: Ludgate Hill.

It wasn't Holborn, but any place above ground seemed like heaven after traveling so long in darkness.

With steadying hands on the wall, Philomena walked on shaking legs until she reached the platform. Though its gaslight beamed to the wall opposite, the platform floor cut light abruptly. Philomena stood at the short stairway below the platform in total darkness. She lifted her chin to a light that did not illuminate her face. Step by step, she ascended into its glory.

CHAPTER 29

MORDECAI

Despite his dirty, disfigured appearance, no one spared Mordecai a glance. The people stepping into the omnibus looked hungry and beaten by life. This gave him a clue to his whereabouts. The station's name, spelled out in blue tile across a white tile wall, confirmed his destination.

In every possible way this place was as far from the Paulsons' posh neighborhood as were the ends of the earth, itself. The train's route ended here.

A solitary figure exited the omnibus, looking quite a contrast to those who had entered it. Mordecai's eyes followed the man whose bearing was authoritative and whose manner of dress hid his identity while proclaiming his purpose.

The plague doctor wore a wide brimmed hat, a long coat, and gloves. His pants tucked into boots that reached to his knees. Every black inch of his attire was made of leather waxed to repel fluids and filth. A hood of brown leather covered him to the shoulders and was stitched to follow in rough facsimile the contours of his head, face, and neck. The man turned his head, showing in profile the hood's long curved beak. Wall sconce gas light flickered across the glass dome set into the leather mask; it and its twin protected the wearer's eyes. He carried a long, stout stick, which he used to lift rank bed linens so that he could examine without troubling himself to touch the wasted bodies of those who lay dying. With this same stick, he directed the invalid's unfortunate relatives, who would likely occupy the same bed within days of its current occupant's death.

Every decade or so, a maverick stepped forward to suggest it was the water that killed. On the surface the claim seemed logical. The river wound like a serpent through every borough of this metropolis from its garden-terraced hilltops to its steamiest pits, but it flowed sluggish and thick as a noxious stew. Eighty thousand citizens emptied their bowels into the sewers, and the sewers emptied into the river. And the slum's populace drank it, having no option other than demon alcohol with which to slake its thirst. One could forgive an educated fool who assumed the water carried death, but it was the air.

Mordecai's lips twisted into a grim smile. Fate was in league with the Paulsons. He'd escaped a hanging death only to die here by the mere act of breathing.

Mordecai would have returned to the relative safety of the tunnels, but their pitch-dark environs stole his sense of direction. Above ground, he'd easily find the seaport at the slum's easternmost boundary, for years of teaching impoverished students in this district had familiarized him with the streets. Mordecai had just enough money to book passage on an East India merchant ship.

No doubt police had set up checkpoints at the port to prevent Charlie St. Claire's murderer fleeing the country by sea. *I must find a way to get past them.* The port presented his nearest chance of escape from unjust conviction of Mrs. Paulson's crime.

As he started up the long flight of stairs, Mordecai's footsteps rang out in the stone and tile cavern of the empty platform. The plague doctor had reached the top stair and disappeared from sight, the echo of his footsteps growing ever more distant.

At the surface level of the subterranean, Mordecai passed the ticket booth. The girl inside it didn't look up from her book.

He entered a labyrinth in search of the street exit, taking a memorized path through intersecting narrow corridors. Gas lamps in caged sconces overhead cast a yellow pall over white tile. He was well into the maze when he stiffened at the echoing sound of running footsteps.

Mordecai stopped to listen, trying to ascertain location and direction of the runner. He'd just registered there was more than one runner – and that they ran ahead, rather than behind him – when a man gave a startled cry. Running footsteps became a scuffle.

Mordecai advanced with shoulders forward and hands clenched. Sounds of violence pierced his awareness so acutely that he could almost see the blows, the struggle. *Two against one, the cowards.* His breath shortened. His molars ground in gathering anger. Ears attuned to direction, he identified the route. He quickened his pace, rounding a corner with a shout.

Two ragged, vicious young men didn't bother looking Mordecai's way, so intent were they on robbing the plague doctor. The glass lenses of the doctor's hood limited his range of vision, and thus his ability to fight back. He focused entirely on keeping his medicine bag, gripping its handle in both gloved hands while one youth tried to wrest it from him. The doctor ignored the second youth's ransacking of his person, the fellow plunging hands into various pockets of his coat.

Mordecai picked the plague doctor's staff off the floor and swung it at the clearest target. Stout wood cracked against the bag thief's skull with enough force to knock the hooligan off his feet. Suddenly free of oppositional force, the plague doctor fell. This left the coat thief standing without cover. Mordecai swung the staff at him with a banshee cry.

The men fled, hooting in triumph. One raised the doctor's bag in a gesture of victory. The other tossed a wallet over his shoulder. It slid emptily across the stone floor.

Mordecai knelt beside the plague doctor. He pulled the beaked hood off his head.

His skin looked gray. His eyelids seemed heavy. Mordecai gave his shoulders a slight shake, commanding sharply, "Look at me." The doctor obeyed with visible effort. One pupil was smaller than the other.

Alarm shot through Mordecai. "Help!" His plea echoed. He waited, heart hammering, for the sound of someone running to his aid. Could the ticket booth girl hear him? Would she investigate, or hadn't she courage? "Help!" No answer but his own echoing cry.

The plague doctor appeared to have fallen asleep.

Mordecai snapped his fingers to wake him. "Where does it hurt? Have they broken a bone?"

The man's eyelids fluttered. "You're ...kind to defend me ..."

Kindness had nothing to do with it. "I'm sick of brutality."

The doctor sank, closing his eyes again.

Mordecai searched his body for injury. Finding none, he placed a palm over the man's heart and felt a ragged beat. *What training have I to save him? Oh God, won't someone come—*

"Help!" Mordecai's shout brought nothing but his own voice in a returning shout.

The ragged heartbeat stopped.

Mordecai cupped a hand over the doctor's nose and felt no breath.

Mordecai sat back and rubbed his eyes.

It was a bloody shame. The plague doctor might have cured someone.

Mordecai had students in the slum whom threat of cholera had forced him to abandon. Some had showed promise. One, in particular, had just begun winning international acclaim as an improbable genius when the epidemic surfaced. Mordecai wished the doctor had lived for this boy's sake, alone. *Most likely, it would have been already too late.* Cholera killed quickly.

With contagion in the slums, every indrawn breath drank poison – unless dried herbs and flowers filtered air through the long beak of a plague doctor's hood. Mordecai had now to consider his own chance at survival. The obvious answer slumped before him.

Mordecai stripped the unfortunate doctor of his coat and donned it. He put on the gloves. He pulled the plague doctor's hood over his own head. It dulled his hearing and narrowed his sight, filling his nostrils with the scent of potpourri. Mordecai settled the hat over his hooded head and took up the stout stick.

He retrieved the dropped wallet. Empty of cash, it contained the plague doctor's identification. He thought of police checking identification at the port. They'd take him to jail if he gave them his own credentials.

Mordecai hesitated. He gazed at the doctor who'd entered this district to cure people at the cost to his own life.

A man oughtn't be found dead without a name, especially this man.

But he needed the plague doctor's identification to get past coppers at the portside checkpoint. Mordecai transferred cash from his wallet to the doctor's wallet. He kept the doctor's wallet and slipped his own into an inner pocket of the dead man's waistcoat. A plague doctor's license and a piano teacher's certification, exchanged. If investigators uncovered the doctor's true identity, they may suppose Mordecai had killed him, but he aimed to sail beyond reach of the law before misapprehensions of that sort could be drawn.

Mordecai walked away through an invisible wall, pushing against the backward force of his guilt and remorse. He'd stolen something more valuable than cash and a medicine bag. He'd taken the plague doctor's good name. He'd left him the dubious blessing of a fugitive's identity.

It's an infamous name, but even so, perhaps better than none at all.

Mordecai stepped out of the omnibus terminal, into the land of cholera.

CHAPTER 30

PHILOMENA

Just a few steps inward from the edge of the subterranean platform stood a framed map that drew Philomena like a magnet. From the circle beside Ludgate Hill, she traced her grimy finger over lines intersecting the district. She'd traced several city blocks on the map when her fingertip stopped on a dot beside the name: Holborn. *Why, it's not so very far!*

Philomena leaned her forehead against the map, eyes closing in a prayer of thanks.

It could be seen as a stroke of luck, but to her it was nothing short of a miracle. No pilgrim upon reaching the promised land could have felt joy greater than hers in that moment.

Holborn!

She stepped away from the map and looked around the Ludgate Hill station.

Men waiting for the train dressed alike, in dark wool suits. A pocket watch chain glinted on every chest. A bowler sat square upon every head. Each man carried a shallow, square leather case.

She thought Charles may not have known Holborn as well as he'd claimed, for ladies did visit the district.

Though not as great in number as the men, they stood all around.

Well ... Philomena amended the first impression.

Her parents wouldn't consider them ladies, but Philomena could see by their neat appearance the women held rightful claim to respectability. They wore jackets in somber colors with matching skirts that fell to the tops of their sensible shoes. Hats with modest ornamentation crowned simple hair styles. Each woman stood with back straight and shoulders level, gloved hands clutching the handle of a shallow, square leather case. Philomena wondered if their cases contained family valuables. Perhaps respectable women needn't contract agents to bargain on their behalf, as ladies like poor Mrs. Rasmussen must do.

Smoke and a chugging rhythm of revolving machinery filled the space around the tracks. At this development, every traveler's posture changed. Shoulders went forward. Legs braced. Heads ducked.

The omnibus filled its space. With screeching and a final belch of smoke from its stacks, it came to a stop. Double doors in its iron side slid open.

Men and women charged forward, gripping the handle of their shallow cases.

Men and women identical to those about to board disembarked.

They looked to Philomena like schools of minnows converging in the shallows at the Cote d'Azure. Identical in appearance and purpose, how busily they swam around each other!

All changed their path to avoid drawing near Philomena. Women viewed her warily. Men glanced her way quickly, a snapping up and down of a gaze filled with distaste before, with a grimace or shake of the head, they dismissed her by looking elsewhere.

It was then she became aware of how she must look, coated in black dust. Her scalp itched. Her hair stood out in grimy tufts. The skin around her eyes stretched taut with worry and lack of sleep, and no doubt the skin beneath them appeared hollow and dark. She imagined bad luck had its own evil miasma as powerful as the stench of her unwashed body. She knew herself the very picture of one without home or connections and thought these respectable people must fear the contagion of her condition perhaps more than they dreaded the inconvenience of her sudden hold upon their arm for the purpose of begging a coin.

As she crossed the platform, the people gave her wide berth. Philomena ignored their disgusted perusal, finding strange pleasure in the space granted to her untouchable state of existence. To inspire such physical distancing, one must inhabit either the highest or lowest class. Philomena chose pretensions to the highest. She held her head up and walked with the condescending grace of a queen. She climbed the long flight of stairs with room before and behind her.

At the subterranean's top floor, people stood in a long queue at the token booth. On the other side of the booth people fed tokens into turnstiles. They avoided her as assiduously as had those on the stairs and platform. Their mass revulsion could not diminish Philomena's triumph. She had found Holborn.

The terminal's landing ran as long as a city block. Iron buttresses arched to cathedral heights in support of a glass ceiling. Morning poured its cold, gray light upon Philomena as all gave way before her.

A glass door framed in wood and brass revolved with a push of her hand and slung her out into the world.

The subterranean's place set into the side of a steep hill displayed multistoried buildings as if invisible hands had lifted the streets for Philomena's perusal. She saw the upper stories of buildings farther up the hill, connected by a footbridge made brilliant by meager sunlight shining on its metal roof. An aeroplane flew above, trailing a banner that read: McAndliss Track Finest Dogs Running! Horse-drawn coaches traveled up and down these slanted streets. Pedestrians crossed traffic anywhere they liked, in a haphazard rush. Kiosks stood along the sidewalks doing brisk business.

Philomena narrowed her focus to keep her wits. The exercise brought her attention to a water pump directly in front of her at the curb.

She rushed to it and began cranking the handle until water flowed into her open hand. Philomena brought her hand again and again to her mouth, lost patience, and put her mouth beneath the stream to drink her fill. She swallowed greedily for several minutes. When her parched throat was finally refreshed, she splashed and rubbed her face in an effort to clean it.

Only upon rising did she notice the dray horses drinking from a water trough placed at the pump for that purpose. *Needs must.* Philomena shrugged away memories of the fine wine in delicate crystal that had once graced her lips.

She'd wet her shirt collar, and its clammy adhesion to her bare neck increased her sensitivity to the chilly air. With a grimace and a tug at her collar, she turned about.

On the other side of the subterranean, two more streets rose up to complete an intersection of five points. People rushed into and out of and around the omnibus terminal, as if the subterranean were the queen's center of the city's hive. Passing Philomena on his way to the entrance, a businessman tossed the morning's edition of The Herald into a metal waste bin before descending the steps at a brisk pace.

She retrieved the newspaper, pulling a few pages from its center to stuff into her collar and get the wet fabric off her neck. Her eyes caught on the banner headline above the fold on the first page.

MAD PIANIST KILLS MINING HEIR

She skimmed past the account of Mordecai stealing a coach belonging to party guests, and of the coach recaptured by police outside a tailor's shop in the entertainment district. Mr. Bloom was not mentioned, by which Philomena understood he'd told them nothing useful. *Bless you,* she thought fervently. *Bless you, kind Mr. Bloom.*

The reporter described the hoverbugs flying over the city in pursuit of the fugitive with their strong gaslights beaming through the night sky, and directed readers to page C16 for a reprint of the handbills the bugs had dropped over the city. Philomena rolled her eyes in scorn at that abominable missive and didn't bother.

Though relieved they hadn't captured Mordecai, she saw with rising dismay passages such as "...all law enforcement involved" and " ...nationwide manhunt." Philomena saw, "...ports and borders closed." She read the warning that Mordecai Michaelson was considered armed and dangerous. *Oh, that's ridiculous!*

Her eyes lifted to the first sentence and she began to read in earnest.

The article hewed close to her grandmother's account. Philomena ground her teeth in anger at every malicious, false detail. Indeed, the Paulsons had embellished the story to assign motive.

> Michaelson accosted Miss Paulson in attempt to abscond with her jewels. In defense of her, Mr. St. Claire sustained massive blows to the head from Michaelson, who made savage use of a heavy candelabra to dash out the young man's brains.

Philomena stared for several moments at the newsprint without seeing it. She saw her grandmother standing over Charles with the bloody candelabra in her hand. She saw her grandmother point at Mordecai and scream,

"Murderer!" She remembered Mordecai's shocked expression as an external replica of her own internal reaction. Philomena's shock had broken first, for she knew the ruthless nature of her clan. She knew it now, with their merciless ambition culminating in every printed word.

> The Paulsons have left the city for an undisclosed retreat in order to provide their daughter privacy and safety in which to mourn a love torn from her side by unspeakable violence.

The brazen lie took her breath away. She wondered what they would do. Her family could not claim to have her without eventually producing her.

Philomena read on.

> Michaelson succeeded in his theft of Miss Paulson's jewels, an array of precious gems worth in excess of —

Yet another lie! Philomena pondered the motivation behind it. She knew her kin well enough to guess. They would trace the jewels publicly as a means of tracing her privately. Of course they must recover her in secret. If society believed a kidnapper had opportunity to ruin her, the damage to her character should prove irreversible. Equally horrid, if not worse – oh, yes, far worse – was discovery of Philomena's false leg unmasking the Paulsons' genetic code as trash. But these considerations swerved wide of the mark.

Without Philomena, it should be the Paulsons' word against Mordecai's as to who had murdered Charles St. Claire.

Philomena was the only witness, and she was on the loose.

A simple revelation presented itself to her. *Oh no, no, no it cannot be*—She wished to close her eyes and pretend she didn't see it but she could not.

The Paulsons didn't want her back to marry her off to a fortune.

They wanted her dead.

The day before yesterday, she'd never have thought them capable.

But then Grandmother killed Charles.

To love horrid people hurt so much when, at last, one knew them completely.

If the jewelry turned up, the Paulsons should know themselves well on their way to apprehending her. They'd not leave such a thing to police, of course. Like Mrs. Rasmussen with her agent, the Paulsons had someone discreet.

"Mother, who is that man?" Philomena had asked so far back in childhood that she still expected honesty from her kin. "The man with a fearsome countenance who waited at the gate, Papa pressed something into his hand."

"We keep no company with those of fearsome countenance, Philomena. You are mistaken, pray do not speak of it again."

But Philomena had seen him again, out of the way, in the shadows, and when his eyes met hers, she always ran away.

Philomena must get as far away from these diamonds as possible, as soon as possible. She'd sell them, for she needed money. Then, she'd find Mordecai before anyone else did.

But first ...

She could see plain as day the reputable jewelers on the three streets that intersected before the subterranean. Perhaps it was this visibility that ladies of reduced circumstances hoped to avoid. She'd do well to follow their example.

Philomena tossed The Herald in the waste bin before setting out for Holborn.

CHAPTER 31

MORDECAI

Mordecai walked a wide dirt street that forked in the middle distance. Traffic and pedestrians so thronged all streets that he moved quickly in a constant attempt to avoid collision. He recoiled from a pig making a panicked escape from the charnel house. He used the plague doctor's stick to fend off curious dogs intent on sniffing his trousers, and stepped around piles of horse manure left in the wake of dray carts.

With stooped backs and arms crossed tightly in defense of the cold, men and women revolved through haberdashers and green grocers, the meat market and tobacconist shops. They had hollow cheeks and haunted eyes. They hid the lower portion of their faces beneath anything that could be found conveniently at hand, be it handkerchief, shawl, or an upturned collar pinched closed over nose and mouth. That this precaution so often proved fruitless caused none to abandon it; perhaps hope against hope was another incurable condition. One never saw the populace in better neighborhoods shielded thus, nor did they suffer in consequence of the omission. Higher classes credited genetic superiority for their unfailing health. Mordecai supposed this an easy perspective to attain within tall houses on high hills surrounded by clean, landscaped thoroughfares.

Here, tanning barns, laundries, and inadequate plumbing turned the air noisome. Garbage fires warmed ragged men gathered around them. Mordecai shuddered to think of the invisible contagion collecting on the surface of his stolen hood as the fragrant herbs stuffed into its great hooked beak filtered the smoke and steam and street dust clouding the choleric air.

The hood's construction inconvenienced his misaligned eyes. Its right goggle lined up to the top half of his vision, its left goggle to his lower half. In consequence, Mordecai saw the slums as a fractured whole, in visual testament to its inhabitants' reality. Children ran after a death cart piled high with bodies bound for the potter's field. Makeshift masks muffled their shrieks and giggles, and their eyes sparkled in the spirit of fun.

Taverns swallowed men into their dark interiors. Mordecai understood their desire for respite from life's relentless and arbitrary assaults. Yet, the prospect of a momentary stop along the way did not tempt him. On foot, he reckoned to reach the port within the span of half an hour's time.

He had not reckoned on the transforming effect that sighting a plague doctor had on people.

It started when one man broke away from his companion to grab Mordecai's arm. The man's eyes leapt in his haggard face. His voice rang out hungry and hoarse, "Come see my Sarah, wasting away. You must cure her!"

This broke the restraint of the others and they rushed forward, clutching handfuls of Mordecai's coat, pulling him this way and that, beseeching him in a babble of immigrant languages the unified language of fear and one message: Save my father, my mother, my wife, my child! And one word in refrain: Cholera!

Cholera.

Cholera.
He's three days down with it ...
Looks to die any moment ...
Just fell sick this morning. Might there be time, then, to save her?
Come, doctor.
Come with me.
Please, this way —
Come!

That he lacked a doctor's bag of medicinals took nothing from his disguise. They pulled him in all different directions. Mordecai wrenched an arm free, only to find his other one captured. He flung them off and was grabbed again, pulled toward opposite avenues.

"I've an appointment," he shouted with cold authority through his leather mask.

But desperate people cannot hear. They grew louder and more violent by the minute as the crowd grew. Dogs barked and chickens scattered. Boys ran to see what the commotion was about. Women ran for the same reason and upon sight of the plague doctor grew frantic.

My husband —
My child —
Sick!
Cholera!

"I've an appointment!" Mordecai boomed in a voice like the thunder of God. He swung the plague doctor's stout stick at them. Despite their efforts, he'd plowed forward against their power in the direction of the river port. He'd made enough progress to see the great ships looming in the distance. He could not be detained while escape was visible before him.

A repetitive note found its way through the verbal tumult of the crowd. Mordecai ignored it as he churned forward, down the street toward the port. But it followed, dancing overhead. Chiming, uplifting. Then downturning.

Then equal through several counts. Voices dulled in his ears, but the ditty started anew. A trilling skip across keys. Piano keys. He mustn't listen.

But his footsteps slowed.

He looked up.

An empty sky met a long flat line of tenement rooftops trimmed with a sentinel row of roosting birds. Beneath that ran the top floor's small windows. His eyes followed his ears. One floor down, a window was improbably open to winter breezes. Out of that open window came the repetitive notes of a singular piano scale.

Five stories below, street dirt churned in yellow clouds around a fitful mob. Mordecai no longer felt their clutching demands. He stood still, looking up, listening, and as he listened, he saw in his mind's eyes, a fist rolling its knuckles across keys, followed by a finger tapping twice. That double tap always sounded impudent to Mordecai, like the wrinkle of a pert nose or the quick dart of a tongue before a laughing chase ensues.

It was the Knuckle Song, the one thing anyone who does not play the piano will play if there is a piano in the room. That he should find it so arresting was an eccentricity of his nature Mordecai could never explain.

The Knuckle Song ended abruptly, as the Knuckle Song does. Then, he heard the childlike pitch of a girl's voice across a distance too vast to distinguish the actual words. But a high note at the end identified an enquiry, and its tone contained sadness and eagerness in equal measure.

Through the obstructive positioning of the hood's eye goggles, Mordecai made out the tenement's address. With a mighty, full-bodied convulsion, he shook off the clutches of multiple hands. He stepped into a tiny vestibule with an uneven floor and crumbling plaster walls. Through the filtering potpourri, Mordecai smelled cooked cabbage and stale piss.

As he ascended the narrow stairs, he asked himself what

the hell he was doing.

She was playing the Knuckle Song again. Each note drew him up another step.

Mordecai heard sobbing behind closed doors at each floor.

The exertion of climbing ten flights shortened his breath. The humidity of his exhalations coated his skin and the sound of his huffing and puffing filled his ears. Mordecai held himself steady with each hand on a wall on either side of him.

The Knuckle Song stopped.

Through the open tenement door, he heard a girl sigh in apology, "It's all I know."

She'd heard better often enough, but the girl had no ear for learning.

Mordecai entered the tiny flat. He saw thin mattresses rolled up and piled against a wall. He saw a small table and mismatched chairs. He saw heaps of soiled bedlinens ready for washing and steam rising from pots of water set to boiling over a stove filled with fire. A worn-looking woman busy with the laundry cast a defeated glance about the room and saw him. She dropped a pot on the cookstove's surface with a startled cry.

A girl of about twelve years old appeared from another room. "Mother?"

"Oh, thank heaven!" The woman rushed toward Mordecai. "He found you! Mary — Papa found the doctor!"

"We've naught to pay him," the girl whispered, then quickly covered her mouth as if to stop the utterance that had already escaped.

The mother steered him with a commanding hand on his back while her voice emoted with enough deference to suit a king, "Oh sir, thank you ever so much for attending our boy. How good you are! You see, he is resting in bed, only resting, for I'm sure you'll have him from bed in a matter of hours. You are so talented and skilled in your craft—"

"Mother, do not prattle so," the girl interrupted in a beseeching undertone. "You mustn't vex him."

"Beg your pardon, sir," the good woman amended with no slowing of speech, "What must you think of us? Where are my manners? May I bring you some tea?"

"We'll bring you some tea," Mary echoed as she pulled her mother back into the front room that served as a sitting room, kitchen, and makeshift bedroom. She had noticed, if her mother had not, the plague doctor's imperious lift of the hand in a silencing gesture.

Mordecai had eyes only for the wasted form on the bed. It signified nothing that he hadn't the plague doctor's bag, for no treatment could save this pitiable creature. His face was sunken and blue with cholera's inherent victory, his lips stretched thin by dehydration. His body lost its moisture in sweat and in waste, which the women of his family kept busy cleaning away. By careful and fixed scrutiny, Mordecai apprehended breath in the faint movement of the invalid's chest, but illness had stolen the strength for any other movement.

Here lay the boy whose improbable genius had sparked international attention. Mordecai's brightest and poorest pupil looked like an effigy fashioned of papier mâché. Had his sister's efforts to cheer him with the Knuckle Song registered at all? He seemed insensible to activity around him. His eyes remained closed but Mordecai remembered they were large and brown, trusting and sweet. If they opened now they would shine with fever but not with intelligence, for Josiah Templeton was considered a half-wit.

He was simple but blessed with the rare gift of perfect memory for pitch and tone. He'd only to hear a composition once to play it with flawless skill. He'd never deviated from the score without the deviation first demonstrated to him, for he hadn't the mental capacity for invention. What the almighty Creator had formed of Josiah was a perfect recorder. When last Mordecai had seen him, the boy was fast on his way to fame. Concert halls were billing him as a sensation, a protégé plucked from idiocy to acclaim. But once cholera caught him in her blue embrace, all doors closed against him. There would be no concerts before the crowned heads of the continent now. Josiah Templeton had been sent home to die.

Pain squeezed Mordecai's heart.

He looked around the small room made smaller by the unusual choice of furnishing; no dresser or table to speak of, but all space sacrificed to an upright piano pushed against the wall opposite Josiah's sweat-soaked bed.

Mordecai sank onto the piano bench. He set aside his stick. He took off his gloves and began to play Philomena's cheeriest composition. The frolicking notes made him realize how soulful and sorrowful most of her compositions were, expressive of her secretive and solitary existence. She'd composed this piece the morning after they'd met by chance in the music room. The notes sang of her joy in the love they'd professed for each other.

The music rose like the sun at daybreak. It filled the sickroom and Mordecai hoped it brought the lift in Josiah's spirits that his sister had tried to inspire with her rendition of the Knuckle Song. When the last clear note floated away, Mordecai noticed Josiah's sister and mother in the doorway. Through the mismatched vantage point of the plague hood's goggles, he saw Mr. Templeton and Josiah's elder brother had arrived home. As one, the family stared at him, stunned and speechless. Then the girl looked to Josiah with a gasp. All heads turned.

Josiah's mouth had opened and was quavering in a visible effort to marshal the strength and energy to speak. There broke from his lips in a hoarse whisper, the word, "Maestro?"

Mordecai took off the plague doctor's hat and hood.

Josiah smiled to see his teacher approach. Mordecai carefully, gently, lifted the boy's weightless, skeletal body into his arms.

Inarticulate cries of confusion erupted from the boy's relatives, but no one prevented Mordecai carrying Josiah to the piano and seating himself with the boy beside him on the bench. Josiah leaned against him within the circle of his embrace. Mordecai supported the sticklike arm that feebly rose.

Josiah's trembling fingers stretched toward the keys. His faint touch replayed the first few bars of Philomena's composition.

His mother broke into sobs.

Josiah's fingers fell from the keys. Mordecai caught the boy's hand. His shoulder and neck cradled Josiah's head. Grief held Mordecai's throat in its teeth.

Footsteps pounding up the tenement stairs, accompanied by shouts, broke the spell that gripped the room. Mr. Templeton and his eldest boy turned their tear-streaked faces to the closed apartment door upon which multiple fists hammered while men yelled for the doctor. The girl disappeared into the other room.

"Don't answer it, Mary." The Templeton men showed no patience for intrusion or for its apparent cause. Their jaws hardened and their brows drew together in twin scowls.

"Leave off!" the eldest son bellowed.

"There's no plague doctor in 'ere!" the father roared.

That was true, enough. Mordecai worried his inability to heal would turn the tenement dwellers violent. If they tore off his hood, they might recognize him as a man with a bounty on his head. That reward was a ticket out of the slum for the man who collected it.

Josiah's mother lifted him from Mordecai's embrace. His sister flew to Mordecai and caught his sleeve. "Make haste, Maestro," Mary said with a strength that belied her slight stature. "I've seen to your exit, and we'll let none intercept you."

CHAPTER 32

PHILOMENA

Between a barber and a laundry stood a small store with the name SHELTON BROS. PAWN arched across the top of its window in fat red letters with a gold drop shadow, and beneath that in plain black: NOTARY. The rest of the window displayed musical instruments, an ermine cape, and an extensive selection of rhinestone jewelry that sparkled in the shade of a striped awning.

Inside the store, a narrow path wound through merchandise toward a counter, behind which sat an old man with outlandish whiskers. Philomena supposed him to be one of the Shelton brothers. He'd crammed a small brass thing that looked like a miniature telescope into his eye socket and peered through it at her diamonds.

Time and again, he paused to consult papers on his desk behind the counter. What printed information could be so important that he should reference it in appraisal of her gems? Philomena's unease made her restless and she took to pacing about the shop.

... Bicycles, scooters, coats, tiaras ...

She found an upright piano, and her fingers began traversing the keys.

The telescope fell from his eye as he raised his head. "A singular composition ..." Shelton mused. "What's it called?"

"I haven't named it." If she didn't keep her fingers busy, she'd bite her cuticles and betray to him her anxiety. "I have but now created it."

He set the jewels aside. His eyebrows matched his whiskers, great fuzzy wings that rose in a shrugging expression, "I could pay ..."

His offer made her laugh in disbelief.

Philomena had some head for the market value of jewels, because they related directly to society's value of the ladies who wore them. During the social season, her mother and grandmother talked of little else. She countered with a sum that made *him* laugh, but Philomena intuited the deliberate nature of his mirth and realized a game of sorts had commenced.

"I should think a fine fellow such as yourself," the pawn broker made pointed reference to her bedraggled appearance with another facial shrug, "cannot have found himself often with such a weight of gemstones."

Philomena parried coolly, "*Weight* has nothing do with value."

"Indeed?" His pale blue eyes sharpened on Philomena as she drew near the counter. "What weight should you assign to the amount of ..." His amended offer topped his original but still fell short.

Philomena did not think it wise to linger in one location too long. She held out a hand. "Perhaps I ought seek a second opinion."

Shelton's large-knuckled hands settled on the diamonds. "Perhaps, I ought do the same with regards to their origin." The insinuation was clear. Grimy young fellows with newspaper stuffed into their collars did not often come into possession of a fortune in diamonds by legitimate means.

"Perhaps you ought." Philomena's arch tone dropped all

pretense the deal taking shape was above board. "A fat sale cannot satisfy so well as knowing you've done the *right thing*."

"What is the *right thing* in this instance, d'you reckon?"

She could not be sure, but she thought it had grown darker inside the shop. In any case, Philomena sensed a shift that was not to her liking. She reached across the counter to retrieve her diamonds.

"All right."

To be certain, Philomena repeated her original price.

His aspect communicated resignation. "You drive a hard bargain, young man."

She knew she had not. What could his capitulation mean? Oh, but to get her hands on the money and leave! Philomena kept one hand over the diamonds and opened the other, palm up.

The old man opened a drawer beneath his desk and began to place money in her open palm, small bill by small bill.

Watching him pay her at glacial speed, Philomena resisted the urge to chew the cuticles on her free hand.

Through the glass case set beneath the counter, she saw the edges of those papers he'd been shuffling through while appraising her jewels, but a display of highly-polished pistols kept her from reading the information printed there.

Her gaze lifted to wander over a colorful collection of fireworks shelved behind the pawn broker. Philomena's attention returned to the currency piling up in her palm. She suppressed an impatient sigh. "Could not you count faster?"

"I could, my dear boy, had I not cause to count so very much."

Philomena thought she heard beneath his words a noise but if it were so, she could see no change in the shop that should account for it. Then, she remembered her earlier impression that the store's interior had dimmed. Philomena turned to see a metal lattice drawn across the whole of the pawn shop's front. She whirled around, eyes wide. "What is the meaning of this?"

"A transaction of such import requires privacy." He lifted each bill high in the air before lowering it into her palm, as if hoping to draw her eye into hypnosis. "A push of a button beneath my desk alerted my stockboy to exit the back way, come around and draw the screen across."

Philomena eyed the man narrowly. "Why should not the boy walk past us?"

"Our business is not his province." The pawn broker continued retrieving bills from a seemingly bottomless drawer. He may only have small bills on the premises. Or, he may have chosen to pay in small bills as a means to detain her as long as possible. Perhaps her suspicion was only a phantom of her overburdened mind, but she could not be sure. Resolved to an abundance of caution, Philomena told him, "I've reconsidered."

His pale eyes rose beneath the bushy brows. "I've not finished paying your price."

Philomena's hands closed over the money already paid. "This will suffice."

"Most irregular."

She walked to the front of the shop and pulled the door open.

The metal lattice across the door would not make way. Philomena pulled it this way and that in a rising panic, pushed outward until it clanged in its frame. A tiny woman in a peacock blue coat glanced briefly her way before moving on.

Stifling fear and confusion, Philomena whirled in defiant fury.

The old man stood in the center of his shop, a smile playing about his lips beneath the bramble of whiskers.

"Let me go!"

"There is no profit in that, Mr. Michaelson."

Surprise and understanding struck a single blow. Mistaken identity caused her imprisonment!

"I should never have guessed had you not composed at my piano." He held up the front page of this morning's Herald with its screaming headline: Mad Pianist Kills Mining Heir.

"Unpleasant business ..." He began a return to his counter, ambling through his merchandise on bent knees and with bent back, touching anything stationary along the way to aid in balance. "I must say, you're nowhere near so hideous as reports indicate."

Philomena followed him, preoccupied with the turn matters had taken. Should she prove by undressing to her corset that she was not Mordecai Michaelson? Images repeated endlessly in Philomena's mind—the red spray, Charles falling, his body twitching as his brains leaked through his bloody hair. The particulars of the murder were not nearly so horrifying as the ease with which her grandmother had committed it. As the only witness, Philomena could not afford to come out of hiding.

"I should like you to know," Mr. Shelton reached his desk with Philomena close behind, "I did intend buying your diamonds. Though stolen, as clearly identified in the missive distributed throughout the district ..." He held up a printed drawing of her pieces.

So, that had been his reference when appraising her jewels!

" ...And though missing a few stones—"

"Which stones?" Philomena snatched the drawing and spread the diamonds out to count and compare. Indeed, the collection had lost several pieces since her tumble from the hansom cab. Though among the smallest gems, their custom cut identified her as the jewelry's owner and each added up to a trail the Paulsons' henchman could follow straight to her.

Shelton ruminated, "I could have the diamonds across

the channel within the hour, in the hands of the highest bidder shortly thereafter."

"You still can," Philomena told him. "They're yours if you let me go."

"But they're already mine, Mr. Michaelson! And there's the matter of the reward." Sifting papers, he found the WANTED handbill and read the bounty's amount aloud with a wondering shake of the head. He lowered it to find she'd snatched a pistol from the display case.

Philomena aimed at his heart. "I'll shoot," she declared in as steady a voice as she could manage, "if you do not release me."

"There's no powder in that pistol," he advised wearily. "To be sure, you artists have so little grasp of practical matters."

His condescension pricked her temper. Out of spite, Philomena tucked the pistol into her trousers' waistband and swept an assortment of fireworks into the crook of her arm.

"See here!"

"You haven't paid me enough for the diamonds."

"The police shall relieve you of the contraband in short order."

"They won't have the chance." Philomena spied a satchel and stuffed the fireworks into it. "I mean to escape."

"Do you? How clever."

Philomena shrugged into a man's greatcoat. Though heavy, she found its weight upon her shoulders reassuring. She swept aside a curtain.

Shelton followed her into a back room. Philomena went to the door at its opposite end.

"Locked," the old man said as she tested his claim, "by my stockboy."

"He's taking rather a long time."

"The boy has my every confidence—"

Insight blazed in her smile. "I don't think he does!"

"He can take til' Hades freezes, for all the advantage it gives you." The old man watched her struggle unsuccessfully with the small window set high in the door. "I could have told you it's painted shut."

Philomena turned circles in the small room made smaller by shelves and boxes, a chair and little table set with a teapot and a sole cup and saucer. She saw no stove or fireplace in which to boil water for tea. The buildings along this street had two stories and that meant— Philomena darted behind the stacked boxes and spied another door.

They both went for it but the boxes impeded his progress and she got there first.

Halfway up the narrow stairs, she forced him back with a swing of the satchel. Philomena managed to reach the door at the top of the steps, shut it behind her, and lock the old man out. She dropped the skeleton key in her trouser pockets.

The pawn broker pounded on his own door, shouting, "You needn't think you're free! The police shall have you in a thrice!" But Philomena's heart raced in triumph.

The grease-spotted little kitchen had a cast iron stove upon which rested the kettle she'd wondered about earlier. On a shelf nearby sat a box of matches that soon disappeared into her satchel.

She pulled drapes from a window and looked out at the rear exteriors of the businesses that faced the back of SHELTON BROS. PAWN. Philomena shoved up on the paint-caked, humidity-swollen sash and climbed out the window onto a metal balcony.

Metal stairs led from this balcony to the cobblestoned alley below. Similar balcony-stair combinations protruded from all the buildings and she supposed these provided escape in case of fire. Escape in case of anything!

Philomena closed her eyes and with a smile, took a deep, celebratory breath of freedom.

153

Then grimaced. Her celebratory breath reeked of garbage overflowing the bins below.

Shrill whistles sounded from the nearest intersection, where traffic moved quickly aside to clear room for a police wagon pulled by horses at a full gallop. In the police wagon's buckboard, a young man in a workman's apron pointed onwards but he was diverted by the pawn broker yelling from the downstairs exit. Through the balcony slats she saw Shelton waving his arms and pointing skyward. "He is upstairs!"

The police horses turned into the alley at full speed, as thoroughbreds round the bend of a race course. Above the clatter of hooves on cobblestone, the stockboy shouted, "I see him!"

Philomena crouched behind the balcony rails and dug bright containers from her satchel.

She had experienced fireworks only as an observer, one of a crowd at the Queen's Jubilee delighted by the visual sensations erupting high in the dark sky. But how did these little boxes become brilliant constellations?

She snatched one up, squinting at tiny lettering that told her little beyond *touch flame to fuse* and *CAUTION! Potential injury if mishandled.*

A bullhorn magnified police orders, "Stand with your arms in the air!" as she tore frantically at the packaging.

Colorful tubes resembling paper candles scattered over the metal floor. Striking a match to metal produced a flame. Philomena lit a wick. Sparks blazed in her eyes. With a shriek of fear, she threw the firework.

BOOM!

The world flared red, then exploded in giant gold flowers that winked and flashed as they showered the alley.

Past the squealing trails of firework noise, she heard men shouting. Philomena lit another firework and threw it. Then another. The alley flashed multicolors through the smoke. The air smelled of sulfur. Her eyes stung and watered.

She tore blindly through a different box, lighting one firework after another without knowing whether she touched flame to fuse or merely set paper exteriors alight before throwing each incendiary into the void. Explosions filled the alley. Colors whirled and whizzed. In their combined reverberations, a fusillade of shots rang out.

Philomena jumped at the loud ping of something striking metal near her face. *They've opened fire!*

She lit something she couldn't see and threw it.

BOOM!

Screaming dragon tails streaked above the rooftops, raining sparks.

Philomena choked as her lungs filled with smoke. The balcony in which she crouched pitched and shook. Grabbing hold of a metal rung, she dragged herself up one of the balcony's high sides.

"Michaelson!" A voice through the bullhorn coughed and bellowed, closer than the street – from the stairs! "Come down with your hands up!"

CHAPTER 33

MORDECAI

Mary led Mordecai back to the kitchen and drew aside a curtain. A glance out the window sent his heart into his throat.
He saw an airshaft, an enclosed space without exit. No balconies or fire escapes attached to exterior walls, for city planners never considered the benefits of these for slum tenants. They'd designed airshafts for the sole purpose of complying with a civil mandate that interior flats have access to air and daylight. Success proved elusive, however; for airshafts blocked breezes and trapped smells wafting up from anything thrown to the ground from a window. Tenants living opposite each other strung clotheslines through pulleys to run between them, and laundry hung in such excess across the airshaft that tenement walls could scarce be seen.
If Mordecai lost his grip, he'd drop six stories.
"I'm so sorry," Mary's tear-strained voice thinned with anxiety. "It's the only way out. But it's so dangerous! I wish—"
"Why, it shall do a treat!" Mordecai interrupted breezily. He did not wish to add his problem to her own. Her hair was damp and frizzy from endless laundering of Josiah's

soiled linens. He saw fatigue in her thin face from lack of sleep over worry for Josiah. Grief in advance of his death haunted her eyes and certainty of more death trapped her. Cholera swept through families. Awareness of this fact dwelled in their shared gaze.

"I can't make him well, no matter how I try!" she blurted. "I can't make Mama rest nor comfort Papa—"

"Of course, you can't!" Thought of her playing the Knuckle Song made his throat hurt again. "You do everything right, Mary." Though she rejected his assertion with a shake of her head, he insisted, "Whatever the odds, try your best and don't let it lick you. That's the right thing, even if it's the only thing you can do."

Tears spilled down her cheeks and a sad smile trembled on her lips. She flinched at a sudden commotion inside and glanced nervously to the door. "They'll break in!"

"I'm off, then." Setting the hat and hood aside, Mordecai climbed over the sill of the open window. He gripped the clothesline tight and flashed a confident smile. "Cheerio!"

"Maestro, wait!" To his surprise, Mary kissed his cheek, muttering forcefully, "You make for that flat across the airshaft." She indicated with a jut of her chin and specified, "second floor, count back four windows from here."

Something slipped past his ears to hang lightly around his neck but he hadn't time to examine or enquire about it, for just then the crowd outside the door broke past its flimsy chain lock. Templeton men rushed at them, shouting, "By Christ, I'll clout you good!" and "Bloody get out!" as Mary slid the curtain across the window.

Releasing his grip on the sill swung him upside down as the world blurred past. Mordecai hung from the clothesline by his bent legs and arms. Blood rushed to his head, building pressure. The plague doctor's coat fit snug from shoulders to waist, but gravity pulled the rest of it inside out.

Mordecai shook his head free of the coat's obstruction to see, beyond his waving hair, a card swaying at the end of a lanyard. He caught the lanyard in his fingers and put the card between his teeth. Mary had given it him for a reason and he should not lose it. Below the six stories of hanging laundry on either side, he saw a thin line of parched ground. *If this line holds so much weight of wet washing, it may yet hold me.* That he hung within reach of the Templetons' unwanted houseguests posed a different danger.

With a care not to *pull* the line, lest he draw it through the pulleys and lose as much ground as he gained, Mordecai moved gloved hand over gloved fist and leg by leg past baby nappies and combinations, shirtwaists and bedclothes.

Pushing past fear, he obsessed over details of his environment. Four clotheslines ran north to south through the airshaft. At the sixth floor, the Templetons' line ran nearest but one to the west side. Two more ran between the Templetons' line and the tenement's east side.

He recalled Mary's instructions. *Make for that flat across the airshaft. Second floor, count back four windows from here.* To reach sanctuary, Mordecai must travel from this clothesline *across* two clotheslines and *down* four lines. At some point in this across-and-down route, he must pull himself southward far enough to reach the correct window on the second floor.

Laundry hung above Mordecai from the seventh floor. His body weight dragged his clothesline below those on either side, where laundry hid him from view of sixth-floor windows at the east and west sides.

Window sashes flew up. Women yelled to each other across the airshaft. Something – they could not see what – sent laundry dancing jerkily in the stagnant air. "Birds?"

"Rats, more like!"

Their imaginations should soon leave off rodents and

land on him. News traveled fast through tenements. It could not be long before they learned a fugitive traversed this very building in a flight from justice. Mordecai had to keep going.

Damp fabrics, by turns heavy or flimsy, chilled his face and clung to his body. He paused within their clammy folds when he thought he'd reached midway. Two windows behind him, two more ahead.

Mordecai began a gingerly sway, increasing it as he dared until he snatched the line running parallel to his. This jerked him to a standstill. Stretched between the two clotheslines, he gathered breath, energy, and strength to continue.

His new line suddenly whizzed north, breaking his hold on the old line.

Frantically, Mordecai slid his arm over the new line to catch it in the crook of his elbow as the Templetons' next-door neighbors reeled him in. Mordecai flung his free arm up and managed to get a hand hold. His body swung in violent jerks as he pulled away from the people trying to catch him on the new line while his legs dragged across pinned washing on the old line. In hopeless frustration, he looked down.

The distance made him nauseous.

As the new line sped toward his captors, Mordecai unpinned a threadbare petticoat and tied it into a solid double knot over the line. He dropped his legs from the old line and descended the petticoat as on a rope. Dragged down by his weight, the fabric shredded halfway across and dropped Mordecai with it.

He hung onto the torn petticoat with one hand as the cotton frayed farther and the line sped north. He made a wild grab for the line below.

And caught it.

He released the torn petticoat.

Mordecai held onto the fifth-floor clothesline for dear

life while swinging his free arm up to catch the line in his hand. His arrested fall had torn connective muscle between arm and shoulder. He endured throbbing pain, gritting his teeth on the card and dragging his body through air in a resumed journey south.

Above and between articles of laundry, he caught glimpses of excited faces.

The housewives earlier shouting, "Birds? Rats!" now shouted, "It's him!"

"The plague doctor?"

"No—he hasn't a hood!"

They speculated at top volume.

"He's that criminal, the one murdered a gentleman!"

"Don't be daft! What would he be doin' here?"

Behind them in soaked bedding lay their dying kin. The mystery of his identity provided distraction from their terrible fear and grief.

Though Mordecai imagined their motivation through natural compassion, he could ill afford to empathize when they attacked him.

"Get him down!"

Food and crockery flew into the airshaft. Coffee grounds, human waste flung from slop buckets, cutlery, and all manner of debris hit the laundry and hit Mordecai. Something struck the back of his head that, on impact, became wet and slid juicily down his neck. A pottery shard gouged his forehead, and blood ran into his eye. Agony exploded in every bone of his hand when a cast iron object struck it with enough force to open his fingers. He nearly lost the line.

Windows.

Ignoring pain, fear, and makeshift artillery, Mordecai counted windows. Exultation seized him when he reached the fourth in the east wall.

Ah, but the window Mary set him toward was on the second floor. Mordecai hung at the fifth floor.

Grunting and grimacing, he traveled south down the line until he happened upon a long, sweat stained combination suit, an undergarment Americans called a *union suit*. With the clothesline in his armpits, he unpinned and tied the combination's sleeves.

The wool stretched and sagged as he descended its length. At last, Mordecai hung by the cuffs of the combination's legs. His toes brushed the fourth floor clothesline. He looked down, gauging the direction of his voluntary fall.

And took his chances.

The fourth floor line caught him in the stomach. He grabbed the line with laundry bouncing all around him. His legs kicked and his elbows danced as he fought to attain a solid hold. Mordecai propelled down the clothesline, the frenetic movement of laundry betraying his position to the mob pursuing him. He chanced upon a thick, fuzzy, wet blanket and knotted it as tightly as he could. He climbed down its length. The blanket held, but the line snapped.

Mordecai fell.

Arms and legs pinwheeling in a blind panic, he grabbed wildly for the third-floor line but missed. His fingers brushed fabric but failed to catch it.

Gravity threw him to earth. His hands clawed for anything.

His fingers closed on twill. He climbed the trouser leg as it slipped in its clothespin. Its waistband snapped free on that side but he'd grabbed the other leg and this he climbed in a race against his own weight. The remaining pin lost its grip on the second-story garment just as Mordecai caught the line.

His eyes closed in relief. Then opened when he felt himself pulled sideways.

One person or many reeled him towards a second-story window. Mordecai craned his neck for a glimpse of his enemy. From behind a bedsheet that hung on the line nearest the east wall, a cane slid into view. Mordecai looked at its curved handle, dumbfounded.

It was the sort of cane used by stagehands to yank a vaudevillian offstage. Perhaps angels of the Almighty had come to yank him from the ludicrous roadshow his life had turned into. Mordecai almost lost the card between his teeth as laughter overtook him.

Philomena should think you a fine fellow in this state. Bear up, man.

Mordecai regained composure and, in consequence, reclaimed self-respect.

And bugger this cane. With a grimace, he swatted it away. It returned.

He grabbed it in a temper. Its owner hooked the handle over the clothesline. *BLAST!* Mordecai could not free the line without losing his grip. The cane drew him into the last line of laundry and ever nearer the east wall. He kicked repeatedly in the direction of the villain hidden behind articles of washing. He glimpsed a broad torso and took vicious aim.

Impervious, the man caught the line in hand. The world pitched on its axis as Mordecai attempted evasion. Strong fingers closed on the plague doctor's coat. A brawny arm swept around Mordecai's back.

Mordecai's foot hit the windowsill. He attempted to push away, but he was pulled through the window into a tenement.

He landed on his knees and staggered to his feet, throwing punches blind. Dizziness drove him against the wall. Pain crushed his bones and his muscles screamed fire. Nausea swept through him. His legs gave out as his vision went dark.

Mordecai had the sensation of rising by some power greater than his own. He hung like a drunk on someone's arm as his vision returned in a series of blinks. He jabbed his elbow into a solid set of ribs, winning his freedom but falling again into the wall. He glared at the man whose stature filled his field of vision, leaving little view of a neat kitchen behind him.

The man's big fists rested on narrow hips. A lantern jaw tilted down as grave eyes observed the fugitive narrowly. "Didn't she tell you?"

Mordecai hadn't strength or will to hide his incomprehension.

"I'm Mary's uncle."

The card fell from Mordecai's teeth to hang from its lanyard. "Is this the second floor, then? Fourth window?"

"She told me to make haste, said I should expect you." The man splashed whiskey into a shot glass and offered it.

In a state of wonder, Mordecai tossed it back. It was cheap and scratched all the way down his throat but warmed his stomach and cleared his head. "My apologies, sir," he gasped. "I'd lost count of the windows and ..."

"Feeling better?"

"I'm much obliged to you, Mr. ..." He hesitated, wondering from which side of the family his rescuer hailed, "Templeton?"

"Clive'll do." Mary's uncle shook his proffered hand. "We best shift ourselves. Friends an' neighbors on their way, you know." He led the way but turned in the tiny hallway, his shoulders brushing the walls. "Have you any money?"

At a loss how to answer, Mordecai belatedly caught the man's true meaning. He did not ask for money but *offered* it. No one here had enough. Still, Templeton offered. Humbled, Mordecai feigned financial ease with a pat of his breast pocket. "Safe in my coat."

Mary's uncle nodded. Neither man acknowledged the coat did not belong to Mordecai.

Outside voices grew louder through thin walls. Clive opened his door and looked out both ways before waving Mordecai forward. "Now or never, mate."

Mordecai followed his swift descent, past the ground floor. They made a sharp turn through a door, down narrow steps into the tenement's dark cellar. Mordecai heard the scratch of a flint, then saw a tiny flame. He followed its bearer to the far wall.

With the flame, Clive indicated a small metal door set high in the wall. "Coal man should be along soon." He illuminated the space beside it, where steps rose to a door that opened to the street. "When the chute opens, you take them stairs."

Mordecai nodded, understanding the plan. Crude though it was, the strategy hid him from the tenement crowd until he could make his getaway. "Mr. Templeton, I owe you a debt—"

"Not a'tall!" the man interrupted with a force that set Mordecai back. "You made our Josiah happy. I heard what they say you done to that mining heir gentleman, and *I* say—" He spit on the floor. "—to that!"

He knows I'm accused of the murder! Mordecai stared in disbelief at the man's generosity. *My God, the reward for turning me in could save them from poverty, from cholera.*

"Risking your life to stop here...to play for our boy!" Emotion thickened Clive's words, "To help him play his last—" He moved the flame from his crumpling face. "I defy anyone tells me a killer does that!"

Stunned and grateful, Mordecai could say no more.

As Clive Templeton climbed from the cellar to the tenement's ground floor, the door suddenly opened. Clive startled, his cry ending on a chuckle that sounded false. "Fair gave me a fright, you did."

A woman asked hungrily, "Is 'e down there?"

"Who? Oh – nah."

Her shadow flowed into the light slanting over him. "Are you sure?"

Templeton asked silkily, "Care to look with me?"

Her gasp did not quite convey the level of shock

propriety demanded.

He stepped back invitingly.

Mordecai froze in the dark.

"Who knows what we could ..." Soft laughter insinuated into his tone, " ...*find*."

"Mr. Templeton!" she breathed, stepping back as he climbed.

"You look so fresh," he purred, "How'dyou manage it?"

"I do my best, I'm sure ..."

Clive shut the cellar door behind him.

CHAPTER 34

PHILOMENA

Philomena tumbled over the metal-slatted wall and landed on the neighboring balcony, her satchel landing heavily on top of her. She reached for the window, thanked heaven it opened, and climbed inside with as much stealth as she could manage. She gently shut the window and drew the curtains.

Philomena regretted the stench of sulfuric smoke filling her nostrils, for she imagined this tidy kitchen must smell sweetly of rice and orange tea. On a red table, a Siamese cat lounged between two place settings. It stood and stretched as Philomena crept past.

She slipped through a door and descended the narrow stair.

Philomena paused before opening the next door, wondering what peril awaited her without. The police would not tarry at the foot of SHELTON BROS. damaged balcony. They would surround the block, invade the commercial spaces in search of her. With a quick sigh, she acknowledged the futility of turning back.

Stepping through the door, she saw white ...

Through a fog of steam that clung to her skin, she saw shuddering panels of white, which her awareness belatedly recognized as undergarments and men's shirts. Audible chaos hidden behind the lines of laundry made weak impression on her ears, for close proximity to exploding fireworks had deafened Philomena. She could just make out the difference in voices by gender: high and frightened female tones beat down by authoritative male tones. She'd wasted precious seconds trying to gain her bearings. The police were inside already! She turned her face away from the laundryworks and opened a second door.

In a small back room, a slim, dark-haired woman watched her from behind a sewing machine. Though Philomena could read no expression in the woman's black almond eyes, she felt they assessed every detail of her person and categorized her in short order. The woman's fingers rested on either side of the machine's needle. Her dainty foot poised over its pedal. A peacock blue coat hung behind her. A dark-haired child pressed himself to her side, his dark eyes wide.

"Little man," Philomena said, too gently to hear her own words, "do not fear."

The woman let out a spate of words that Philomena couldn't hear, but she saw by the strain in her throat, they carried a shrill imperative. She obeyed the woman's command by instinct, turning back through the door from whence she'd come.

Philomena descended the stairs to the laundry's cellar. A door opposite beckoned. Philomena stepped through this door into the pawn shop's cellar. She passed bales of merchandise until she found this cellar's opposite door.

The next cellar held instruments of the barber trade. Philomena reasoned connections between shops existed in groups of three, for she found no door leading to a fourth cellar. The only door remaining led to the shop upstairs. However, the course of her search revealed a curious inventory stocked behind the outermost shelves.

What need had a barber for so many pistols and rifles?

For what purpose did he keep crates of empty bottles? A few rags might suffice to dust an establishment. Why store sacks full? Behind a tall shelf filled with combs, clippers, and hair tonics, Philomena spied a contraption of wood and metal. She ran her fingers across a series of metal blocks individually embossed with letters, considering the obvious. It was a printing press. What manner of literature required seclusion to produce? She tried opening several boxes near the press but found them locked.

Her curiosity frustrated, Philomena returned to her immediate predicament. She had to elude police and find Mordecai. That she hadn't a clue where to start looking for him mustn't discourage her. Inspiration would strike; she was sure of it. Philomena hastened upstairs and nearly collided with a man standing at the top.

In his shadow, she looked up, up, up. His height and breadth of shoulder filled the door frame. The dome of his big head bristled with hair that glinted in the meager light. Indeed, his entire mien seemed to bristle, for he had the air of a man who'd arrived at the top of the stairs in a hurry. His broad nose seemed out of joint for reasons additional to the old injury that had bent its bridge. His light eyes flashed. His upper lip curled back from a long incisor. "AMOS!"

Philomena's shoulders jerked. Her ears popped and hearing returned.

A man instantly appeared, trepidation in his, "Yeah, boss?"

In the boss's face, temper roiled like a monster turning over in the sea before sinking into the depths. He said with studied calm, "See to the lock on that cellar door, won't you?"

"I could've sworn I–"

Boss seemed to grow taller, while Amos shrank.

The chagrined employee slid past the unmoving monolith in human form. When he passed Philomena, she flattened against the wall.

Her eyes lifted worriedly to Boss, whose head had lowered on his bull neck to peruse her more closely. Most of his mouth didn't move but the corners angled up like wings. "You're a good deal smaller than St. Claire. How'd you manage to brain him with a candlestick?"

She was too surprised by his initial words to protest innocence. "You knew Charles?"

"Seen him. Know his type."

"I thought I knew him until ..." Philomena remembered the contempt Charles had shown her at their betrothal ball. "Still," she mused, "one mustn't speak ill of the dead."

"Oh, aye," came the dry rejoinder. "With one blow, you made your point. Why belabor it?"

Philomena closed her eyes in pain, seeing her grandmother throwing the bloody weapon in Mordecai's path. "Oh, you don't know anything!"

"I know Shelton's loss is our gain." Now he smiled with his whole mouth. "You'll fetch us a pretty penny, Mr. Michaelson!"

Philomena resisted with a desperate look and a shake of her head, leaning away from Boss and bumping into Amos, who yanked her greatcoat inside out down her arms.

Boss pulled the pistol from her waistband.

Amos completed his confiscation of greatcoat and satchel.

"Come along," Boss said, as if inviting her to tea.

Though Philomena couldn't see past her lead captor's brawny form, she heard another man ask, "Everythin' all right, Boss? Coppers'r tossing every shop on the street. They say it's Michaelson shot off them fireworks – hang on!" He'd just seen Philomena as the trio joined him in the empty barber shop.

"And you wondered how we'd fund our next objective," Boss chided. "Didn't I tell it always comes right?"

"You did, indeed!" With his hands on his thighs and his

head stuck out, the third barber bent to inspect Philomena. "Sure, he's a wee fellah, to be killin' folks."

"There's not much to the likes of Mr. Charles St. Claire, *esquire*," Amos intoned the honorific in a top-drawer accent. "Killin' him musta' been like swatting a fly."

Philomena pursed her lips to hear him mocked, for though he'd treated her shamefully, she'd once liked Charles and no one deserved to be murdered.

"They buy their muscle," Boss said. "Never forget it, lads. They only keep power by keeping the rest of us down."

"But they're *perfect!*" Amos sneered in falsetto. "Innit right, Cyril?"

"Not a crip or a halfwit among 'em!" The third barber declared, "Better genetics makes 'em better, Amos – ya must know that!"

"Why, it's a privilege sendin' our wee'uns down their mines," Amos opined in mock humility. "A right pleasure to work in their factories for slave wages, on machines that slice an' crush for want of proper maintenance."

"Sure, proper maintenance," Cyril scoffed. "Why pay for that when Miss Philomena Paulson wants another diamond necklace?"

Philomena fought back tears. *Is this what people think of us?*

"Shut up, you two," Boss muttered, staring through his storefront at the unrest outside. "He's been down the cellar."

"He won't tell 'em what he's seen," Amos said on a defensive note. After all, he'd been the one who forgot to lock the adjoining cellar door. "He'll be too intent on tellin' 'em he's innocent."

"Yer innocent, Mr. Michaelson!" Cyril proclaimed brightly, his face too close to Philomena's. "And we're just barbers!"

When a bell chimed above the barber shop door, every

aspect of Boss's demeanor changed. Philomena could not have described the change, for he'd been tense before and he was tense now. But it was a different kind of tension. She looked around the mocking barbers to see what manner of person drew the boss forward so quickly.

A long peacock blue coat conformed to her slender figure. A simple hat adorned her sleek black hair. A black-haired little boy held her hand. Philomena recognized the seamstress and realized this was the woman passing by the pawn shop who'd glanced her way as she'd rattled the locked metal lattice across Mr. Shelton's door.

Boss bent slightly, clasping his hands as if he'd just whipped a hat off his head. The seamstress spoke in her inscrutable tongue. To Philomena's astonishment, Boss answered in her native language. He drew very slightly nearer. A note of enquiry, a tone of disbelief; these transcend language. The seamstress gave him her firm reply.

Boss glanced sideways in Philomena's direction. "Cyril, give young master Cho a trim up, will you?"

"I just cut it yester—"

Light eyes darkened.

"Sure, boss, sure ..."

The seamstress took a seat as the little boy clambered up into the barber's chair and Cyril swept a drape around his tiny shoulders.

Police approached the barbershop.

Boss told Amos, "Mr. Michealson could do with a shave."

Philomena's struggles amounted to nothing against their combined strength as they hustled her into a chair.

The glass storefront filled with so many policemen, their dark blue uniforms seemed to meld them into one predatory force. The old pawn broker did his best to keep up with them. And ahead of him, another man in plain clothes moved with the singular purpose of a lone hunter.

Amos tied the cape's collar around her neck. Philomena felt like she was choking, but it was her throat swelling, her gorge rising, that constricted her breathing as fear overwhelmed her.

She knew the hunter's craggy features.

She cringed in sudden blindness when Boss dropped something warm, and wet over her face. A panicked noise escaped her tight lips.

"Be still," Boss ordered, rearranging folds.

Through effort of will, Philomena breathed in measured draughts the humid air trapped inside the towel that covered her entire face. She felt Amos pulling the drape down, smoothing it over her legs. He froze.

"Boss."

"Not now."

The bell above the shop door jangled.

She heard the men enter, felt their presence change the energy of the room.

She heard the pawn broker say, "Remember, I found the fugitive Michaelson."

"May we help you, officers?" Boss enquired on a genial note.

"Mordecai Michaelson is reported to be in the vicinity," the policeman in charge stated.

"I reported it!" the pawn broker cut in. "It was my shop he entered—"

"He's escaped," the policeman said, "and is at large."

Philomena hoped that when the barbers removed the wet towel from her face, the police took her before the Paulsons' henchman saw past the shorn head and men's clothes and recognized her. *When they raise the towel, I shall insist I am Mordecai, no matter what he says. I cannot fall into his hands!* If she had to choose between two bad outcomes, she hoped for the police.

"Has Michaelson entered your shop?"

"No," Boss said.

What?

"P'raps he's passed by?"

"I've not seen him," Boss said. "Amos? Cyril?"

The barbers answered in the negative, while Philomena's mind raced. They had only moments ago anticipated the fat reward offered for delivering Mordecai. What could Boss mean by his change of plan?

The pawn broker said, "Well, we'll be off then, won't we officer? Michaelson's not here. I found him."

"And lost him," the policeman retorted. "Have another look ..." Philomena heard a rustling of paper. "Sure you haven't seen him?"

Boss gave a derisive chuckle. "I'd've noticed that misaligned visage. I wonder his mother could stand to gaze upon it."

Philomena's face grew hot with temper, as it always did when someone insulted Mordecai.

"Let us away," the pawn broker urged. "He is elsewhere and gaining distance from us, I'll be bound."

No one moved.

"O' *Shau-ne-ssey...*" the policeman drew out the synonyms.

"It's my name," Boss said, with an undertone of danger.

"Brady and Fitzgerald."

No one confirmed the barbers' names in the tense silence that gripped the room.

Cyril cut the little boy's hair with exaggerated care—*Snip.* Pause. *Snip.* Pause. Pause. *Snip*—as police began moving through the shop.

The lead lawman continued, "There's an infamous confederacy whose members answer to those surnames."

"The Barbers' Guild has a fair number," Boss said easily, then snapped, "that's far enough, unless you've a warrant." Officers halted near the door to the back room.

"It's not barbers I'm thinking of but another group, entirely," the lead officer replied. "One that should find a fugitive of this sort a fair prize to hold in its grievance against the Crown."

"I hope it's not treason you're accusing me of," Boss said with soft malice. "Common surname don't mean common cause."

"It does all too often," the lawman said. "Let's have a lift of that towel."

"I'll lift you through that window!" he blazed. "That's a customer beneath a towel. It's my livelihood you're playin' with."

"I do not play," the lawman said with quite force. "I'm telling you—"

"He's tellin' me, lads! D'you hear that?"

Cyril laughed softly. *Snip.* Pause. *Snip.*

"D'you think I'm hiding him?" Boss enquired in tones of incredulity. "Sure, why should I miss a chance to grab Shelton's reward? It'd go a sight farther between three barbers than if we shared it with any – *confederacy*, as you call it."

"He's not here." Impatience thinned the pawn broker's voice, "Let us away!"

"Listen to my neighbor," Boss laughed, "seeing his money go up in a puff o' smoke while you loiter in my shop."

The lawman relented with a terse, "All right, Shelton."

Boss wished the departing police, "a good day to you, sirs," with a gaiety their leader received with ill grace.

There was hurt pride in his parting shot. "I may come back with that warrant, yet."

"By all means, do," Boss called after him, "and stay for a trim o' that tumbleweed you call a beard!"

The barbers laughed as the bell above the door jangled.

Cyril whisked the drape away and the little boy hopped from the barber chair.

"We keep sweeties for our best customers, do we not?"

"We do, boss."

Philomena heard the child's cry of delight. She freed her face from the towel in time to see the pair leave. Boss bade them good-bye in their native tongue, with a tenderness they perhaps could not hear for the jingle above the door.

"Whyn't you ask the widow Cho to supper one night, eh, boss? Take her to a show?"

"Sweep up, Cyril."

With the police gone, Philomena felt a frantic temptation to attempt escape, but Amos clamped a hand on her shoulder. "He's got a wooden leg."

"Get that towel back on."

"It don't say nowhere he's got a wooden leg." Amos hastily arranged the clammy fabric over her eyes. She had just enough time to see the Paulsons' henchman returning to the shop at a brisk pace.

CHAPTER 35

He'd come back for her. Philomena could barely breathe. Fear frazzled her wits so completely that she hardly comprehended the verbal interchange that commenced as the bell chimed again.

"Mr. Higgleson," Boss greeted. "Come back for a haircut, have you?"

"I'm paid too well to favor this place."

"One should hardly think it by the state o' you."

"Still trying to bring down the oppressors?"

"You still licking their boots?"

They know each other! The barber's antagonism gave Philomena no cause to hope, for she sensed mutual contempt formed a bond of sorts between the two men. They locked horns in competition that made sport of nefarious transactions. Philomena saw now the reason Boss had kept her from the police. He believed himself capable of wrestling from Higgleston a sum greater than the publicized reward.

"I'd like a look beneath that towel," the henchman said.

"Would you, indeed?" Boss derided in his first strategic block. "T'aint him."

"I know that, you idjit," Higgleston parried. "Your ...*customer*, as you call him ...is Michaelson's accomplice."

So, that's what he's calling me! While at large, I'm no

daughter but an accomplice.

"Well, now!" That Boss enjoyed this exchange was evident in his tone. "I read nothing of an accomplice in The Herald. Amos, did you?"

"Not a word, boss."

"Cyril, anything in that handbill about such?"

"No, boss."

"Well!" Boss marveled, "The Paulsons are powerful keen to keep this accomplice to themselves!"

Amusement overtook the barbers entirely.

"I should think anarchy a dull vocation in the main," Higgleston surmised, "if you're this desperate for a laugh."

"You bein' desperate makes us laugh!" Boss sobered with only partial success. "It's a fine errand they sent you on this time, innit?"

"To be sure, it was almost too easy." Higgleston sounded bored. "He left a trail of clues leading me to this very street."

Oh, those cursed diamonds!

"Let us be certain," Boss suggested. "Does your man possess any distinguishing characteristics?"

The henchman's answer sounded dragged out of him, "…A wooden leg."

Boss slapped the counter smartly. "Our man's got a wooden leg! But – hang on a minute! There's scores of lads back from war with a wooden leg."

"The accomplice is no soldier." Higgleston betrayed annoyance with a sarcastic show of patience. "I'll recognize him, when the spirit moves you to … lift the towel?"

No, no, no!

Boss said, "Amos, do the honors."

Philomena cringed inside the barber's cape. Too soon, Amos lifted the last of the wet fabric away. She turned her face toward the back of the shop, but she could feel the henchman's evil presence drawing ever closer. In a flare of defiance, she whipped her head around. Philomena expressed the full force of her anger and fear in a murderous glare.

Impervious, the man searched her face.

Philomena searched his as well, for in all her life it was her first opportunity to scrutinize this shadowy figure openly. She saw a whip-thin body emanating leashed ferocity, a face bladed by sharp bones, eyes beady and penetrating.

He tried to see beyond the grime and fatigue masking her soft features. He stepped back and perused the whole of her slight form in the big chair. When his gaze rose to her patchy head, his mouth twisted in disgust. "Was it you butchered his hair? He's a right disgrace."

"Is he *yours?*" Boss demanded. "Is this your accomplice?"

"*Mordecai Michaelson's* accomplice," Higgleston corrected. He drew a fat wallet from his waistcoat.

"Put that away," Boss derided. "I want none of your allowance."

Higgleston's teeth flashed in a thin-lipped retort. "They are large bills, O' Shaunnessey, enough to keep your people in potatoes and whiskey til' Christ returns, if you were so inclined to redirect your budget."

"I'll shove potatoes up yer arse!" Amos yelled.

"And drop that wallet down your neck once I've separated yer head from it!" Cyril shouted.

"Easy, lads," Boss said mildly. "What I mean Mr. Higgleston to know is, I'll not take a reward from him but only from Theodore Paulson."

Higgleston gave a neat shake of the head. "It won't do. My client has commissioned *me* to make the exchange." He drew his arms wide, one hand holding out the wallet like a steak to junkyard dogs. "Right here. Right now. No questions asked."

"At the Puggle and Poke," Boss said with narrowed

eyes. "Four o'clock. Bring your employer with you or there'll be no exchange."

"You obstinate mick," Higgleston insulted tiredly.

"Paulson don't care beans for the murderer. It's the accomplice he wants, else he'd not have sent you out in secrecy to find him." The corners of his mouth jabbed upward. "He's tipped your hand, clear. You can't blame me for the blunder."

Higgleston shoved his wallet back into his waistcoat. "I'll see you at the Puggle and Poke—"

"With Paulson," Boss said.

"Four o'clock," the henchman said as the bell jangled above him.

Philomena's mind raced in pursuit of a plan to escape during the brief delay her captors had bargained for. If she could somehow get to the back room without their notice, she could grab her satchel and pistol. She could— She could—

Boss said, "Mind the lass. She looks about to bolt."

"Lass?" Amos exclaimed. "Have you gone barmy?"

"Mrs. Cho can size up a body in a second, no matter how it's dressed." Boss raked Philomena with a glance. "She came to tell me the fugitive was no Mordecai Michaelson."

Philomena found her voice. "He didn't do it!"

Dark amusement warmed his eyes. "Love him, do you?"

"Yes!"

"More's the pity." The corners turned up independent of his level mouth. "Blowin' your way out with fireworks, you're a credit to him. Don't see as he credits you, if I'm honest."

"You know nothing about him!" Philomena countered hotly.

"Was it a pact you made with him," Cyril asked, "to die together?"

"Certainly not!"

"Sure, you'd not be the first to make such a pact," Amos said, "though I could think of a nobler cause f'rit than thievin' and murderin'."

"Ah, but who was it they thieved?" Cyril asked. "Who was it they murdered?"

"We didn't!"

"Shame to see 'em hang for that!" Amos said.

Boss sighed, "Well, each can think o' t'other when drawin' their last; it's the best we can promise. Clean her up, lads. I'll not give her over lookin' like *shite*."

They pulled the newspaper from her collar, pushed her into a chair and whirled her around. Philomena felt exceedingly vulnerable with her head over a sink and her throat bared to the ceiling. "Just so I'm clear ..."

They paused, Amos with his hands clawed above her scalp and Cyril tilting a pitcher of water.

"You'd be sorry to see anyone hanged for killing Mr. St. Claire?"

"We'd thank him, at least."

She heard pure hatred in Cyril's voice just before he poured water gently over her scalp. It felt wonderful and soothing, completely at odds with the fate in store for her. "Higgleston means to kill me—oh, you must know that! What else would he do, lock me up in a tower?"

She tried to catch their eyes, but they'd have none of that.

"By all means," she persisted, "kill *me* as an accomplice to killing Mr. St. Claire – whom you despise. Does it bother you none at all?"

Amos rubbed soap into her short hair, scrubbing gently with an air of professional indifference. Aside from their scars and broken bones healed badly, she saw smooth skin and even a few spots. They couldn't be much older than she. "I'm a lass!" She used their slang, hoping to form a connection. "Should you allow your sworn enemy to kill a lass?" Cyril rinsed her scalp. Amos threw a towel over her head. Cyril raised her up and Amos rubbed her head briskly. "Let me alone!" she cried in sudden anger, swatting at them and grabbing the towel. "I'm a lass not yet twenty."

"Amos, d'you know any lass twenty years of age who'd wager on seeing twenty-one?"

"I do not, Cyril." Amos began snipping Philomena's hair to even up the spiky tufts. "But, p'raps our lass is a lady's maid and only been among our betters."

"Oh, our betters, aye. That's a different story altogether." Cyril rubbed pomade between his palms. "They don't see the grave til' they're ninety, and then don't look a day over thirty."

"Is that it, lass?" Amos taunted. "Sheltered, are you?"

"Do I look it?" Philomena slapped dust off her borrowed clothes. "It's a cowardly thing, sending a lass off to be killed. What should your mothers say?"

"My mother?" Amos snapped the scissors closed, his white knuckled fist clutching them like a dagger. "My mam says naught, now she's died breathin' cotton dust in a Paulson mill!"

Philomena stared, aghast. She knew nothing of the mills, but she knew she'd been wrong to plead mercy on the basis of her youth and innocence.

"A St. Claire mine collapsed on my brothers," Cyril seethed.

She could not tell lads with no hope of growing old that she feared dying.

"They'll not take me that way," Amos vowed.

"Nor I, by God," Cyril grated, "I'll die fighting before I let 'em kill *me* for the sake of a wage!"

"Enough!" Boss shouldered them aside. "She's done your heads in."

He looked down at her with eyes as pale and hard as stones. He gave her that strange, level-mouthed, corner-tilted smile. "We're not buzzin' off seeing you killed, lass, but a deal's a deal."

Philomena saw she must try another angle. If she could not appeal to compassion, she could appeal to their cause. "You're selling me cheap, Mr. O'Shaunnessey."

"'Pon my soul," he joked, deadpan. "We've a broker in our midst, lads." He took the scissors from Amos' loosening fingers. Philomena noticed the easing of tension, how the barbers relaxed under the influence of their leader's nonchalance.

She focused on him. "Why should they send their lackey for an accomplice instead of the murderer?"

Boss shrugged as he trimmed Philomena's hair. "P'haps *you're* the murderer."

"I am a witness to murder," Philomena told him. "I know …' Her throat locked up. Could she really accuse her own grandmother of murder, even if it was the truth? She was a cruel old woman but Philomena had loved her.

Cyril raked pomade through Philomena's hair while Boss studied the conflicting emotions disturbing her face.

She drew a breath. "I know who killed Charles."

CHAPTER 36

"We all know who killed him," Boss remarked with a satirical gleam in his eyes. "Sure, didn't The Herald tell us?"

"Mordecai didn't do it!"

Whisking her neck and shoulders with a soft brush, Amos asked, "Who, then?"

Cyril suggested, "Philomena Paulson?"

"Even she couldn't stick him!" Amos snorted. They fell against each other, laughing.

If Philomena was deaf, she'd think pain distorted their features, for humor scratched lines in their hard faces and pulled their lips back from their teeth. Unfortunately, she wasn't deaf. The ever-increasingly ridiculous and salacious reasons they suggested for Miss Paulson finding Mr. St. Claire insupportable as a lover made her flush with mortification and rage.

"Now, lads, no cause for that!" Boss chided at the same time Philomena, provoked beyond endurance, shouted, "*I am Philomena Paulson!*"

"Sure, I'm the Queen of England," Boss said.

"Oh, Your Majesty!" Amos squealed.

"Your Royal Highness!" Cyril shrilled.

They curtsied clumsily, trying to kiss Boss's hands.

He slapped them away. "Get up, you loonies."

Amos held a hand to his heaving chest. Cyril rubbed his moist eyes.

"I'll thank you to watch your language," Philomena said icily.

They regarded the shorn head and grubby, ill-fitting men's clothes so at odds with her feminine outrage.

"A plummy accent don't make you a lady," Boss said.

"My birth does."

"That wooden leg says different," Amos said.

"It don't happen to them," Cyril said.

"It does," Philomena told them. "And it did." Her eyes returned to Boss as she related the secrecy of her upbringing and the truth of Charles' murder. The barbers kept silent, letting their leader express the incredulity writ large across their faces.

"You're telling me," Boss interrupted, "an old lady struck a man dead with one blow?"

"She's not a sweet old lady. She's a battleax."

"He's a fine catch for a girl, is St. Claire. Why'd she kill him?"

"He saw my wooden leg. He wasn't supposed to know about that until—" Her eyes fell. She blushed. "Until our wedding night. Then it would be too late, you see."

"Couldn't he divorce you then?"

"Oh goodness, no!" She laughed at the very idea. Her eyes fell again. She said quietly, "That's not how any of this works."

She could feel them looking at her. They might try to understand but they never could, and she might try to explain it but she couldn't.

Presently, Boss said, "He sees your wooden leg before the wedding, and if he's a mind to tell—"

"It should be our ruin," Philomena whispered. She was born damaged. She was living proof that her people were inferior. She was to have pulled them up to higher ground by marrying well, but she'd failed. The weight of shame threatened to pull her through the floor.

Amos grinned. "Well, that's something, innit?"

"Lovely stuff," Cyril agreed.

They laughed through their noses.

Amos's shoulders shook. "Ah, God ..."

"Jesus," Cyril muttered.

Philomena cried, "You think it's funny?"

They collapsed in gales of laughter.

Anger flamed through her. *They* could laugh. If either of them was missing a leg, no one should think twice about it. No one expected them to be perfect so everyone beneath them knew their place.

Suddenly, inspiration struck.

She had known it would. She had hoped it would. She had needed a plan. Now she had one.

Philomena raised her voice. "Do you think I told you my darkest secret for your benefit?"

Boss turned, still laughing. "And whose benefit must I consider but my own?"

"Mordecai Michaelson's." The cellar's secret inventory flashed through her mind. Guns. A printing press. Locked cabinets. Rags – *flammable* rags. "You're a sight more than a barber."

His grin faded.

The barbers moaned in residual hilarity as they held their sides and tried to stand.

Philomena rolled her eyes at them. "You've more than these two."

His gaze narrowed.

"You've got people working everywhere. Soldiers, spies—"

"Employees."

"I dare say they are, in a way." Philomena said, "They'd find Mordecai by four o'clock if you set them to it."

Cyril and Amos came out of their laughing fit as the tension between their boss and their captive dawned on them.

"S'pose they find him," Boss said. "Then, what?"

"Bring him to me."

Cyril snorted, "Bring him back to be caught?"

"P'raps he'll kiss you farewell as they carry him off," Amos scoffed.

"You needn't reunite us in a public place," she retorted. "We'll slip away in secret."

The barbers burst out laughing.

Even Boss had to smile. "And what would I have to show for it?" He sank to his knees beside her chair and trapped her with his cool gray eyes. "*You* are what I'm trading, lass."

A pang struck her stomach. Philomena's idea carried endless repercussions and relentless exposure. She knew a moment's wild temptation to ask, *Could you not trade, instead, on knowing Grandmother is a murderer?* But the courts would never take his word against a lady's. Philomena mustered courage. "I've something far better to trade."

"You had a secret." Boss tapped her wooden leg. "Now I have it. Once your papa knows I have it, he'll pay any price."

"To keep you quiet?" Philomena challenged. "Isn't that the problem? You don't want to tell him about my leg."

"Don't I?"

"You want me to tell the world."

CHAPTER 37

MORDECAI

Sunlight danced on green wavelets with a brilliance that made Mordecai squint. He stepped into the shade cast by the ship docked before him.

What he'd taken for a card attached to the lanyard Mary had hung around his neck was, in fact, passage on any East India merchant ship owned by the Star Company.

The ticket gave no departure time or date. It did not specify identity of the ticket holder. Exploring the packet further, Mordecai discovered with sadness those additional tickets bought for Josiah's kin. The happy family had once anticipated his triumphant concert tour through the farthest reaches of the Queen's empire. But with a slip of the lanyard around Mordecai's neck, Mary had bade farewell to their future.

Mordecai lifted eyes filmed by sudden tears.

Midnight Star looked a beauty of a ship. Her furled masts rose like church spires in the gray sunlight. Sailors loaded the last of her commercial cargo up her ramps. On an East Indiaman, Mordecai knew he'd escape notice. Merchant Marines intent on their commercial duties took scant interest in passengers, and the thrifty passengers cared more for reaching their destinations than for socializing with strangers.

Though a ticket might be held by anyone, the ticket holder need submit proof of identity upon boarding any ship leaving port. Mordecai examined the plague doctor's identification. That its thumbnail-sized daguerreotype was too low in quality to bear more than passing resemblance to the doctor proved lucky, indeed. Mordecai could claim the grainy and blurry image as his own until he reached a safe harbor.

Mordecai hardly dared to relax, but at present there seemed no immediate threat to his safety. Though fairly crowded, the populace in this vicinity went about their business, with no more interest in Mordecai save the usual recoil from his ugliness. To be sure, his misadventures had roughened his appearance still further but this did not excite suspicion from the few constables present. If anything, they looked bored with their routine posts. Where was the manhunt that had driven him through the city?

His skin itched with dried sweat and grime. His face felt constricted beneath a crust of blood. Whatever soft foodstuff had slid down his neck had turned sticky. His coat seemed tighter across his chest and pain throbbed from his shoulder down his arm. His stomach growled. He could do with a bath and a meal.

Mordecai consulted the posted timetables for the day's arrivals and departures. He saw *Midnight Star* was not scheduled to admit passengers for a while yet.

At a public bathhouse, Mordecai braced for someone to raise the alarm upon sight of him and a new manhunt to commence. Instead, the bath porter sold him soap, towel, and a razor.

A painful stiffness in his right side made undressing a clumsy endeavor. Mordecai pressed gingerly on the swollen pectoral muscle and shoulder. Catching a clothesline as he hurtled to earth had saved him but it had done so at a price. Bending his right arm made him wince.

Favoring the injury, Mordecai bathed. Soon, he emerged from the bathhouse clean and fresh – in dirty clothes and still in pain, to be sure, but feeling a new man entirely.

Mordecai wondered if he might chance things a bit further by getting a bite to eat. A church bell tolled the hour of three o'clock. He could put down a chop and a glass of port and still board the East Indian according to schedule.

Mordecai seated himself at a sidewalk table, for he knew he should feel trapped if he dined inside the public house, itself. He thought entirely reasonable the uneasy undercurrent running beneath his newfound sense of wellbeing. Though not under threat in the moment, last night's mob had shown him how quickly events could turn.

Indeed, he thought the streets uncommonly busy at this hour. It was not quitting time for everyday working men and women. Still, there seemed to be plenty of them rushing by.

"People seem much preoccupied," he remarked as the bar maid set his meal before him.

"God, aye," she said, "they're after that murderer."

Mordecai kept a neutral countenance. "Is it that fugitive, the one who killed the gentleman?"

Her averted eyes grew wide. "The very one, sir. Horrible ugly, he is! Oh—" her gaze flicked in his direction before flying away again. Though she found him ugly, he saw she did not like to offend him with any reference to ugliness. "Beg pardon, sir," she said.

"Quite all right," Mordecai reassured her. "I assume they make haste for the subterranean, but may I also assume they've a destination in mind? It's very curious."

"Word is they sighted him in Holborn."

He affected mild interest. "Holborn?"

"Oh yes, sir!" Though she looked into the pub's doorway in pained recognition she'd be missed by patrons inside, she could not resist lingering to report, "He tried to fence them diamonds he stole from the gentleman's fiancée."

Mordecai stared at the mutton chop on his plate as he reasoned his way through this report. He hadn't stolen diamonds. He'd bade Philomena hide them in the parcel containing his newly tailored clothes. He'd put Philomena and the parcel in a hansom and sent her home. "Curious, indeed," he mused aloud.

"Well, sir, it was the jeweler, himself, raised the alarm."

Philomena has the diamonds. Except, perhaps a jeweler had them now.

"It's all in The Herald Extra," the barmaid remarked with the empty tray at her hip. "I wonder they don't read it for themselves, and be done with it." She sighed. "But some folks are all for experience. Them out there ..." she waved a finger at the pedestrians rushing for the nearest subterranean, "must hope to see the mad pianist dragged into the gaol." She hesitated before going in. "Anything else at the moment, sir?"

Mordecai shook his head. His troubled gaze wandered as he considered the barmaid's account.

At the nearest table, a thin sheet of newsprint fluttered in the breeze, its corner trapped beneath a tea cup. Mordecai retrieved it and saw that it was The Herald's Extra, a slim midday edition printed whenever news broke on events obsessing the public. This missive felt damp from recent printing, its ink smearing at the touch.

FIERY STANDOFF

Mordecai probed the inflammatory language for bare facts and learned this: Independent of police, an agent of the Paulsons had distributed to jewelers and pawn shops a detailed description of Philomina's betrothal diamonds. The Extra gave no description of the man who'd tried to sell them in Holborn; no mention of the normal features, so at odds with Mordecai's abnormal features, that should have exonerated him on the spot. Apparently, mere possession of such distinctive jewels identified the seller as the maestro-turned-murderer. The pawn broker had sent for the police while keeping the man locked up in his shop. The "pianist" had blasted his way out with the broker's own fireworks.

Mordecai chewed the tough chop in contemplation. Had this man with the diamonds accosted Philomena? *I saw her safely into a hansom!* She must have arrived without incident, for The Herald Extra reported Philomena was at home. Had she forgotten the parcel, left it behind in the cab? *Yes, that must be it.* Her wits had been scattered by events, and she'd left the parcel. Perhaps the hansom cab driver had taken it. *Poor sod, he may hang for the impulse, mistaken for me!*

Mordecai was about to wash the chop down with a swallow of porter when a thought struck him. *The diamonds are insured.* Paulson would file a claim, rather than attempt recovering the gems and further highlight his daughter's involvement in the dreadful scandal of murder. *To be sure,* Mordecai amended, *he might attempt recovery, if the diamonds were a family heirloom.* But the Paulsons were not a sentimental clan.

But she's home, The Herald says so! Mordecai clung to that reported fact.

Except …

It had long been his opinion that The Herald's claims to veracity hardly stood beyond reproach. For example, it reported that he'd murdered Charlie St. Claire, though it had no corroborating evidence to support the Paulsons' account of it.

The Herald reported Philomena was home. Was she?

Mordecai tried a reconstruction. *Philomena gets out of the coach.*

Why? Where?

Never mind that. She gets out. A man steals the parcel. She boards the coach again? That made no sense.

His mind traveled a different route. *Philomena departs the coach. A man steals the parcel.*

A man steals the parcel.

And she does not make it home.

His gut clenched of its own accord. He pressed a fist to his mouth as he forced shut the multiple doors in his brain that opened to show the multiple ways Philomena could be harmed. If he could get his hands around that jewel thief's neck, then Mordecai knew he should truly be guilty of murder.

With effort, he composed himself. He wondered why, if Philomena were from home, the Extra should report otherwise. *The Paulsons' agent must be tracking the diamonds as a means of finding her without drawing undue publicity. Well, they should know by now that Philomena and the diamonds have parted company.*

Mordecai tossed back the port. Its flavor rose to burn his nostrils. As he took a moment to recover, he finished the Extra article.

> "He played the piano in my shop," Mr. Shelton related, "a singular composition, one he owned was of his devising. And sir, he played with virtuosity. It was then I knew I had the mad and murderous pianist in my very presence!"

Mordecai's scalp prickled icily.

Leaving enough money to pay for his repast and the bar maid's service, he hastened to the subterranean. Church bells tolled the hour, alerting him that *Midnight Star* would soon begin admitting passengers. He cared nothing for that, only that he board the next omnibus for Holborn.

Philomena, what have you done?

CHAPTER 38

A festive atmosphere filled the omnibus car as people wagered on whether the coppers had caught the mad pianist and what punishment awaited him once he'd been convicted. With every word, they insulted Mordecai Michaelson, but Mordecai – somehow passing unnoticed among them – didn't care what they said.

As the omnibus rushed into a black tunnel, Mordecai stared through his reflection in the window. His thoughts revolved around Philomena.

He feared her delicacy of manners. Clearly, she was not delicate of spirit. She had donned his clothing and passed herself off as a man sufficient to fool those she encountered. But once police caught her, Philomena's shyness and a lifetime of maidenly protocol would bind her to continued subterfuge. Her sheltered upbringing could have given her no understanding of prison routines, no preparation for the moment they stripped the new inmate and discovered her true gender.

That Mordecai had earned respectability through his musical talent in no way blinded him to how the world treated those outside respectability. Life for such unfortunates held no security or safety. Philomena's adventure was no girlish lark. In the eyes of society at every level, she had abandoned herself.

The rough men employed in prison work would have no

hesitation in taking every liberty with Philomena they wished, in accord with the common belief that a woman's conduct sets the standard by which others treat her. Philomena's brutal admission to prison presented not a finite event but an introduction to lifelong degradation. The tunnel's darkness was nothing to the darkness of his fears for her.

I shall confess. There can be no doubt to identity; my singularities confirm it.

It stood to reason they'd take Philomena to the nearest jail. If captured in Holborn, there would she be imprisoned. *I must intercept them before they take her inside. Once jailed, she is lost.*

The Paulsons would shun her. Mordecai had no money to give her. *But she has such beautiful hair.* He imagined she must have tucked it very snugly inside a hat to complete her disguise. If she sold her hair to a wigmaker, she'd have a little money to carry her a little while. Perhaps, Mr. Bloom could be prevailed upon to give her work, however humble, for Mordecai's sake.

Without such charity, a fresh young female fell prey to the false motherliness of an enterprising procuress. Houses run by such women aged girls to hags within a few years. Once past her prime, a girl landed in the streets. By day, she slept in the streets. By night, she plied her only trade. She put her earnings toward a dram of rotgut spirits or a night's lodging. She could afford one or the other, never both at once. All too often, such women threw themselves into the Thames, finding eternal peace in the river's embrace. Mordecai shuddered.

No, it must not come to that. I shall see it does not.

First, he must confirm The Herald Extra's report that police had apprehended Philomena. If the newspaper's report proved false, Mordecai could occupy those shackles before they had a chance to close around her wrists. As long as The Herald promoted the Paulsons' myth that

Philomena remained with them, she might have a chance to run home with no one outside ever learning she had left.

Mordecai disembarked at the Ludgate Hill station with his fellow passengers, whose frivolity startled those waiting on the platform. Businessmen, secretaries, and errand girls soon reverted to type, boarding at a brisk pace, intent on their purpose.

The new arrivals rushed for the stairs, waving the handbill bearing Mordecai's likeness. He wondered they did not see its striking resemblance to the twisted man ascending the steps alongside them. Did excitement blind them? Would they only recognize him in the place they imagined he already occupied – chained, between guards, at the prison gates?

Passing a mirrored advertisement for a popular brand of gin, he caught a fleeting glimpse of a man of his height who kept pace with him. A second later Mordecai realized this man was himself. He turned back. To anyone else, he appeared to be reading the tagline praising the gin's quality. But Mordecai gazed at himself in the advertisement's mirrored surface.

Amazing, the alterations wrought by the last twenty-four hours! He no longer resembled the maestro pictured in the handbill. Misadventure had cost him his false monocle and moustache. His heavy makeup had worn away. Without these elements of disguise, Mordecai looked closer to his true age. Added to that change, the glass reflected a general strength in his features he'd never seen before. He could not apprehend the source of this impression without careful study of his features. He'd no time for that.

Philomena did not look like the wanted man either, yet her possession of Paulson diamonds and her singular talent as pianist and composer promoted false assumption. Mordecai must take back his identity. Upon this, Philomena's life depended.

Mordecai dismissed his reflection to resume his climb,

and in this moment's transition, his peripheral vision recorded someone several steps below. Mordecai could not account for the frisson of alarm that ran through his frame upon sight of this man who was but one stranger among many. Nothing distinguished him, unless one counted his garish plaid waistcoat made visible by his unbuttoned jacket. Yet ...

Mordecai sought him out but did not find him again.

He cannot disappear. Once on the stairs, there you remain until you reach the top.

But it seemed the man had melted into the multitude ascending the stair. Mordecai frowned, shrugged inwardly. The disappearing stranger was of no consequence.

At the subterranean's street level, late afternoon sun glared through the glass ceiling. Mordecai felt its heat as a shrinking of his scalp – or perhaps the sensation owed to his feeling that someone followed him. He looked over his shoulder for the man he'd seen on the stairs.

There.

The nondescript wearer of the garish plaid waistcoat was purchasing an issue of The Herald Extra from a newsboy. Behind him stood a man who reached his arm forward, over the plaid-waistcoated man's shoulder, to push a coin before the newsboy's face. This posture pulled back the open lapels of his jacket, revealing a scarlet waistcoat with white dots. Mordecai saw nothing overtly threatening in this commonplace activity. Feeling suspicious nonetheless, he hastened to a revolving door.

As the door swept him into its rotation, Mordecai turned his head to look through its glass into the subterranean gallery. The men had gotten their copies of The Herald Extra and moved on. In the scant time afforded him by the revolving door, Mordecai didn't see them anywhere else. Resolved to put distractions behind him, Mordecai stepped out into the vast, teeming cityscape of Ludgate Hill – a place comprised of innumerable and simultaneous distractions.

Dray horses' shod hooves clip-clopped as the wooden wheels of the carts they pulled rattled on cobblestone. Trolleys rolled by with a ringing of bells. Storefronts glinted and skyscrapers towered above, joined by skywalk bridges. An aeroplane flew noisily overhead, trailing a pennant advertising a miracle hair tonic. Immediately before him, tethered horses drank from a trough and business people tossed on-the-go dinner wrappings and The Herald Extra into an overflowing iron-girded wastebin.

Mordecai took a deep breath of horse-scented air and let it out in a heavy sigh. He did not expect to look upon this sight again. Strange, that it should hold his fancy now. Imminent loss of his freedom to stop here at will made him sentimental for the place. Then the thought of Philomena gripped in jailors' hands swept all concern for himself aside. With a lifelong familiarity for the streets of this district, he set out toward the Holborn jail.

No one respected the automated Stop-Go signs. Traffic of all kinds flowed around each other, or stalled and honked horns and shouted insults while others tried their best to circumnavigate the conflict. Mordecai darted around lorries and dray carts to the best of his ability.

Reaching the other side of the street alive and unhurt demanded panoramic awareness. Half a block distant, a rangy fellow appeared in Mordecai's peripheral vision. It was the very man who'd waited impatiently for his chance to buy The Herald Extra. Mordecai recognized him by the white pindot pattern of his scarlet silk waistcoat. Now he ran an obstacle course in parallel to Mordecai, his long legs reaching for the safety of the sidewalk. Then a swerving lorry blocked view of him. Nothing in the pedestrian's errand should cause alarm. Why did the fine hairs lift on Mordecai's arms?

He scanned the routine chaos of the Ludgate Hill

thoroughfare, on alert for the other man who'd purchased the Extra, he whose tartan plaid waistcoat in clashing colors gave injury to the casual gaze.

Garish plaid. Pindot white on scarlet. What did a man's waistcoat matter? It did not, but for a small talisman pinned just above the top button of each waistcoat, a speck too inconspicuous to warrant notice that created commonality between seeming strangers.

Mordecai should not have discerned the tiny article were it not for the sharpened awareness characteristic of his fugitive status. In the split second it had registered, his mind's eye had likened the talisman's shape to that of a small black bird.

Mordecai altered his planned route, cresting a hill and taking a sharp right behind a bookseller's outdoor shelves. He grabbed a volume, opened and lifted it to obscure his face. Lingering in apparent assessment of the book's worthiness for purchase, he peered beyond its edges for the men in fancy waistcoats. Mordecai replaced the book to its shelf and resumed his trek, going on instinct as his eyes watched for the men. When he found himself traversing narrow streets that dog-legged and angled strangely, he realized he'd reached Holborn.

Choosing an alley, he made his way between waste bins and beneath metal fire escapes. He ran yet another phalanx of vehicles at a crossroad before darting into another alley. His nose wrinkled at the strong smell of gunpowder. A moment later, his throat convulsed on a dry cough. A haze of smoke still lingered faintly.

Mordecai walked the alley in a state of wonder at the waterlogged destruction of a recent fire. His feet trod over damp stones and crunched foil wrapping. He picked up colorful scraps of packaging. He read a torn label to ascertain the scraps had once enclosed fireworks. Could this be the place where Philomena had made her spectacular escape this morning? It must be.

With new understanding, he perused the alley and the backsides of business establishments. He read faded lettering on a metal door to his right: SHELTON BROS. PAWN.

A young man leaning against the pawnshop's wastebin and smoking a cigarette watched Mordecai narrowly. From the white apron tied around his neck, Mordecai took him for a stockboy on break.

Nodding to the youth as he strolled on, Mordecai tuned his ears for the sound of footsteps behind him. Hearing none, he forced himself to relax.

His nerves had deceived his intellect. Though recent events had contrived to keep Mordecai on guard, he counseled himself to remain calm so long as circumstance warranted calm. Otherwise, he'd lose ability to react effectively when a true threat presented itself.

Mordecai cast a parting glance into the alley Philomena had set alight with the holiday spectacle of fireworks. The shopboy had gone, his break evidently over.

Mordecai set out toward his original destination.

At the corner of Delancey and Rubicon, a young man in a green and orange striped waistcoat flicked a cigarette to the gutter and set out in Mordecai's direction.

Mordecai told himself to reserve judgment – if not of his haberdashery, at least of his purpose. Not every man showing questionable taste had questionable intent. After weaving through traffic over the span of several city blocks without seeing the man in the striped waistcoat again, Mordecai dismissed his initial impression. He'd enough concerns without concocting new ones.

CHAPTER 39

At last the central tower for which the Holborn jail was famed came into view. A fortress surrounded the tower, fronted by a large stone courtyard, with the whole of this establishment barricaded behind a high iron fence. A large crowd filled the square facing the fenced jail. Mordecai had just stepped onto the square when someone shoved an image of Philomena into his face.

"Tuppence, going cheap!" The man flipped the card on its stick to show Charlie St. Claire's likeness on the other side. "The doomed lovers—"

A woman grabbed the card.

The busker snatched her coin, pulling another card from the tray suspended from his neck and shouting, "Tuppence, cheap!"

Mordecai pushed past people waving souvenir cards and WANTED handbills high over their heads. Images of Philomena, Charlie, and Mordecai flipped and swayed energetically as people jumped up and down, yelling for justice.

"Show 'im!"

"Show the murderer!"

Perhaps people expected the warden to produce the criminal for their approval. Mordecai thought he might do just that. The Crown liked that. See here, citizens: we always get our man.

Within the vocal chaos surrounding him rose a unified chant, "BRING! HIM! OUT!"

Mordecai closed his eyes and fought dizziness. While he struggled with his emotions, his feet shuffled over the littered pavement as the crowd's collective movement carried him along. The ringing in his ears could not block out the bloodthirsty words:

"BRING! HIM! OUT!"

He'd got close enough to the tall iron fence to catch glimpses of the courtyard behind it. Beyond the courtyard rose the institution, itself. Rows of similar barred windows and seemingly miles of cut stone in the jail's façade left no distinguishing milestone with which Mordecai could gauge his position. He began to fight his way to the iron fence.

His name, screamed by unified voices, ceased to be his name and became a battle cry.

"Michaelson! Mordecai Michaelson! BRING! HIM! OUT!"

At last, his fingers closed on the fence. Slammed into the bars and lifted off his feet by the force of pressing bodies, Mordecai strained for a view of prison gates. He must reach the guards stationed there. It was only then, and only to the guards, that he could make himself known.

"Hang him now!" the crowd shouted.

"Cut off his murderin' hands!"

"Let us have him! By God, we'll see it done!"

If he announced too soon, they would tear him limb from limb.

That his life had come to this grieved him in the moment, but he felt no regret for the moments in Philomena's company that had led him to this end. His inner ear replayed a nocturne composed from the depths of her genius. Her whispered declaration of love carried more resonance than the clamor presently around him. Mordecai deliberately released all the irrational desires of his heart. That he should ever hold her again, inhale her scent, and share a duet or a smile; these hopes he exchanged for the singular hope to win for her the life she'd unwittingly thrown away.

The guards' tall, black-furred helmets showed above the heads of the people mobbing the gates. Mordecai caught glimpses of their red coats between the shifting figures that stood in his way. With effort, he brought himself within reach of the guard nearest him.

The official gave no reaction to the spittle flying at his face when they shouted, "BRING! HIM! OUT!" He stood ramrod straight, hand on the rifle at his side.

Mordecai stretched his arm, fingers straining to touch the guard's sleeve. "I am Mordecai Michaelson!"

But his own name rose in shouts all around him as the crowd called for sight of the prisoner. It roared like thunder from a hundred throats, "Mordecai! Michaelson!"

Mordecai tried to scream above them, "I am Mordecai Michaelson!"

The crowd's chant drowned his voice, "BRING! HIM! OUT!"

Mordecai tugged on the sleeve so insistently that finally the guard broke character and turned his way, displeasure on the countenance shadowed by the enormous black fur hat. Mordecai shouted to his face, "I am Mordecai Michaelson!"

The crowd's sway toward the fence broke his hold on the guard's sleeve.

A striped waistcoat of orange and green filled Mordecai's view.

"You don't understand!" Mordecai screamed over the man's shoulder to the expressionless guards. "I'm turning myself in!" He was knocked sideways. A black bird talisman flew across his vision. "I'm Mordecai —"

"We know, mate," said a calm male voice.

Said another, "Best kept to ourselves, though, eh?"

"For now." A tartan plaid waistcoat hitched in a laugh.

Mordecai drove his shoulder into the pindot swathed chest.

A shadow swooped over his face a second before the blow to his ear knocked him out.

CHAPTER 40

When the world returned to Mordecai, it swayed rhythmically. Pain pounded at his temple. He smelled leather and Bay Rum and tobacco. Mordecai opened bleary eyes to perceive a row of knees in tight breeches. His gaze lifted to a row of patterned waistcoats. Left to right: tartan, pindot, stripes. At each lapel: black bird, black bird, black bird.

One of the brotherhood snatched Mordecai by the hair, forcing his head sideways. This served as introduction to the man in shirtsleeves who shared Mordecai's seat in the moving coach. The first thing Mordecai noted was yet another little black bird near the lapel of a waistcoat. The talisman formed a void in a kaleidoscopic clash of colors that coalesced into paisley formation. The white shirt inside the paisley waistcoat seemed mild, but an old-fashioned stock tie knotted flamboyantly beneath its high collar harkened to past eras. Mordecai's broader perusal identified the wearer of this eccentric costume as the stockboy he'd passed outside the rear door of SHELTON BROS. PAWN.

The youth had bunched his apron behind his blonde head. He leaned back against the hansom door with his arms crossed, a posture that caused one side of his waistcoat to bulge jaggedly. Blue eyes gleamed beneath long blonde lashes. A hand-rolled cigarette dangled from a babyish mouth. The mouth suddenly twisted in disgust.

"That ain't him."

"He said he was!" the young man wearing scarlet pindot silk protested. "We heard him plain as anything screamin' at the guards, 'I'm Mordecai Michaelson!'"

The stockboy snatched the fag from his mouth to snarl, "I seen Mordecai Michaelson and this ain't him!"

His compatriots sat in their miserable row of loud-patterned waistcoats.

The stockboy swept them with a scathing look, enunciating, "I seen him! Ol' man Shelton had him like a bird in a cage but he pulled a legger out the fire escape. I seen him and I told you *exactly* what he *looks* like …" Sing-song diction emphasized his contempt.

The wearer of green and orange stripes yelled, "You said he was a gimp, and we followed him all over the Hill and Holborn to make sure!"

Tartan plaid backed him up. "You said, 'don't pay no attention to the handbill.' You said, 'it don't look nothin' like him.'"

"And he's a right messed up ol' fella, ain't he?" The pindot dandy gestured to Mordecai while the stockboy waved his head about with a roll of his eyes and a drag on his fag. "Didn't you tell us, look at the walk?"

"Did *you* get a look at his walk, Callum?" the striped gentleman pressed, and noting Callum's hesitation, drove it home, "Or did you read The Herald and tell us from that? Maybe you don't know so very much about him, neither—" He finished on a scream as Callum's cigarette burned into his cheek.

Stripes swung at Callum with a knotted sock of coins that had most likely been the instrument used to render Mordecai insensible – while evading Callum's jabs with the lit cigarette. Trying their best to maim each other as Pindot and Tartan fought to restrain them caused the hansom to pitch crazily. Holborn appeared to bounce outside the rear window. Mordecai noted from this view that the cab had not traveled so very far from the jail, caught in heavy traffic as it was.

"Jesus, Callum, you bugger." Stripes held his burnt face. Callum's fag jumped in his angry baby mouth, "Want another go?"

With a warning shove from Pindot and Tartan, Stripes shook his head.

This satisfied Callum, who grabbed his stockboy apron, bunching it behind his head and leaning back against the door.

Mordecai glanced from the aggrieved dandies to their ringleader. "I am Mordecai Michaelson."

Callum considered him beneath doll-length lashes.

"You ought take me back to Holborn jail this instant."

"Yer a loony wants to hang," Callum said around his cigarette. "I'll hang you. I'm mad enough to do it for laughs. But first, I want. The. Real. Bloke!" He banged his head on the last three words, causing a flurry of concerned pleadings from the waistcoats.

"Ah! Don't hurt yer head, Callum. Yer ma never got over droppin' ya—"

"Shut up." Callum sat up straight to catch Mordecai's eye. "Listen, you loony."

He'd every physical advantage, and all the confidence of every bully Mordecai had once feared and now despised.

"You gimps hang together?"

"It's a bond unknown to those who are whole."

"Any chance you could lead me to him?"

None in Hell. Mordecai said, "I'd need some clue to start. Are you sure he remains at large?"

"Shelton ain't got his reward." As if that settled it, Callum took a long drag.

Mordecai tried not to get his hopes up. "The Herald Extra implied the police—"

"Bollocks."

Tartan elaborated on Callum's smoke-plumed response,

"The Herald rushed to press in advance of confirmation."

Could the sheltered girl have proven canny enough to evade police?

Yes.

Mordecai saw this now. Others appraising her as weak – that was always their mistake. He counted himself among the deceived. Philomena had known when to advance on him and when to draw him forward by retreating. She'd known to seduce him with a piano composition, her exposed shoulder appearing incidental to the matter.

You are a sly one, he thought with pride.

She'd donned his clothes and sold her jewels, but how had Philomena known to come to Holborn on the errand? Mordecai remembered their first confidential conversation. She'd known the one spot in her country estate where they could not be overheard. Lifelong practice of eavesdropping on servants and family had given her a spymaster's skill. Last night in Piccadilly, Philomena should have had no trouble gleaning from a mob's chatter that Mordecai had boarded an omnibus for Holborn.

She followed me.

Callum's baby face went beet red. "I want Mordecai Michaelson!"

You shortsighted git. "You seek the reward for yourself?"

"Don't say nothin, ol' sod," Stripes advised Mordecai, still clutching his burnt face. "It's a bit of a sore point with—"

"I want the rest," Callum told Mordecai.

"The rest of what?"

"THE DIAMONDS!"

Tartan comforted, "Aye, to be sure, you got most of 'em, Callum,"

"I want all," Callum seethed.

In the chaos, Mordecai could well imagine Philomena had dropped or damaged and lost a few diamonds. With their cut as distinctive as a signature, the Paulsons' agent must have tracked them as a means of finding her. Mordecai had resources less than diamond sharp — the brains of these criminal dandies — with which to find her. "Someone gave your employer a drawing of the gems, I believe."

"Sure, he came 'round this morning," Callum related, "told the old man, 'if a beautiful girl comes in 'ere with diamonds to sell ... well, you don' say nothin' to the coppers but come straight to me. I get the girl, you get the diamonds.'"

"He visited all such shops in the district. Then all he has to do," Pindot suggested, "is bide his time at the Puggle and Poke waiting for news she turned up."

"It weren't no girl, but a bloke come in with diamonds," Callum said. "Ol' Shelton musta thought t'was our mad piano fella. He presses a button beneath the counter what rings this little bell in the back room."

"Callum legs it to the coppers —"

"I'm tellin' it!" Callum glared at Tartan. "Was you there? No! Coppers followed *me* back."

Mordecai struggled to suppress impatience. "Did you see the fugitive?"

"Shelton pointed to the fire escape. I seen a little kid. A kid! Mind you, there's some on the street I'd not turn my back to."

Mordecai doubted Philomena had ever seen a fire escape in her life.

"Just then—" Callum made explosive noises and threw his arms up. "Aw, t'was magical!"

Philomena had no expertise in handling incendiaries. What chance had she of escaping the encounter uninjured? "Did you see the fugitive move through the smoke?"

Callum gave no answer. His doll eyes gleamed in a faraway gaze, as if still enjoying the spectacle.

Mordecai raised his voice. "Did you see where he went?"

Ripped from reverie, Callum twisted his lips into a pout. Mordecai pictured her up there. Frightened. Hurt. Lost. Alone. Had anyone bothered finding her? He glared at this stupid boy. "Did you check the fire escape?"

Callum's gaze wandered.

"I knew it!" Mordecai shot across the seat and grabbed Callum's lapels, shouting into his shocked face, "You didn't even bother!"

Callum snatched the fag from his mouth. "Let go of my waistcoat—"

"Someone should have helped him!"

"*Helped him?*" Callum laughed. "I helped myself to a fortune in diamonds!"

"You bloody—" Mordecai twisted the lapels of Callum's waistcoat in a spasm of rage. "—waste of *breath!*" The sound of tearing fabric barely registered.

Callum's fist landed four knuckles deep in Mordecai's eye.

Mordecai's head flew back and fell forward. He grabbed the stockboy's neckwear, seeing Philomena past the dancing lights in his eye, imagining her terror in the noise and smoke. "You got your bloody diamonds—" Mordecai pulled the ends of the stock tie in opposite directions. "You enjoyed a fag by the bin—"

A curse strangled in Callum's throat.

"—While she lay hurt up there!"

"*She?*" Callum croaked. His face swelled and reddened. He jabbed the lit fag at Mordecai's face.

Mordecai rose out of range to crouch over him. Ignoring the burns Callum inflicted on his gloves, he wound the tie around his knuckles as he pulled it tighter.

"Mates!" Callum choked.

Mordecai felt the dandies pulling and shoving him, but he gave them no attention in his single-minded assault upon their leader. Philomena suffering, while this foolish fop stole diamonds, made him want to kill. Mordecai knew he'd hang anyway for Charlie St. Claire. He may as well hang to avenge Philomena on the boy who'd never bothered to climb a stair to look for her.

Fresh air ruffled through his hair as Callum fell away from him. Mordecai tumbled through the door opening behind Callum's back. Callum crashed to the street and Mordecai landed on him.

The thug pulled out from under him, clutching his throat and drawing hoarse breaths as he staggered through foot and horse drawn traffic.

Mordecai chased him, driven by thoughts of Philomena. "You're going to help me find her!"

"*Her?*" Callum's features roiled with defensive rage. Holding his waistcoat together at its torn seams, he fled Mordecai. "You're mad! — Mates!"

Mordecai had some peripheral awareness of the dandies in pursuit, but only he was close enough to see Callum collide with a stone wall.

"Have a care!" Mordecai yelled, reaching for him.

"Stay away from me!" Fury flashed in Callum's wild blue eyes. He scrambled up the wall as he fought to loosen Mordecai's fingers from his waistcoat, the struggle rending fabric still further. "Mind the silk!"

Mordecai kept hold, trying to pull the insensible youth to safety. "Come down off the wall!"

But Callum thrashed his limbs in all direction, mindful only of doing Mordecai injury and getting free of him. He fell backwards. Only Mordecai's hold on his waistcoat kept him from hurtling over the side. Callum looked down and saw the Thames flowing fifty feet below. "Mates!"

"Here, Callum," Stripes reassured him with an embrace, fingers gaining purchase in the paisley waistcoat.

Callum cursed pleadingly, his blue eyes wide with terror.

Mordecai felt in the way, now Callum's mate had caught him.

Stripes met Mordecai's eye while sliding an arm under Callum's legs. "Let go."

Stepping back, Mordecai released one side of Callum's waistcoat. He was about to release the other side when Stripes' sudden turn of Callum's body trapped Mordecai's fingers in the paisley silk.

"I said," Stripes snarled at him, "Let go!"

"I cannot!" Mordecai slid over the rampart, his fingers strangled in the tightening folds of Callum's waistcoat. He braced his own body against the wall in an effort to save himself going over the side as the falling man flailed for Stripes.

Cheap silk shredded in Mordecai's fingers. He fell to the street.

On the other side, a scream diminished with distance and disappeared in a splash.

Dazedly, Mordecai shoved a bulky scrap of torn paisley silk into an inner pocket of the plague doctor's coat.

"Oh my gawd, mate!" Stripes shouted over the bridge wall. "I tried to save you!" He lifted a torn portion of Callum's waistcoat to his face, sobbing loudly into it as his fingers searched its folds. Then he brought it swiftly down, head turning in a fury.

But Mordecai had retreated out of sight into the incident's reactive chaos – stalled coaches with doors thrown open and their passengers running toward the scene. Women leaning over the bridge wall screamed as men ran down the embankment.

Pindot and Tartan pummeled Stripes, who flung them off.

"Are you mad?" Pindot shrieked.

Mordecai didn't hear Stripes' rejoinder, but he did see a man wearing a floral waistcoat run past and heard his muttering growl, "You'll hang for this."

Sirens bleating in the distance grew louder by the second.

From a heightened vantage point, Mordecai heard Tartan's panicked, "We've got to get out of here!"

The floral waistcoat dandy shouted, "Oi, my coach!"

It careened around stalled vehicles, the startled horse leaping when Mordecai cracked the whip.

CHAPTER 41

The horse tossed its head and nosed between the cobblestone for errant weeds to eat. Mordecai studied the broken fire escape above him. Colorful bits of singed paper hung from the wrenched metal. The air resonated with the stench of sulfur. Brick walls bore scorch marks from Philomena's low-thrown fireworks. Dirty water pooled in every depression. The fire brigade had done its job. Beyond the alley, commerce had rallied to its normal pitch, as if spectacle had never interrupted it.

Where are you?

If he'd recaptured her, Mr. Shelton would have produced her to collect his ransom. Mordecai reasoned the laundry didn't have her, for he could ill imagine a group of immigrants daring to apprehend a British citizen.

He considered the back alley exit of the pawn broker's other neighbor. No sign identified the business within, but if memory served, Mordecai believed it to be O'Shaunessey's barber shop.

A peripheral awareness he wasn't alone crept in. His eyes roved the fire escapes. Above the laundry, a Chinese woman watched him between parted curtains.

Mordecai reboarded the coach and set off to scrutinize the rest of the alley for signs of Philomena's direction of escape. He saw none. Could she remain here even now, having somehow evaded discovery by police searching the buildings?

The barber shop stayed in his mind. The reputation of its owner did nothing to ease his mind regarding Philomena's safety.

Boss O'Shaunessey's Christian name had long vanished from collective memory in favor of the underworld honorific, while the national origin of his surname provoked scrutiny of his political dealings. Authorities suspected his legitimate business masked a network with connections running from the criminal to the seditious.

He could see O'Shaunessey's barbers pulling Philomena from the smoky ruin of the fire escape. They'd enjoy hiding a fugitive while the Crown searched high and low. Whether mistaken for Mordecai or revealed to be an heiress, Philomena embodied a commodity in high demand. Anyone in possession of her had bargaining power, indeed.

Mordecai slowed in front of O' SHAUNESSEY, BARBER. He knew the district treated the shop almost as a social club whose doors never closed. Yet at this early hour, a CLOSED sign hung in its window with the curtains drawn.

Mordecai ground his teeth, considering his options. He could break in and fight the barbers to free Philomena but in such a conflict, he held the physical disadvantage. The alternative, reporting a possible abduction to police, should only expose Philomena's activities and hasten her ruin. No, he could not extricate her without doing her injury, but Mordecai thought of someone who could: the Paulsons' henchman.

The Paulsons wanted Philomena back without incurring scandal. The henchman hoped the diamonds would lead him to her. Mordecai had the diamonds. Bundled in the torn scrap of Callum's silk waistcoat, they filled the inside pocket of the plague doctor's coat. With every moment he grew more certain of Philomena's whereabouts. He would use the Paulsons' man to rescue her.

Mordecai recalled Callum's story of the henchman alerting brokers to watch for the jewels. No doubt, he still waited in Holborn for word. *Bided his time at the Puggle and Poke,* Pindot had said.

Though its ownership remained a mystery, the pub's hospitality was famous. Holborn favored The Puggle at the end of a work day, merchants and laborers finding equal welcome in its dark and hop-scented environs. People with few prospects who had coin for a pint found themselves tolerated to make it last hours. The henchman might have done so, waiting for those diamonds to turn up and lead him to Philomena. With a grim smile, Mordecai patted the silk-wrapped bulk in his pocket and spared a moment for hope.

Then, he reined the hansom's horse toward the Puggle and Poke.

In time, he drew the hansom abreast of a plain brick building without windows, sparing a glance for the large wooden sign hung above the door.

A squash-faced dog of indeterminate breed glared at a boy jabbing it with a stick. This painting left no room, or need, for the pub's name. On the sidewalk stood a placard emblazoned with the words DUELING PIANOS.

Mordecai had no idea what the Paulsons' henchman looked like, but few pubs had many patrons at this late-afternoon hour, and he thought it should not prove difficult to discern a man with an air of purpose from a few day drinkers who had nowhere else to go.

To his surprise, Mordecai could hardly shoulder himself inside for the number of patrons.

Clerks appearing fresh from the office in their cheap but respectable suits downed shots of whiskey. Shop girls sipped cordials and laborers gripped pints of foaming lager. People conversed at a shout to be heard.

Above the din, he heard a woman ask, "What'dyou

fancy?" Turning, he realized the enquiry was for him.

A barmaid held a tray filled with various libations. "On the house!"

Mordecai chuckled. "Did Hell freeze over?" With everyone reaching for free drinks at once, Mordecai asked, "What is the occasion?" But the barmaid had turned without hearing him and in the next instant disappeared into the fray. Only her tray, held high and now empty, could be seen above the crowd.

People sang with tuneless abandon in support of two different popular songs banged out on two pianos at the same time. Mordecai winced as the singing grew louder, in a competition between songs. Combatants singing on either side of him threatened to burst his eardrums and drive him mad.

One camp screamed its way to victory. The winning pianist finished with a flourish, jumped atop his bench and waved his cap to the cheering crowd. Spotting Mordecai, Percy winked in greeting. What he said to the other pianist could not be heard above the din, but his fellow leapt atop his own bench and searched the throng. Spotting Mordecai, Jimmy bowed to his maestro.

The pianists fell in synchronized unison to their benches and plunged into another duel with two clashing music hall favorites that set the crowd roaring. Mordecai shook his head in equal parts pleasure and resignation of the peculiar niche in which his former students made their fortune.

Returning to mission, Mordecai turned his gaze from the wall where Jimmy and Percy played. Opposite the pianos' location, a bar ran the length of a wall until it met two swinging doors leading to a kitchen. Behind the bar, bottles glinted in mellow light while a bartender worked his magic before silver-flaked mirrors. Musical instruments of all type hung from the wall between the pianos' end of the room and the bar's end. The pub's street entrance continually opened behind Mordecai, bringing frosty air and more customers.

Again, he had to wonder at the unprecedented attendance at this time of day. Barmaids continued to dispense free drinks, and the revelry showed the effects of this largesse. Mordecai watched a photographer set up his camera equipment in front of the kitchen's double doors.

What occasioned this merriment, he couldn't fathom, but he mustn't let it distract him. Mordecai searched the crowd for any glimpse of a man who looked out of place. What qualities identified such a man? Mordecai supposed he would be the only fellow in the Puggle, besides himself, who was not drinking.

A hand on his shoulder broke Mordecai's concentration. He looked back to find Stripes had outpaced his blackbird brothers in catching up to him. The brotherhood's hansom tethered outside must have confirmed Mordecai's whereabouts.

"I'll take the coat, if you please." The hoodlum grinned. "I've a taste for the contents of its pockets."

Mordecai needed the diamonds to verify himself to the henchman. His elbow shot backwards.

Stripes doubled over with a pained exhalation.

Patrons closely surrounding the pair rolled with this motion, too distracted by free drinks to notice the combative nature of it.

Grimacing in pain, Stripes kept a grip on the plague doctor's coat. Rage flushed his pock-marked cheeks and glittered in his eyes. "I killed Callum for them diamonds," he muttered for Mordecai's ears alone. "I don't mind killin' again."

Mordecai's lips parted on a yell, but a knife point to his ribs told him to be silent.

Stripe's cuff and the folds of the plague doctor's coat hid the knife from view. Revelers in the crush could not distinguish ordinary jostling from a robbery in progress.

The killer's fingers flew down the front of the coat,

freeing buttons and halting another counterattack with a quick reposition of the knife. Unless he fancied losing his entrails, Mordecai had to surrender. He knew to those around him, the theft appeared as nothing more than a loan of his coat to a friend. Heavy with diamonds, it fell from his shoulders and his plan to rescue Philomena fell with it.

Catching the coat in the crook of his arm, Stripes cracked a thin smile. "Much obliged." Mordecai suspected he'd no intention of sharing the diamonds with his brotherhood. The criminal hastened out the Puggle's door, no doubt to retrieve the hansom for a swift getaway.

Mordecai fought despair, determined to continue his search of the henchman. He'd no material means by which to facilitate Philomena's liberation, but he still had his wits. He must use them.

To gain a better view of the pub, Mordecai stepped up onto a banquette seat already claimed by a group of friends.

"Sod off!" the nearest occupant protested.

Mordecai snagged a lager from a barmaid's passing tray and handed it to the man.

"Oh, cheers! Thanks a lot. Have a seat."

"I shall stand."

"As you please."

Drinks passed as Mordecai plucked them from the tray and handed them down amid a chorus of thanks.

His new friend said, "Ask her if she'll pass a menu …"

The barmaid answered, "Kitchen's closed."

The photographer kept his box camera and tripod positioned directly in front of the kitchen's double doors. On alert, the man held the camera's drape, ready to dive under it. He held the flash high. Mordecai held his gaze on him.

Whatever mystery accounted for the generosity of the house would be solved when those kitchen doors opened.

CHAPTER 42

PHILOMENA

Philomena could barely see Mordecai's identification through her tears. She'd been crying ever since Boss gave her Mordecai's wallet. Beside his name and profession, the card displayed a small photograph of Mordecai's face. It blurred in her vision.

Boss's men had found him dead in a deserted subterranean. They were bringing his body back to the barbershop, back to her. The police weren't to have him, of that she'd been assured.

"Put the wallet away, lass," Boss ordered gently. "We've business here."

Here was the kitchen of a public house. They sat across from each other at a small table, while Amos and Cyril stood near the door through which she and the barbers had entered from the alley.

"Find out who killed him," Philomena grated.

"Business first."

"Promise me!" Her eyes flashed. "For that, I'll tell them—" she indicated the pub beyond the kitchen's double doors "—anything you want."

"You need say nothing but the truth."

Her thumb gently caressed Mordecai's likeness.

Philomena marveled that only a few months ago, she hadn't known him at all. When he'd arrived to be her tutor, she'd actually thought the sum of Mordecai Michaelson amounted to no more than these two words printed upon the card: Pianist, Instructor. Philomena swallowed past a great lump of pain. She felt Boss's eyes on her.

"I'll find his murderer. You've my word."

A knock on the alley door prompted Cyril to open it. Outside, a sentry hunched against the bone-chilling gusts that reddened his lean face. Expressionless, he beckoned visitors inside.

Higgleston entered, but Philomena's grief flattened any fear he'd once inspired in her. Next, her father stepped inside. Philomena glared at him. Then, an unexpected third party entered.

The black-garbed woman whose veil hid her identity presented a surprise and a mystery to her host, two qualities never welcome at a business transaction. "The lady will keep her hands aloft that I may see them at all times," Boss intoned with displeasure.

She felt the widow's stare, as fixed as a raptor's gaze behind the black veil. *She knows me.* And though she'd donned the widow disguise to hide her identity while slumming through Holborn, the woman couldn't fool Philomena. *I'd know that ramrod posture, however garbed.*

Boss looked to Philomena for enlightenment.

"It's Grandmother," she told him in a poisonous undertone. "Mordecai's accuser."

Cyril searched Papa with an insolent thoroughness that made him scowl.

Higgleston took Amos' frisk in stride, taking it as an opportunity to assess their new environment.

The trio's arrival had shaken Philomena's apathy regarding her surroundings. She followed Higgleston's gaze and took note of the place.

Few mansions had electricity installed, but this pub

kitchen of white tile and stainless steel glowed beneath the cold light of bulbs screwed into uncovered fixtures. Only the light above the double sink did not appear to work. It was dark and loose in its socket, like a dead eye gazing down upon a skinny man who worked elbow deep in suds. A fat man spread sizzling oil across an empty griddle as flames danced beneath it. A woman wearing a bloody apron cleaved pork into chops at a merciless rate. None looked up from their tasks.

Opposite the alley door, double doors gave view of the Puggle and Poke's public room through their porthole windows. It was near these doors that Philomena sat with Boss, a new bottle of whiskey and a few clean shot glasses between them.

Philomena slipped Mordecai's wallet inside the greatcoat she'd taken from SHELTON BROS. PAWN. It swamped her. She tucked her chin into its collar, clenching her hands inside its sleeves. She drew her feet beneath its hem. This inward posture kept her from flying at her kinfolk in a fit of rage. Mordecai, dead. *It's their fault.*

Grandmother boxed Cyril's ear hard enough to make him wince. "Unhand me!"

"Mr. Higgleston, reassure the lady," Boss instructed.

Higgleston muttered inaudibly into her ear. She relented to the search, seething.

"The hat." Boss reminded his lads.

Feeling around under its brim, Amos slid a long hat pin free.

Grandmother grabbed the hat before he could dislodge the veil.

As the barbers piled weapons at his elbow, Boss grinned a wide welcome. "Mr. Paulson, approach. Do!"

His guest glared, without moving.

"We are honored, indeed! Are we not, lads?"

The barbers' lips twitched with stifled laughter.

Angry color flushed Papa's cheeks. Contempt glittered

in his eyes.

With a side glance, Higgleston read his employer's mood. He prodded Boss. "We are come as you directed for the person in question."

"You shall have him," Boss reassured easily, turning to Philomena with a complaisant air. "There he sits. Though near the doors, he shows no inclination to escape."

The lead barber spoke rightly on that score. Philomena felt keenly the activity beyond those double doors, the buzzing of conversation and clinking of glasses and most of all; the inexplicable presence of two pianists playing two different tunes, each beginning overlapping the other's ending to discordant effect. Beneath her leaden grief, curiosity stirred and she wondered why on earth they played in opposition instead of in concert.

Then her grief smoldered again into anger. In the barbershop, she had bargained with Boss as a means to reunite with Mordecai. Now that it could never be, her purpose turned to vengeance. Society would pay for the fallacy of perfection that cast Mordecai down. Grandmother would pay for accusing him. Her family would pay for putting the power of its influence into hunting him. But for the Paulsons, Mordecai should never have found himself in the subterranean facing a murderer. *It's their fault.*

"Look upon the object of our transaction, Mr. Paulson," Boss invited, amusement warming his tone. "You may tell me, is he quite all you expected?"

Theodore Paulson's narrowed eyes looked Philomena up and down without a shred of recognition.

Perhaps this could be expected, even if Higgleston had prepared him to face her short hair and men's clothes. And a storm of weeping had distorted her features. Still, was he not a parent?

Sneering at the waste of his time, Paulson turned to the alley door without another word.

The widow caught his arm.

Why did Grandmother condescend to accompany Papa? Perhaps, and rightly so, she did not trust him to know me.

Higgleston whispered in his ear.

Boss laughed. "The lackey apprehends what you do not. For shame, Mr. Paulson! Do not you recognize your own …" he paused to relish the term, " …*accomplice?*"

Paulson's eyes slashed his henchman.

Higgleston expressed his employer's ire. "Have a care with the phrasing. That's no accomplice of his."

"Complicit these nineteen years, Mr. Paulson!" Boss reached for the bottle sitting before the pile of weapons and used the hat pin to break its seal. "Now, that's an accomplice I'd treasure were I so lucky as you, sir. I surely would." He poured whiskey into a shot glass and held it forward. "Let us drink together, Mr. Paulson, and toast the discretion of intimates."

Paulson did not move to take it. His lip curled. "You play a farce."

"Do I?" Laughing eyes lit on Philomena. "Do I?"

She glared at Theodore Paulson. "T'is I, Papa."

He recoiled, blinking.

The secret of so many years, now revealed, hung in the air.

Paulson insisted, "Philomena remains at home."

"Oh dear, oh dear," Boss mourned playfully.

"Any boy may sound like a girl!" Paulson argued, "and say any words you put in his mouth."

"I see you need proof." Boss shook his head in mock regret. "And I thought sure you'd wish to avoid it." He encouraged Philomena with a soft glance and a jut of his chin.

She stood and, taking a few steps to give them an unobstructed view of her, she bent. Gathering fabric carefully, Philomena slowly revealed her false leg past the jointed ball of the knee.

"T'is fine workmanship, is it not?" Boss purred. "As delicately crafted as one could wish for one's – dare I suppose *only* ...? *Legitimate—*"

"Shut up!"

"—child?"

The whites of Paulson's eyes surrounded his pupils.

Boss's eyes nearly closed from the extent of his pleasure. "Come, come," he enticed, holding out the shot glass.

The noise in the public house had risen, the music gone rowdy.

Her father took a step, eyes on the shot glass.

Boss caused the whiskey to swirl silkily in its shallow depths.

Paulson grabbed and threw the whiskey back. His throat convulsed. His eyes reddened.

Boss took his empty glass with a gentle clutch of its base and set it on the table. "You can have no hesitation now."

Paulson barked, "What do you want?"

Boss named a sum.

Higgleston burst out frustratedly, "That's exactly what I had in the wallet you refused!"

"I'll accept, now I've achieved my desire—" His eyes roved Theodore Paulson's rigid form— "to have a fine gentleman consent to share a drink with me."

Higgleston removed the wallet from his coat's inner pocket.

Boss smiled his tip-tilted level smile. "Amos, take it."

Amos did so, while the dishwasher shelved the last dish and dried his hands thoroughly.

"Now. Cyril, show our guests out through the kitchen doors, if you please."

The Paulsons recoiled. Philomena could imagine their horror at the prospect of impending contact with the low grade populace currently making merry beyond the double doors. How irretrievably damning to their social position, were their brief sojourn at the Puggle and Poke discovered. Grandmother and Papa rooted in place, heads turning to their hired man.

"We'll leave as we came." Higgleston opened the alley door to find the outdoor sentry sighting him down the barrel of a rifle.

Higgleston slammed the door.

Boss laughed. "He'll not take a bullet for you, Mr. Paulson. How's that?" He ignored the widow gliding silently around the perimeter of the room. "Now we know where loyalty ends."

Paulson snarled at his henchman, "Do something!"

Higgleston made a dive for the weapons on the table. The dishwasher pulled the dead bulb free. Fake it was; attached by a long cord that seemed to grow out of the ceiling as it sailed through the air to catch around Higgleston's neck. When the dishwasher snapped the cord tight, the henchman's back arched. Choking while his employer watched in disbelief, Higgleston reached impotently for the purloined arsenal, fingers straining far short of the mark.

Boss contemplated Paulson's empty shot glass, moving it in lazy circles on the table's surface.

The cook stopped Grandmother with a raised spatula to her veiled face. Sizzling grease dripped from the instrument, burning holes in the linoleum floor.

Boss held the shot glass to his eye.

Papa hesitated, trapped by the butcher woman's strange fixed smile as she chopped bloodstained wood in relentless metronome.

Boss turned the shot glass so the whiskey's amber residue gleamed in the flickering light of the real electric bulbs. The moist application of Papa's lips on the rim of the glass had left it slightly cloudy. "Sure, there's only one way forward."

Papa gestured toward Philomena. "I'll not be seen in public with ..." He grimaced. "With *that* ..."

"You'll have some respect!" Boss flared.

"Oh, he cannot help himself," Philomena sighed.

"Higgleston," Boss jibed, "you stay with your new friend. We'll see the Paulsons out."

By linking arms, Philomena pulled her grandmother and father close. Boss and his lads stood close behind. Philomena marched her unwilling kinfolk through the swinging doors.

As soon as she entered the pub, a white flash blinded her. Philomena's ears resonated with the muffled explosion of the camera and the incoherent cheering of a crowd.

"Quiet, all! Quiet! Quiet!" Boss boomed.

The patrons fell silent. The pianists stopped playing.

Green squares danced in Philomena's blinking vision as the photographer threw aside the black drape with his free hand. The other still held the flash high, as he braced to go under the drape again. He was Boss's man. A tweed-suited gentleman scribbling in a notebook she took for a journalist sympathetic to Boss's concerns.

Grandmother and Papa pulled against Philomena's tight embrace. She guessed Cyril and Amos grabbed them, because their escape suddenly ended. They stood, arms still linked with Philomena's. She felt them quivering with outrage.

As green squares in her eyes diminished to dots, Philomena spotted two grand pianos, nose to nose. Then, she saw Percy! It pleased Philomena to know the theater was not Percy's only employer. At least at the Puggle and Poke, he need not double as an extra in a donkey costume.

"A most distinguished personage has stopped by the Puggle and Poke tonight." Boss proclaimed.

Scanning the crowd for their reaction, her gaze found one face that made all others vanish.

Shock paralyzed her heart. Then it lurched painfully to

frantic life, sending joy spiraling through her. She had his wallet in her coat – retrieved from his dead body, so she'd been told.
Yet, here he is!

CHAPTER 43

MORDECAI & PHILOMENA

From his stand on the banquette, Mordecai observed the boy who stood between Theodore Paulson and a woman whose steel-spined posture identified her to him as the dowager Mrs. Paulson. A man's overcoat swamped the boy's slim form. His short golden-brown hair, brushed sideways and set in place with pomade, appeared groomed for church. The ruddy swelling that always comes of a violent fit of weeping subsumed the boy's delicate features. Yet, joy shone through this disfiguration. Mordecai felt fixed in place by the boy's rapturous gaze.
Why does this child stare at me, so? Disbelief dissolved, leaving Mordecai dizzy as realization dawned. *It is Philomena!* Although someone or something had obviously upset her, she appeared otherwise unharmed. Relief swept through him. *But she is here. Why?*
Philomena turned to look up at Boss. Had he known Mordecai was alive? It appeared he hadn't, for he looked just as surprised as she was.
They were mistaken! Weak-kneed with relief and stunned by happiness, Philomena could barely catch her breath. She longed to clasp Mordecai in her arms and tend his injuries. He'd a blackened eye, swollen shut. Cuts and

bruises! But she'd wager his antagonist had taken a strong dose of reciprocal medicine. There was steel in the angle of Mordecai's jaw, self assurance in the set of his shoulders that she'd never seen before. The glint in his eyes ought to serve as warning to anyone challenging him in future.

Then Mordecai smiled, dispelling the impression of danger inherent in his features. Warmth bloomed in Philomena's heart. She'd banked everything on finding him. He had found her!

Mordecai smiled to hide his concern. In truth, previous misadventures compared nothing to the danger presented by this singular situation—

The Paulsons, here!

People of their class did not frequent public houses for any reason. Mordecai had expected the henchman to retrieve Philomena from the barbers at a price, and bear her home in secrecy. Yet two rough-looking characters physically held Theodore Paulson and his mother in place, displaying them like exotics at a zoo.

A big man with a confident air stood behind Philomena. Mordecai sensed an odd familiarity between the two. He saw her flinch when the man proclaimed, "We are fortunate to entertain Mr. Theodore Paulson – the great mill master and tycoon!"

Philomena steeled herself to follow through with her part of the bargain.

Mordecai wondered the purpose of the man's plan.

People clapped uncertainly.

Boss taunted the crowd. "Is that all the welcome you have for a man superior to us in every foreseeable way?"

Philomena snuck a glance left and right. Her father looked angry. Her Grandmother's rigid form conveyed extreme displeasure. Their moods had affected her for so many years. Their power intimidated her. *Well, we're not at home now,* Philomena reminded herself, *and everything is about to change.*

Mordecai saw willful resolve in the set of Philomena's features. Her eyes left his in a turn of the head that seemed evasive. *Whatever his plan, she plays a part.*

The big man goaded, "Is Mr. Paulson not a prime example of his class?"

People seemed unwilling to agree.

A woman hollered playfully, "If he's so prime, why d'you hold him, Boss?"

They call him Boss. Mordecai mulled it over. *This is the barber suspected of criminal and treasonous activities. He must own the Puggle and Poke, else how could he make so free with the place?*

Boss favored Paulson with a casual glance. "I've no right to hold him, though by commerce and law he may hold *us* for want of a coin. He's better than us and may do as he likes."

The man nearest Mordecai at the table shouted, "Better?"

O'Shaunessey gives them free drink to hold them here, and bend emotion to his will.

Snorts, insults, rude gestures and noises erupted all around Mordecai and someone answered from across the pub, "He lives better, aye!" and still another yelled, "He owns better!"

Above the rowdy displeasure of the crowd someone cried, "By those accounts, he's better!"

"Nay, not upon those accounts!" Boss affected to calm with a placatory lift of his hands. "Fortune favors them on account of genetics. Admit it, friends."

The Puggle fell silent. It seemed no one liked to be compared unfavorably to Theodore Paulson.

Into this quiet, Mordecai heard, distinctly as everyone else, those accepted truisms no one below upper class liked to hear. The men holding the Paulsons in place spat the ugly words.

"There's not a crip or a halfwit among 'em."

"It don't happen to them."

"Ain't we always been told t'is so?" Boss purred, "Is that not justification for the sorrows that plague us, alone?"

A mood gripped the place, palpable in its malignancy.

"Well, my friends – you must know I hold him ..." The big man's lips drew back from his teeth in a dry snarl. "To account for a lie!"

Mordecai's companions responded in like fashion to the rest in the pub, with heads lifted, in confusion and consultation among themselves. "Lie?" they asked one another. "What lie?"

Boss pressed his point. "I've proof."

Philomena knew her part in the performance was fast approaching and felt growing excitement.

Dread settled upon Mordecai's shoulders, for he had an uneasy sense of where Boss O'Shaunessey led them.

Boss pointed to Theodore Paulson. "He and his lady wife had one child – *with one leg!*"

Mordecai's table companions coughed on dry laughter, in utter disbelief. Mordecai gave no outward indication of his inner turmoil.

Beside her, Grandmother said, "I'm leaving." But Cyril held the struggling widow in place.

"Take your hands off my mother!"

Philomena gasped, for Papa's outburst unmasked Grandmother.

She growled from behind her veil, "Shut up, Teddy!"

Mordecai's tablemates hooted and clapped hands and quaffed their drinks with gusto. A female among them chided, "Oh, we ought not laugh, with his daughter's fiancé murdered!" but her exhortation sobered no one.

"Come now, men! Have you never run afoul of your mothers?" Boss joked as laughter overtook the place. "He's not so different from us, as you'll soon see, for we've three generations of Paulson with us today."

Three generations! The pub buzzed with this, all eyes on

the boy between the captive Paulsons. The man nearest Mordecai, muttered, "Didn't know he had a son."

He doesn't. Mordecai felt sure the impression would soon be corrected. That he still could not catch Philomena's eye increased his sense of foreboding.

Boss promised, "The child between them shall prove the lie that's kept you accepting the least of life's rewards."

Mordecai's foreboding hardened to a knot in his stomach. Here was the reason Boss O'Shuanessey lured or coerced Theodore Paulson to the Puggle and Poke. *He's using Philomena to launch a revolution.*

Grandmother seized her arm in a threatening vice. Philomena took a sharp breath, for courage. She looked at Mordecai.

His eyes gave warning.

Hers begged understanding.

The photographer held his flash high, as he hunched under the drape to take the shot of her proclamation.

The journalist poised his pen above his notepad.

Philomena scanned the expectant faces of the crowd, relishing the turning point between before and after. *You'll all be free from delusion in a moment, and so will I.*

As she began unbuttoning the coat, Mordecai schemed wildly for some way to prevent her revelation.

Philomena saw the pub's front door open, though few others noticed this because all eyes trained on her. The identity of the new arrivals dried Philomena's throat to dust. Indecision split her between two options. Speak the words prescribed by her bargain with Boss? Or invent a code of warning for Mordecai's ears alone?

Mordecai watched her struggle to reveal her identity and the truth of her disability. He knew of only one way to stop her confession – with his own.

In a flash of intuition, she saw his intent. She must stop him.

Philomena shouted, "I'm Mordecai Michaelson!"

CHAPTER 44

Grandmother dropped her arm.
"We agreed what you'd say," Boss growled.
"I'm Mordecai Michaelson!" Philomena shouted as policeman flowed into the pub. "I'm Mordecai Michaelson!"

"You've put my bullet in your brain," Boss muttered in a fury. "Goddamn you for it."

Philomena believed him, but couldn't heed his threat with Mordecai in danger.

"Police!" Theodore Paulson yelled. "These hooligans accosted us and hold us prisoner!"

"Don't attract attention!" Grandmother hissed. Pointing in Mordecai's direction, she declared loudly, "Look there!" with such command in her tone the police obeyed.

"No!" Philomena shouted. "Arrest me!" Philomena caught Mordecai's eye. *Run, Mordecai!*

Mordecai shook his head. "Over here!" he yelled. "I'm the murderer!"

His tablemates thought this a fine joke, laughs all around.

Desperate to draw the police off Mordecai, Philomena cried, "I tell you, *I'm* Mordecai Michaelson!" She had Mordecai's identification in her coat. Would that she could use it, but it bore his likeness, which held no resemblance to her. "The pawn broker knows me! Fetch Mr. Shelton!"

"A man threw Shelton's stockboy off a bridge," a constable retorted.

Philomena blinked in confusion. Another murder?

The lawman scanned the room with an authoritative eye. "We've word he stopped here. Anyone seen a man wearing a plague doctor's coat?"

"No!" Boss barked. "Get out!"

Mordecai gave a grim smile. In point of fact, he had seen a man in a plague doctor's coat. He called the lawman over with a gesture. "I've information for you—" But he hadn't anticipated Philomena's single-minded fear for him.

She screamed the place down, "I'm Mordecai Michaelson!"

"IMPOSTER!" Mordecai roared, wincing inwardly at the stunned hurt on her face in response to his shouting *at her*. He told the police, "*I* am Michaelson." He nodded to the dual pianos. "Percy will confirm it."

Percy told them, "I've never seen this man before in my life."

Mordecai snapped at the other pianist. "Jimmy!"

Jimmy flinched when Percy's flicked cigarette hit his nose in a shower of embers. Percy held his gaze. Jimmy's head dropped and his fingers plunged the keys. He murdered a song, getting louder and faster.

Percy destroyed a different tune at top volume.

The effect was madness and the crowd loved it. Everyone sang whichever song they liked best, voices rising in audible chaos.

"I'll show you I'm Mordecai Michaelson!" Mordecai pushed people out of his way, dislodged Percy at his bench and began to play with such skill that Jimmy's ditty trailed off in a few feeble notes and the pub grew silent.

Men emerged from shadowed corners. Philomena noticed them because they did not sing. Their faces held no expression. They moved silently through the crowd, reminding Philomena of the kitchen help who seemed innocuous at first but turned deadly on command. She saw them narrow in on Mordecai. "Call them back," she begged.

"He distracts you," Boss said. "I can't be doin' with that."

If she declared herself to be Mordecai, Boss's shadow men would take him. But if she declared herself to be Philomena, the police would take him. There seemed no good outcome, but remaining in place solved nothing.

Philomena suddenly broke away and plunged into the fray.

Boss yelled, "Stop that lad!" but no customers could distinguish which lad among their number he intended they catch. His shadow men couldn't stop Philomena, for they focused on Mordecai. The close press of drunken patrons unbalanced her continually but she kept on.

When Mordecai drew his masterpiece to a close, the pub's patrons stood transfixed.

"Gor …" a woman whispered, clutching a pint to her chest, "S, beautiful …"

Mordecai turned with satisfaction to the open-mouthed policemen and cocked an eyebrow. "I think we know who the real mad pianist—"

"AMATEUR!"

Heads turned in Philomena's direction.

She slid into place beside Jimmy. Her fingers flew over the keys, devising a fast-paced number inspired by the tumult of her recent adventures. Her composition brought to mind sea battles, invasions, dragons slain on the point of a lance. It stirred the blood and brightened the eyes.

Mouths fell open. "I say!" a man marveled. Another man began pounding the bar in time to the music. Then, everyone at the bar joined him. Those standing stomped their feet. Those at tables rapped the surface.

Philomena finished on a crescendo that brought the house down.

Hands caught her beneath the armpits, surprising her. She found herself lifted by Jimmy to stand on the bench and heard him urge, "Take a bow!"

Heart racing and breathless, Philomena received the adulation of the crowd. A stupefied grin spread across her face. She turned incredulous eyes to Mordecai.

He watched her darkly. *Crowds change.* Mordecai remembered the mobs he encountered in previous hours. Philomena didn't know the dark changeability of a hive mind. He wanted to warn her but just then, Philomena's expression changed from joy to alarm. Percy gave a shout of warning a second too late. Fingers dug into Mordecai's inflamed shoulders and arms. He shouted from the pain.

As shadow men pulled Mordecai from the bench, Philomena shot a blazing look at Boss. Her message: *I shan't tell my secret; I'll tell yours.*

His eyes narrowed.

I've seen what you keep in the cellar.

Of the police presence in his pub, Boss needed no reminding. "Stop!"

His outburst confused the cheering crowd.

His men released Mordecai.

Police moved in on Philomena, evidently convinced by her playing that here was the real Mordecai Michaelson.

Determined to change their minds, Mordecai plunged into a raucous number, spurring drunken revelers into song. The police halted. *That's right. Come to me.*

Following his gaze, Philomena looked over her shoulder and saw the police. *Stay away from him. Come to me.*

With Jimmy's help, she scrambled down onto the bench and played from the open songbook above the keys. Half the pub launched into the tune with such belligerent joy, they came close to drowning out those singing Mordecai's number.

Each duelist played as if spurred on by the devil, for winning the duel proved the victor guilty – and the loser innocent – of being the mad pianist who'd murdered Charlie St. Claire.

Playing, Mordecai glanced at Boss O'Shaunessey, who was flanked by minions still holding the Paulsons in place by the kitchen doors. The man scowled at Philomena, clearly furious that she'd stolen his audience and thwarted his plan. Boss had reminded people of their unhappiness, but Philomena had given them fun. *She might yet escape, under cover of this carnival atmosphere.*

Playing, Philomena cast worried looks at the police frustrated by the energetic crowd. *With the pub in pandemonium, Mordecai might make his escape.* She caught his eye, mouthing, "Go!"

With a quick shake of the head, he mouthed, "You go!"

Philomena began to sing, her beautiful voice rising above the chaos with such clarity and perfect pitch it drew gasps and cries of pleasure from the crowd.

"Bless him!" A woman gushed with maternal delight, "Still so young, his voice ain't changed."

Philomena's fans sang her song with boisterous abandon.

Percy jabbed Mordecai in the ribs. "He's raised the stakes!"

Mordecai met Philomena's challenge by singing at his loudest, unapologetically off key. His crowd followed him joyously off a tuneless cliff.

In dueling call-and-response, the patrons of the Puggle and Poke reached jamboree volume. Everyone embodied the loose-limbed frolic of their favorite song as they linked arms, whirling each other about in crazy-leg jigs.

Philomena laughed to see a constable sneaking the last lager from a passing tray. She could not fear anyone just now, with people singing and dancing all around her. Nor could Papa's disapproving frown discourage her. Philomena's shoulders danced.

Mordecai's gaze returned to Boss O'Shaunessey. There

was a calculating stillness to the big man's posture. *He knows as well as I the shifting loyalty of crowds, and is biding his time.*

Philomena leaned over the keyboard, and sang to Mordecai, "Somebody loves you ..."[i]

Her crowd picked up, "Yes, they do! Yes, they do! Yes they do!"

Mordecai warned her with his eyes. They had yet to find a way out of this mess. He sang, "Picture a girl ..."[ii]

Mordecai's crowd sang back, "A beautiful girl —"

Philomena's crowd sang louder, "Someone is wild about you —"

"—Someone who'd never doubt you!" She blew Mordecai a kiss.

He tried not to smile.

Suddenly, horns wailed. Percy and Jimmy shot to their feet, grinning.

Jimmy collapsed to roll on one hip and shout in Philomena's ear, "They've emptied the wall!"

It was indeed bare, patrons having taken down any instrument they knew how to play. Rattles and tambourines shook. A strange instrument of wood and corrugated metal clattered beneath thimble-encased fingers. Strings thrummed bass, while anyone still seated made a drum of the nearest surface.

Mordecai sang above the cacophony, "Picture a boy—"

His crowd bellowed, "A wonderful boy!"

Philomena sang, "Somebody loves you!"

Her camp blared, "Only you! Only you! Only you!" They spun each other around, waving hands in the air.

Mordecai's fans shout-sang, "If this wonderful girl wed this wonderful boy!"

"And they started to live in a house filled of joy!" Mordecai sang at full volume, eyes darting over the crowd and his expression turning anxious.

He'd seen Boss O'Shaunessey motion to the lead

constable in a gesture that appeared to say *round them up.* And the lead constable – lead in name only, it seemed – signaled his men to the pianos with a wave of his nightstick.

Philomena followed Mordecai's gaze to police, who had split ranks. Two sides surged toward the pianos with obvious intent of apprehending both suspects.

It was too soon for the crowd. A rageful cry erupted over the clash of songs, instruments and dueling pianos, "You'll not take the Mordecais!"

It spread through the pub like a battle cry, "You'll not take 'em!" Chopping the dueling songs to discordant notes, they stopped singing and started yelling, "Save the Mordecais!" Which dueling pianist was the real Mordecai Michaelson mattered nothing at all. Police spoiling everything – it was an outrage! Someone smashed a guitar over a copper's head. The cop swung his bully club. A shadow man landed a punch in the copper's gut, and the brawl was on.

Jimmy and Percy took over dueling pianos as glass flew overhead and combatants crashed and rolled around them.

Now's our chance, Mordecai realized. He caught Philomena's eye.

Yes, she agreed with his visual cue, *while everyone's distracted.*

Mordecai rose, beckoning her.

Philomena wanted nothing more than to take his hand and make their escape, but something halted her.

She understood Boss would track her down and kill her for abandoning their agreement, else he risked appearing weak to the vast network of subversives that jumped at his command. The police wouldn't rest until they brought the accused murderer of Charles St. Claire to justice. Setting things right was no longer a matter of vengeance to Philomena, but of freedom. "Close the piano, Jimmy."

"But I'll lose the duel!"

"Please!"

Percy shot his opponent a quizzical glance as Jimmy closed the lid on his grand piano.

With Jimmy's help, Philomena climbed atop its broad surface.

"It's not safe!" Mordecai flung an arm up in defense against an airborne glass. It shattered on impact against her piano. Reaching, he beseeched her, "Get down!"

Ducking beneath flying debris, Philomena hastily unbuttoned and shrugged off the big coat. Then she stood, hands on hips as chaos reigned all around her.

Perhaps nature hates a vacuum. Her stillness distracted them. Her appearance made them forget to dodge blows or hit back.

Percy and Jimmy gaped up at her, forgetting to play.

Catching a bar stool midair, a man yelled, "Mind the lass!"

A cotton blouse and plain wool skirt belted at the waist accentuated Philomena's curves. She felt embarrassed to have so much bosom on display before nine o'clock in the evening, but she had to admit it proved a point.

She didn't even need to raise her voice. "I am Philomena Paulson."

Boss bellowed, "I've genetic material to prove it!"

Heads swung his way.

"I cut her hair myself." Boss held up a glass jar filled with Philomena's hair clippings. In the other hand, he raised the shot glass. "And her father took a drink with me in this very kitchen."

"She's no daughter of mine!" Theodore Paulson shouted. "I do not know her!"

Philomena tensed against his rejection. One day it would cease to pain her. She met her father's defiant glare. "I daresay, Mr. O'Shaunessey has found a reputable laboratory that will prove our connection."

The police stared at her, brows drawn in consternation.

I'll clear up their confusion. "There is your murderer, in the widow's disguise." Philomena pointed to the old woman who had ruled her life with her iron will. "Grandmother killed Charles!"

A collective breath sucked all the air in the room.

"And this is why."

Guessing her intention, Mordecai muttered painfully, "Philomena, don't!"

She met his eyes. *I'm done pretending.*

They won't forgive you. Mordecai wasn't thinking of the Paulsons but of the lower classes kept down by lies.

Philomena bent and drew the hem of her skirt up past her lady's boot. She continued up the leg that wore no stocking. She listened to the hiss and murmur of conversation as it became apparent the leg was made of wood. Biting her lip and fighting a lifelong taboo, she exposed the wooden leg to its edge. She revealed the suspenders holding it to the firm flesh of her thigh. "I was born with only one ..."

White light flashed as the photographer's camera caught the moment. Blinded and blinking, Philomena felt exposed. She had thought telling the truth would free her, but she wished to hide now more than ever.

"God almighty," a man breathed.

There was no going back now. "Charles saw my wooden leg. Grandmother hit him with a candlestick to keep him telling anyone."

The police coalesced into a line, pushing its way through the crowd to advance on her family.

Patrons turned toward the kitchen doors in disbelief to see people of quality apprehended. Uneasily, they looked back to Philomena.

Mordecai raked his fingers through his hair. Philomena had no understanding of people, of the comfort they found in nursing a grievance through generations. *You've turned their world upside down. They'll look for someone to blame and they'll find you.*

Philomena told them, "Now, you know our secret."

Mordecai lifted worried eyes.

"It does happen to us!"

They stared at her wooden leg, grappling with the implications.

Philomena's questioning gaze found Boss.

He smiled and nodded.

She released her skirts. Linen and wool skimmed down her false leg. She drew herself up to full height, her shoulders going back and her chin up. In demeanor and posture, she appeared to be exactly what she was – every inch a lady.

But she did not feel the confidence she exuded. Philomena swallowed a great lump of fear and sorrow, and once dislodged it gave no resistance to the raw shout that burst out of her, "I'm a crip, I guess!"

Philomena shivered in the atmosphere of stunned silence.

Then, a woman yelled from the bar, "Yer gorgeous, luv!"

The compliment drained the strength from her flesh-and-blood leg. Philomena fell to one side.

People rushed to catch her. "There you go now, lass," they said. "You're right as rain." They helped Mordecai lower her gently to the floor. "On your feet ..." they encouraged. "Both your feet, and one of 'em just as good as the other."

When at last, she stood in strength and steadiness, her eyes wandered to Mordecai.

His fingers trailed a little melody across the keys.

Philomena's played a counter melody.

"I think we can make a duel out of that," Percy said.

EPILOGUE

Morning found the hotel's tea room a peaceful place of muted conversation and general contentment. Guests lingered over breakfast, while sun shone through large windows. Gentle breezes, warm with the promise of spring, stirred gossamer curtains. Through French doors, one could see the terrace, where flowers bloomed in clay pots and a ginger cat snoozed on the slate floor.

Seated outside, Philomena gazed in pleased wonder at the quaint town with its white-walled, red-roofed buildings clinging to hillsides that descended to the deep blue sea. Mordecai's attention lingered on her, noting with pleasure the transformation wrought by a few months. Her shorn hair had grown to curl gently at her jawline. Self-confidence had replaced her formerly solemn and secretive demeanor. Philomena's lively expression conveyed joy and curiosity. In this moment, she held a torn morsel of a croissant to her smiling mouth but had forgotten it, distracted by the view.

Mordecai resumed reading aloud the newspaper newly arrived from England in this morning's post, concluding with, "Their wedding is set for May 23rd." It seemed Mr. O'Shaunessey had finally asked Mrs. Cho out to dinner and a show. In short order, he'd made bold to ask a good deal more. "And they'll honeymoon in Peking."

The word *honeymoon* brought a blush to Philomena's cheeks for reasons that had nothing to do with the O'Shaunesseys. "How lovely," she sighed, popping the last of the croissant into her mouth.

Continuing in silence, Mordecai read about the case against Terrence Mulhoney, whom he knew as Stripes. Multiple eyewitnesses identified him as the man who had thrown the pawn broker's stockboy over a bridge into the Thames. Being caught in possession of the Paulson diamonds tied Mulhoney to an obvious motive for killing his friend. Prospects for acquittal seemed long odds, indeed.

Mordecai read another article that reported the subterranean murder as a case closed, with the mystery victim revealed to have been a plague doctor set upon by thieves. Tipped off by underworld contacts, police had identified the murderers, only to discover that cholera had already sentenced them to death.

Holding The Herald open in front of his face revealed its front page to Philomena. The photo of her baring her false leg to the patrons of the Puggle and Poke dominated, beneath the headline: "IT DOES HAPPEN TO US" in a point size usually reserved for declarations of war.

And it *was* a declaration of war – against any claims to innate superiority that allowed the powerful to hold the lowly in subjugation. Here was proof that disabilities happened at all levels of society. Yet, even with photographs and newspaper accounts, Philomena feared some people would simply refuse to believe the truth she had revealed.

"They'll believe it in time," Boss had predicted. "They cannot help doubting what they *used* to believe, and in that direction lies progress." As *Midnight Star's* sister ship sailed away, Boss and his lads had waved, grinning and yelling from the dock, "Bon Voyage!"

On this morning, in a sunny land far from the chill of a

lingering English winter, Mordecai folded The Herald back to reach another section. This motion presented to Philomena an article concerning Grandmother's arrest and upcoming trial. Beneath that article, another was headlined: Heiress to be Crown's Witness. *That's months away*, she reminded herself. "Do lower the paper. It hides your handsome face."

Mordecai snapped it closed with an impish grin.

Philomena took unabashed pleasure in the features he no longer sought to hide beneath makeup, monocle, and false moustache. She enjoyed what view of his figure newspaper and table did not obstruct, and thanked heaven his recent injuries had healed.

Their eyes met, shining in mutual affection.

The sudden arrival of a waiter surprised them. The formally attired, white-aproned servant made room among the remains of their breakfast for a steaming China pot and two new cups.

Mordecai told him, "We didn't order anything."

"No sir," the waiter replied, glancing into the tea room, "but Miss Paulson's admirers thought you'd enjoy some chocolate."

"Oh!" She and Mordecai exchanged smiles.

"And if you could, miss ..." The waiter produced a pen and a concert program. "I wondered if you'd condescend ... if you'd be so kind to autograph ..."

"Of course!" Philomena took the program and poised the pen between her studio portrait and the concert title: Philomena Paulson, Composer and Pianist Debut Tour. "Whom shall I address?"

The waiter cleared his throat. "Sidney Melino." As she wrote, he babbled, "Your original compositions are sublime; in particular, Miss Paulson, the nocturne titled Moonlight Falling on the House of the Owl transcends ...transports me ..." He trailed off, blushing furiously in the light of her gentle smile.

"Thank you, Mr. Melino. I feel rather transcended, myself."

After the waiter had tucked the autographed program safely away and carried off some of their dishes, Mordecai refolded The Herald. He set it down and tapped the article headlined: Philomena Paulson Conquers Continent. "How are you enjoying conquest, Miss Paulson?"

"Nay, Mordecai," she protested teasingly. "Do not address me as such!" She reached her left hand across the table.

Laughing, he threaded his fingers through hers.

"Paulson is the name fame and family pressed upon me," Philomena chided playfully as he lifted her hand to his lips. "Call me by the name I chose!"

"Very well, Mrs. Michaelson," he chuckled, with a kiss on her slim gold ring.

ABOUT THE AUTHOR

Naima Haviland writes novels and short stories in which a person is confronted by evil, be it external or internal, supernatural or human. Her subject matter is often dark, but writing and sharing stories uplifts her and brings in the light. She hopes that you, dear reader, will find your creative voice in whatever medium excites you, and be uplifted. It is never too late to start. Or to start again.

You can connect with Naima on most social media platforms, especially at naimahaviland.com and facebook.com/Books.by.Naima.Haviland.

THE FAVOR OF A REVIEW

If you enjoyed The Name I Chose, please rate and review it on social and online media. It really helps!

ACKNOWLEDGMENTS

I proudly acknowledge the actual composer of Moonlight Falling on the House of the Owl, my talented sister, Rachel Rose. Next, I'd like to thank my writer buddies. Reading your work and sharing mine, talking shop, and seeing your pets or kids pop into a Zoom room are experiences that enrich my life and keep my solitary occupation from turning into an echo chamber. Many thanks to Janet and Todd, who helped coordinate the beta reading phase. I'm deeply grateful to the beta readers and to my editor, Fritze Roberts, for guiding me around my blind spots toward revisions that made the story believable and whole. Always – acknowledgment to my Creator, Who likes giving me ideas while I sleep. This particular dream, about naïve and disadvantaged lovers running away together, became a pencil-written short story in a notebook, then a possible novella, and finally a published novel.

---

[i] Somebody Loves You written by Seymour A. Brown, with soprano vocalist Ada Jones

[ii] What a Wonderful Love That Would Be written by Alfred Doyle with lyrics by George Whiting and Paul Cunningham

Made in the USA
Columbia, SC
03 January 2024